THE SLEEPERS OF ERIN

'Yes. I'm a divvie.'

They exhaled simultaneously, exchanging a glance.

'Then you are the one we . . . desire, Lovejoy.'

That ambiguous line from Lena. I said, 'Me? What for?'

'A little trip. To find something old and valuable in the ground.'

'Lena, my dear,' Kurt warned.

'Trip? Where to?'

'You will be told as soon as you are fit.' She smiled. 'Foreign, but you need no passport.'

'I'm going nowhere, luv.'

That smile moved its wet mouth and I heard, 'Then I'll phone Detective-Sergeant Ledger and tell him you blackmailed me into providing your alibi.'

'Blackmailed how?'

'I'll think of something, Lovejoy. A woman's always believed when she makes an accusation concerning sex or money.' We all paused, considering. Hardly a proposition from Wittgenstein, but still food for thought.

Also in Arrow by Jonathan Gash

THE GRAIL TREE
THE JUDAS PAIR
PEARLHANGER
SPEND GAME
FIREFLY GADROON
GOLD FOR GEMINI
THE TARTAN RINGERS
THE VATICAN RIP

THE SLEEPERS OF ERIN

A Lovejoy narrative

Jonathan Gash

ARROW BOOKS

Arrow Books Limited
62-65 Chandos Place, London WC2N 4NW

An imprint of Century Hutchinson Limited

London Melbourne Sydney Auckland
Johannesburg and agencies throughout
the world

First published by Collins (The Crime Club) 1983
Hamlyn Paperbacks edition 1984
Arrow edition 1986
Reprinted 1987 (twice)

Printed and bound in Great Britain by
Anchor Brendon Limited, Tiptree, Essex

ISBN 0 09 934300 2

A story for Freda and hers, for Susan, Glen, Babs, and
Yvonne who wanted such a start.

This book is dedicated as a humble offering to the memory of the ancient Chinese god T'ai Sui, who afflicts with poverty and pestilence all those who do not dedicate humble offerings to his memory.

Lovejoy

CHAPTER 1

Everybody wants them.

You want them. I want them. Everybody. The poor in
the gutter, famous actresses, millionaires on yachts,
robbers clinging to drainpipes, dreamers, hookers, killers.
Everybody.

And what are they, these things?

They are exquisite. Beautiful. Breathtaking, crammed
with soul and love. They also happen to be inflation-
proof. They resist monetary devaluation and wars,
plagues, famines, holocausts and the Great Crash.

They're antiques.

The trouble is, there's blood on most. I should know,
because I'm an antique dealer. Yes, your actual quiet,
friendly, placid bloke who sells you old pots and paintings
and things in perfect tranquillity.

This story starts where I'm bleeding to death.

Hospitals always stink of ether, though they say it's not
used much now. Like in most places, nothing ever really
changes. The ceilings whizzing past overhead looked
cracked and unpainted, the bulbs and fluorescents
grubby, not a lampshade in sight. All those big lagged
pipes still there. The swing doors in Emergency had been
replaced by flexible flaps since last time, but they came
together with an appalling crash just the same. Hospitals
kill me. The nurses had the same massive watches pinned
to their bosoms, to put your eye out when they lean over
you. I tried telling the prettiest one it was only an
accident, honest, and not to call the police.

'You shut up,' she said crossly. 'I've had quite enough
from you in the ambulance. There's blood everywhere.

It'll take hours clearing up.'

A detached voice said, 'Is this the injured tramp?'

'Bloody cheek,' I croaked.

'You shut up,' the nurse said again.

'How did it happen?' that detached voice demanded.

I said, 'I fell.'

'You shut up,' the nurse said.

A house doctor looking like a knackered teenager said bitterly, 'The bastard's O rhesus negative.'

Five faces glared hate down at me, as if blood groups are anybody's fault. An older voice, just as tired, said anyway it would have to be operating theatre and to call out the anaesthetist. 'Take him into Number Three. Another plasma, and do a rapid crossmatch.'

It sounded horrible. 'Look,' I said upwards, trying to be helpful. 'Don't go to a lot of trouble—'

They all said together, 'You shut up.' Manners no different, either.

I woke up some time during the night feeling sick. Somebody had a tin thing under my chin. A fob watch donged my eyeball. Skilled hands mangled my damaged arm so I almost screamed with the pain. A light seared into my skull. Torture's gentler.

'Yes, he's conscious,' a bird's voice said.

A pleasant-looking bloke was standing patiently by when finally I came to. He tiptoed solicitously forward.

'Lovejoy?' The kindest voice I'd heard yet.

'Mmmmh?'

He smiled, full of compassion. 'You're under arrest,' he said. That brought a wash of memory. It made me groan.

'You shut up,' the nurse said.

Fingringhoe Church is out on the sea-marshes. Miles from anywhere. In fact, it's even miles from Fingringhoe, which only goes to prove something or other.

I'd been in this lonely church, kipping on one of the

rear pews after Sal had gone home, and thinking myself alone. A voice woke me, echoing.

'It's okay!' it said. 'All clear.'

Clarkie's voice was instantly recognizable. Sensibly, I kept still so I made no noise. Clarkie always was stupid, hadn't the sense to suss the church casually as if he were just admiring the stained glass windows. I lay on the pew, tired out after Sal but amused at listening to Clarkie's ponderous footfalls in the aisle. He's subtle as a salvo.

'Fasten that bleeding door, Sam.'

The church door boomed to, sending echoes round the interior. He must have his partner Sam Veston with him, a no-hope knife man if ever there was one. Talk about antique dealers. They say they're experts on pre-Victorian domestic furniture, which is hilarious. They're thick.

'What we do first, Clarkie?' Sam sounded nervous.

'Silver. There'll be a safe in here somewhere.'

They were somewhere down the church now. I sat up quietly to watch Clarkie and Sam set to work on the vestry door.

Sam asked, 'Whose was that frigging great Bentley?'

'Dunno. Some bird doing the church flowers.'

'She took long enough,' Sam grumbled.

I smiled. That would have been Sal, leaving for home. Clarkie and Sam must have waited in the hedgerows while Sal and I made love on the back pew. I'd come earlier on foot so they'd assumed Sal was alone. Incidentally, don't go thinking that loving in church is the height of blasphemy. It's God's full-time occupation. Anyway, Sal has an influential husband who would see me off if we were rumbled.

This infamous pair were interesting. I'd never seen anybody (else, that is) carrying out a robbery in person before. Clarkie had tried the vestry door and was standing to one side while Sam rummaged in the lock with a spider—that's an improvised key made of bent wires. You shape it as you go. Very much trial-and-error, but that's all you can expect from antique dealers these days. Now, if Sam had taken the trouble to learn how a splendid three-centuries-old lock was constructed, or had the slightest inkling of the beautiful workmanship which had gone into it when the ancient locksmith crafted it . . . I sighed. Antique dealers haven't a clue. Pathetic. God knows why, but dealers always want to prove that ignorance really is bliss. It honestly beats me. I could have turned that lock without breaking my stride. Clarkie is a minor antique dealer who 'specializes' in everything. He hangs hopefully on the coat-tails of any dealer rumoured to have a cerebral cortex, and picks up the odd trade swap now and then. Thick as a plank, the biggest deal he'd ever done was a quarter share in a piece of Derby, that costly John Milton figure holding a scroll. (You'll still occasionally come across Derby pieces in junk shops, but not as often as you used to.) I saw it, a luscious gold-touched white about 1776 or so. It was genuine, but that was entirely miscalculation on Clarkie's part. He is your actual average antique dealer, which is to say an incompetent, acerebral buffoon whose idea of research is somewhere to the left of guesswork. That deal was a year ago and I knew Clarkie was now on his uppers, though I had never known him do a church over before. It was an interesting sidelight on my colleagues, and I observed their progress with delighted fascination.

'What about a hammer and chisel, Clarkie?' Sam asked.

'Right. Smash the bloody thing.'

I wasn't having that. 'You dare,' I said.

They yelped. Clarkie dropped his bag of tools with a crash. Sam had sprinted half way to the door before they realized it was only me and screeched to a stop.

'It's Lovejoy,' Clarkie gasped.

'Christ.' Sam was grey-faced from fright. 'I thought it was the Old Bill.'

'You silly sod, Lovejoy.' Clarkie mopped his face. 'Made me come over queer. What you doing here?'

I scoffed, 'I wouldn't pay you in marbles, Clarkie.'

'We're just . . . just doing a lift,' Clarkie said apologetically. Sam looked from Clarkie to me and began to edge towards the church door. That was in case I ran out yelling for the peelers.

'And you're not going to stop us,' Sam added. He pulled out his knife and held it loosely at waist height, a really sinister threat calculated to strike terror into the most savage nun. You have to laugh. No wonder antique dealers have a bad name.

'Piss off, Sam,' I said, getting up and walking past him to join Clarkie, my footsteps echoing from the stone-flagged flooring. I noticed the church was not as bright now. The daylight was seeping from the sky and the hard sun shadows were ashed into a sad grey.

Clarkie backed off as I approached. 'Now, Lovejoy, mate,' he began nervously. 'This scam's nothing to do with you.'

'You're right.' I toed his bag of tools. It clanked like a shunting yard. They must have brought every tool they owned. 'And it's nothing to do with you, either.'

'What do you mean?'

'I mean get lost, Clarkie.' I grinned. 'I'll count to ten and you hide, eh?'

Sam spoke up. 'It's only a cloth job, for Chrissakes.' I should have listened to the despair in his voice and saved myself an operation, but maybe I was too clapped out. Anyway, I didn't. 'Cloth job' means robbing a church, an enterprise with a very respectable history if you think about it. Nowadays it's so common it's almost routine. There's hardly an antique dealer in England who bothers to ask any more where you got that old chalice or ciborium. Auctioneers are twice as bad, having no reputation to lose.

'Not today, Sam,' I told him. Honestly, to this day I don't know why I was taking this attitude, especially over a run-of-the-mill cloth job. Even priests are hard at it, flogging their own church silver on the side. Maybe it was the lingering sense of Sal's loving, whatever. Anyway, right or wrong I decided not to let them do it.

'You know we've *got* to, Clarkie,' Sam wailed. Which should have alerted me even more.

'You've got *not* to, Clarkie,' I corrected. 'Because I say so.'

'Erm . . .' He swallowed, eyed me.

I was honestly surprised, yet another warning bleep. Clarkie had seen me angry once, and I know for a fact he was very, very glad to be neutral on that occasion.

'Clarkie,' I warned gently, and he nodded. The bag clonked against his thigh as he picked it up and walked towards the door.

'For Christ's *sake*!' Sam squawked, but he trotted obediently after Clarkie. Smiling, I shut the door gently behind us and crossed the gravel with them to where their old van was parked. They must have left it in a lay-by up the lane towards the village until Sal left.

'Now, lads,' I said as the engine coughed into action. 'You two nellies leave this place alone, right?' I shook a warning finger at them as the van began to roll. 'I'll count the teaspoons. Cheers, Clarkie.'

'Cheers,' Clarkie muttered, but I could see he was dismayed. I wouldn't have thought a mere interruption would have him terrified as all that, but then I wasn't thinking.

I'd actually turned away when I heard Sam yell, 'You bastard, Lovejoy!' Like a nerk I paused affably, and felt a searing pain swipe through my left arm above the elbow. Sam bawled, 'Off, Clarkie!' The van scattered gravel. Its wheels spun and the engine roared, and there I was, left standing in a country churchyard fifty million miles from anywhere, staring stupidly at my arm with my brilliant scarlet blood spurting out into the air in front of me going *shish-shish-shish*.

For one instant I was quite unconcerned, wondering mildly what had happened and casually touching my arm where the blood was spouting. There was no further pain. Then, in a horrid cold terror, I realized. Sam had flung his knife. My artery was cut — *my* fucking *artery* was *cut* and I was frigging *dying*.

I tore off my jacket, blood going everywhere, ripped off my shirt sleeve and wrapped it round in a clumsy knot and got the blood stopped. I went back inside and used a candlestick to wind the tourniquet tighter, then ran.

About three minutes later, I reeled into the church organist's cottage in a worse state than China but alive. The old geezer had a certificate in first aid. He had a high old time, and nearly killed me enjoying himself doing complicated splints and knots until the ambulance came and took me prisoner and nurses were saying you just shut up.

CHAPTER 2

The police gave me two days before I was officially charged. It was quite a ceremony. My arm was sutured, the artery repaired, thank God. The nurses were behaving abominably, as if I'd done myself an injury on purpose just to annoy them. They'd hardly said a word to me, slamming about the ward and heaving me about like a sack of nuisance.

The chap in the next bed was a misanthrope, a real prophet of doom called Smith, accused of osteoarthritis.

A worse temper, and he could have slipped on to the hospital staff unnoticed. Opposite me was a cheerful little bloke with a gastric ulcer. It was old Smith told me I would be charged that morning.

'You're for the high jump, old son,' he said with relish. 'Nicking stuff from churches.'

'That can't be right.' I was so confident. I was a hero. (I'd prevented a crime, right?)

'You wait.'

'Tell 'em the tale, Lovejoy,' the gastric ulcer called across. 'I'll alibi you for fifty quid.' He fell about at this witticism.

Sister Morrison, our ward sister, came in then to tell us to shut up. I liked her, really, a quiet if bossy Irish lass, mid-thirties, in dark blue. She brought two coppers in and stood formally aside while they did their thing.

'Lovejoy?'

'Yes.'

'We're police officers,' the older one said. 'I'm Detective-Sergeant Ledger.'

'Congratulations. What's this arrest bit?'

'Theft of church property.'

'Please can you be a little more specific?' I asked politely.

He smiled a wintry smile over a notebook. 'More specifically, two chalices, two patens, one ciborium and one monstrance. All precious metals. And,' he added with relish, 'one brass candlestick.'

There was a protracted silence, enjoyed by some more than others. I cleared my throat.

'Erm, wasn't the vestry door locked?'

'Opened by a skilled hand,' Ledger said. 'Yours.'

I thought, well, well. Odderer and odderer. And I thought I'd been a hero.

'You're a long shot, Lovejoy,' he continued. 'What with

your record, and that paten being found in your cottage.'

'Lovejoy,' Gastric Ulcer cracked, 'our alibi deal's off.'

'You've had it, son,' Smith prophesied. A nurse hissed at him to shut up.

Sister Morrison was looking at me. 'Are you all right, Lovejoy?'

'Mmmmh?' I'd been thinking. 'Oh, yes, ta.'

The Old Bill was in his element. 'You will be brought to trial—'

'Sure, sure. Look,' I said, because you can't help worrying about small things. 'Don't mind my asking, but *what* paten in my cottage?'

'The one in your cistern.'

'We had a search warrant,' the assistant peeler said with pride.

'Well done,' I said absently. 'And the rest of the stuff?'

'Only you know the answer to that, Lovejoy.'

'It's disgraceful!' Sister Morrison snapped. 'A grown man robbing an unprotected church!'

I ignored her and spoke directly to the Old Bill. 'What's your theory, Ledger? That I sliced my arm, ran home in daylight carrying a load of church silver, buried the loot, carefully put one piece in the cistern—the first place you lot would look—then caught the bus back to get a candlestick for a tourniquet? Something like that?'

'Accomplice,' Ledger said.

'I trust antiques, not people.'

'True, Lovejoy.' He was really enjoying himself, better than a birthday. 'The trouble is, what were you doing in a lonely church if you weren't robbing it?'

Smiling, I drew breath to answer, then said nothing. I'd been there to make surreptitious love with Sal. Sister Morrison was looking again. 'There is that, Ledger,' I said at last.

They went about eleven o'clock. I'd no idea there was

so much paperwork to getting arrested. Nothing but forms. Last time they'd only had handcuffs.

'See you in court, Lovejoy,' Ledger said from the door.

'It's a date,' I called cheerily back, trying to be pleasant. At least they hadn't told me to shut up.

Sister Morrison was oddly terse, silencing my two companions and drawing my bed screens when I said I was tired. She sent some atrocious nosh along at noon but otherwise saw to it that I was left alone apart from one frantic episode in the early afternoon when a gang of nurses invaded my sanctuary, hoovered me and reemed me out, then flung me back gasping like a flounder while they went to punish old Smith in the same way.

All that day I thought hard. My mind was still a bit soggy from the anæsthetic but it began firing on the odd cylinder at last. What had seemed an innocent—well, nearly innocent—dust-up with Clarkie and his tame knife-throwing goon Sam was now disturbingly complicated. Worse, it had become two separate problems. First, I was under arrest for theft. That bit I could understand. But the second bit was crammed full of evil vibes I hated even more.

To start with, Clarkie normally wouldn't get in my way at any price. And Sam Veston for all his bravado with his pet knife usually walked very carefully round me, after a slight disagreement he and I had had in an auction room two years ago when I'd cracked a few of his ribs. Yet Clarkie had actually hesitated, foolhardy youth, when I'd told him to scarper. And Sam had dared to do me untold harm. The point is that normally neither of them would have dared anything of the kind. I remembered that look of despair on Sam's face, and his plaintive cry, 'We've *got* to, Clarkie!' Why? Antique dealers don't *have* to do anything, except survive.

Of course I'd have to crease Clarkie and Sam when I

got sprung from hospital, human nature being what it is. An antique dealer of zero resources just can't afford to be knocked about without at least grumbling a little. Weakness is all very admirable — in others. Nothing teaches you this like the antiques trade. But somebody — somebody 'skilled', Ledger had told me — had opened the vestry door and presumably cracked the safe in there, ferried off the church plate, entered my cottage, popped a patten in the cistern, then bubbled me to the Old Bill. Again, why? But most of all, what was *I* doing in all this mess?

At four o'clock I thought, right. When the rest of the ward were watching the match on telly I got Sister Morrison to let me use the trolley phone in the anteroom. She sent a nurse to wheel me down. I knew the number well enough. Naturally with my luck it was good old Geoffrey who picked up the receiver.

'Horsham Furniture here,' I said briskly. 'Could I speak to Mrs Dayson, please?'

'I'll get her.'

A door closed, then Sal came on, puzzled but guarded.

'It's me,' I said. 'Listen, love —'

'Don't you "love" me!' she blazed. Obviously good old Geoffrey was now elsewhere. 'Where have you been, Lovejoy? If you've been with that bitch again, I'll —'

'That bitch' was Helen, an antique dealer I'm, er, friendly with — or any other woman Sal cares to think of in the same context. There wasn't time for one of Sal's special one-way discussions so I broke in and told her I was in hospital. The beeps went twice until she came down through the superstrata.

'Listen, love,' I said urgently when she was coherent. 'This is important. Did anybody see you leaving the church?'

'No, darling. Oh God. What have they been doing to you?'

'What about Geoffrey? Did he . . . ?'

'No. He was in court,' she said impatiently. 'Oh, darling—'

'Eh?'

'He sits on the bench. Stay there. I'm on my way.' I thought, now she tells me. That was all I needed, Sal's old man the local magistrate. I'd be lucky not to get shot.

I rang round three pubs before I got Tinker at the Queen's Head.

'That you, Lovejoy?' he croaked blearily into the phone against the taproom noise. 'Where the bleedin' hell you bin? Everybody's goin' daft lookin' for you. I've got one of them carved wooden geezers carrying two ducks waitin' up Sudbury way—'

'Jesus.' The moan came out involuntarily. There had been rumours for months about a German limewood figure. They're worth a fortune, if you can lay hands on them. Tinker's my barker, the best sniffer-out of antiques in the business. Now he finds it.

'I can't hold her for ever, Lovejoy,' Tinker gravelled out. I heard somebody shout across the bar if that was Lovejoy on the blower. 'Yes,' Tinker bawled back. 'Here, Lovejoy. I've found a Yankee Windsor chair, I reckon, but funny wood—'

'Shut it, Tinker. Listen. Get over to the County Hospital, Charrington Ward—no!' I almost shouted the command to stop his repeating the instruction all over the pub. 'Say nothing. Just drink up and get over here. But one thing. Find out where Clarkie and Sam Veston have disappeared to. I'm going to dust them over on the quiet.'

'Right, Lovejoy.' He gave a gulp. 'Where'll you be?'

'Waiting,' I said sourly and rang off.

It was when I was reaching up to ring the bell to be wheeled back to bed when I noticed there was an open wall hatch ajar nearby. Through the gap I could see Sister Morrison's head bent over the day's reports in the ward office. Quickly I wondered if she could hear. Not touching the bell, I said carefully, almost in an undertone. 'Sister, please.'

'Yes?' She didn't look up.

'I'm ready to go back now.'

'I'll take you.' She got up and walked round to come for me. She must have heard every word.

Her face was ice. Great, I thought bitterly. Now I was not only a church plunderer, but a self-confessed adulterer and a murderous revenge-seeker as well. Win friends the easy way, I always say.

The rest of that day was not too good so I won't dwell on it. Sal came in, lovely and perfumed and dressed to the nines, frantic with worry and demanding to know every detail. She wept a bit like they do, and told the staff nurse that no expense was to be spared. 'Thank you,' Sal got frostily back, 'but Lovejoy is being paid for out of our taxes.' Surreptitiously she gave me a handful of notes in case I needed to send out for anything. The trouble was she became distinctly cool when I said what had happened.

'Police?' she gasped faintly. 'You mean, really? In actual court?'

'Yes, love. Somebody must have planted a piece at my cottage to bubble me.'

Sal said, 'Oh, darling,' but it wasn't her usual voice, full of possessiveness and humour. It sounded ominously like the sailor's elbow. 'Not . . . not in the *news*papers?'

'It's okay,' I reassured her cheerfully. 'I'll sort it out —'

She fingered her red amber beads, Chinese nineteenth-century. I'd got them for her fairly cheap in a local antiques auction before Sac Freres dragged them off to their Bond Street lair.

Sal is beautiful, really stylish. I was so proud of her there in the ward with the nurses enviously eyeing her gear and Sister Morrison going thin-lipped at the sight of such glamour. I mean, after all Sal was *my* visitor. The only good thing to have happened to me for ages. To my dismay Sal suddenly discovered she had to be going. She kissed me, full of courage about it but clearly taking to the hills. She said she would phone morning and evening, that final psychotherapy of a departing lover putting the boot in. I watched her go, saw her pause and wave from the door before the flaps swung to. Over and out.

In contrast Tinker's appearance can only be called earthy. He stood there, peering hesitantly into the ward. Imagine an unshaven, clog-shod old stick of a bloke approximately attired in an old army greatcoat, holed mittens and a soiled cloth cap, looking every inch a right scruff. Now double it, add an evil stench and you have Tinker Dill. Sister Morrison was instantly hovering on guard against mobile filth. I could tell that plagues and other epidemics had sprung to mind. I admit he's no oil painting but I still wasn't having anybody taking the mickey, so when Gastric Ulcer opposite exclaimed, 'Gawd almighty!' I smiled one of my specials and clicked an imaginary pistol gently at him, which perforated his next witticism. He looked away.

Antique dealers have barkers like armies have skirmishers — to nip around and suss out the scene. Boozy and shabby Tinker may be, but I wouldn't swap him for a gold clock. He sat beside my bed, ponging to high heaven and toothily agog at the ward bustle and the nurses, but mostly at the spectacle of me with my limb trussed up.

'Gawd, Lovejoy,' he croaked out. 'What the bleedin' hell you done? I thought we were doin' a deal.'

'Wotcher, Tinker. Sam and Clarkie.'

'Eh? Oh, aye. Gone to King's Lynn.'

'Wise lads,' I said. 'You tell me the minute they're back, right?'

'What if they don't come?'

I grinned. 'Then I'll go and get them.'

'Like that, is it?' He lowered his head confidentially for his favourite phrase. 'Here, Lovejoy. We in trouble?'

I told him the glad tidings step by step, him groaning and muttering every inch of the tale. When I came to the bit about Sam slinging the knife at me he stared.

'Sam? Him? Gawd, I thought he knew better than try you, Lovejoy.'

'You've spotted it, Tinker.' I listed the mysteries one after the other. 'Neither Sam Veston nor Clarkie would push their luck that far. Then there's the question who actually *did* do the cloth job. And why they bubbled me for it.'

Tinker ahemed at that and glanced about. We were speaking softly because we always do in the antiques game. Old Smith in the next bed was apparently dozing and the bloke to my left had been gruesomely cocooned in a crinkly transparent tent full of tubes ever since I'd arrived, but Tinker was right to be careful.

'Here, Lovejoy,' Tinker muttered. 'You didn't do it, right?'

'Right.'

He thought a minute. 'Then who did?'

'Whoever's got the rest of the church silver, you thick burke,' I explained wearily, getting out the notes Sal had left. 'Look. Here's some gelt. You'll have to manage till I'm out. See Helen, and Margaret Dainty. And Jason in the Arcade. You're looking for *any* church silver, okay?'

'Somebody new, or somebody old?'

That was a point. 'I reckon it's a newcomer. A clever antique collector.'

'How do you work that out?'

I asked, 'What's the least expensive church silver, Tinker? Chalice, ciborium, monstrance, patten?'

'Patten,' he said straight away. 'Only weighs a twentieth of a chalice at most.'

'So he drops the cheapest on me, and keeps the rest,

Tinker. See? Couldn't bear to part with it.'

I sent him off after telling him to check my cottage now and again till they let me go. Not that there's anything valuable in it. Things had been bad lately in the antiques game. It was one of those times when everything seems to be owned by everyone else.

One funny thing happened as he rose to say so-long. Sister Morrison came up and said there was a cup of tea and some cake in the ward office for Tinker if he wanted. Now, this really was odd because women usually want to get rid of him as fast as possible. He went all queer at the invitation because non-alcoholic fluids send him giddy but I gave him the bent eye and he accepted.

'See you, Lovejoy, mate,' he croaked and shuffled off after her.

'Cheers, Tinker.'

Sister Morrison kept Tinker in the office, pouring for him and talking. I could see them through the ward glass. She didn't even make him take his mittens off when passing him the biscuits, an all-time first. I saw him wipe his mitts on his cuffs the way he always does and she didn't even wince. They took a hell of a time over one measly cup of tea, so long in fact that I began to get edgy. I've never known Tinker miss the pubs opening and time was getting on. Maybe she was giving him a talk on hygiene or something. Irritated, I buzzed my buzzer but only got the staff nurse who came and gave me an injection with a syringe like a howitzer. When my bum had been rubbed sore and I was allowed to sit up Tinker was not there any more and Sister Morrison had gone off duty.

Next morning the newspapers were full of it. I was a celebrity.

Not a hero, but definitely a celebrity.

CHAPTER 3

Being stuck in hospital is grim enough. Being the baddie in the black hat as well is terrible. For some days they gave me the full treatment. Even Gastric Ulcer opposite sent me to Coventry, while old Smith read out loud ever-worsening reports about me in the local rag.

It was a real gas. Nurses belligerent, physiotherapists sadistic. The X-ray people who did my arteriogram were obviously disgruntled at having to handle so repellent a specimen of degraded humanity. The surgeons were unchanged, though, merely concentrating when they came round on my repaired artery and telling me to shut up. It was a hell of a life, relieved only by Tinker's somewhat erratic appearances when he called to report the problems in the normal antiques world outside. Curiously, in all this only Sister Morrison showed any sort of balance about me. Her attitude came to light in a way I found embarrassing but it brought her into the problem on my side so I'd better tell it as it happened.

It was on a Tuesday morning when the library lady came round. By then I was desperate for anything on antiques. Tinker had failed at the town library because they'd slung him out for being filthy and having no fixed abode, and I was re-reading a bundle of old issues of the *Antique Collector*. These glossy magazines give me heartburn at some of the careless things people say about antiques. They speak of them almost as if antiques have no soul, which only goes to show.

The promised visit of the library trolley finally came, to my delight, with a splendidly plump matronly bird, all tweeds and blue rinse, parading grandly down the ward dispensing books right and left. I was in ecstasy, because

I'd asked for a text on Ming underglaze blue of the Wan-Li period and the new monograph on the London Clockmakers' Company in Queen Anne's reign. You can guess the state I was in, excitedly watching the elegant lady trundle nearer and nearer between the rows of beds. She came, smiling and chatting, handing out the books and writing her little green cards which said who wanted what for next time. A real Lady Bountiful. She gave Gastric Ulcer his, a thing on greyhounds, and left old Smith his book about pigeon breeding. Then she turned away and went on.

I'd been left.

Apprehensive, I called, 'Erm, excuse me, please.'

'Yes?' she managed, preoccupied with the books and her list. She didn't look up.

'Erm, have you any for me?'

'Subject?' she said absently, still not a glance.

I felt my face redden but got out, 'Antiques, please.'

'I'll check,' she said smoothly, still so very busy. Then she went on to the next bed. Not a word.

Great. Umpteen days trapped in a rotten bed, no antiques anywhere and me suffering withdrawal symptoms worse than any addict. I turned my face away. Bloody hospitals. The difference was that heroin addicts and alcoholics would be kneedeep in intense young sociologists, empathizing like mad, but I was a pariah.

Then a gentle Irish voice uttered my name. 'Have you Lovejoy's books, Mrs Williams?'

'I must have forgotten them, Sister.' Determinedly casual.

'Really, Mrs Williams?' The voice was still soft and enquiring. 'And will you have time to bring them?'

The ward's customary din went quiet. The nurses froze. A couple of old blokes woke up in alarm at the unexpected silence.

'I'll have to see, Sister.' The reply was offhand, but with

that familiar flint-hard core of self-righteous sadism only the pure at heart can manage.

The gentle voice became a bandsaw. '*Nurse*!'
Feet pattered. 'Yes, Sister?' dimply little Nurse Swainson bleated.

'Collect *all* the patients' books this *instant*, and escort that person from the ward — *now*!'

'Yes, Sister!'

Nervously I sat up again. Already the centre of World War Three, the last thing I wanted was the fourth to happen along so quickly. Sister Morrison was calmly dialling at the central phone.

'Excuse me, Sister,' I called nervously. 'Can't we leave it, erm — ?'

'Shut up, Lovejoy.'

Her pleasant voice returned. 'Hello? Sister Morrison here, Charrington Ward. Why have my patients been ignored by the library services, please?'

'*Sister*!' Mrs Williams exclaimed, scandalized.

'Erm, Sister,' I pleaded in a quaver, thinking, Oh Christ. Little Swainson and another junior nurse were scampering about the ward snatching everybody's books and flinging them back on the trolley. It was pandemonium. The two old geezers, relieved the ward's usual cacophony was back, nodded off happily again.

'My charges,' Sister Morrison continued, 'are no better and no worse than any others in this hospital. If you are not able to provide . . .' It went savagely on for a full minute, about ten lifetimes. Finally she slammed the receiver down and turned.

'Nurse Swainson, Nurse Barton, Nurse French,' that alarming voice rasped. 'I thought I told you to escort that *person* out forthwith!'

'Yes, Sister!' voices chowith a trolley rumbled. Books flew and thumped. We cowered in abject terror. Old Smith grumbled to a fraught Nurse Swainson and practically got castrated for his pains as his pigeon book was ripped out of his hands.

Mrs Williams, as she was being bundled unceremoniously out of the place by a gaggle of nurses, tried a last desperate rearguard action. 'I'll complain to the highest authorities about your conduct, Sister!' But she lost that one as well.

'The best possible thing you can do, Mrs Williams! Lies are not the sole prerogative of the hospital library! Kindly *go!*'

I heard Mrs Williams being scandalized all the way to the lift which ran down through the hospital to the Voluntary Services division two floors below.

'Lovejoy!' I looked up as the bandsaw rasped out my name. 'Lovejoy.' The lilting voice was back again, gentle as ever. 'Please accept our hospital's apologies.'

I must have been a bit down, because I couldn't raise much of an answer to that.

The book trolley came creeping back an hour later. An apprehensive young Red Cross volunteer shakily dished books out in total silence. From fright, we'd all forgotten what we'd asked for and took anything she gave us, but my books were among them. Through the whole episode Sister Morrison was calmly writing out the ward report in her office, ever so innocent. The volunteer finally wheeled her trolley past the ward office when leaving, hugging the corridor wall in a wide curve as if the office was radioactive.

She leapt a mile when Sister Morrison quietly called her name. 'Yes, Sister?' she yelped, white-faced.

Sister Morrison smiled. 'Thank you,' she said sweetly, and let her go.

And hospitals are supposed to be there for your peace of mind. They're not there for your health, that's for sure.

You get 'discharged' from bankruptcies, armies and

hospitals. It was two weeks to the day when I got clearance from the consultant surgeon. I'd displeased him by calling him 'doctor'.

'Surgeons are addressed as Mister,' he told me testily, scribbling my clearance. 'Physicians are addressed as Doctor.'

'Sorry, er, sir.'

'Never been the same since that Yank hospital series on telly in the 'sixties,' he grumbled. He tore off a paper and handed it to Sister Morrison. 'Surgical Outpatients next week, Sister.'

He left the office, leaving me to be documented out. I watched her as she slipped my instructions into an envelope and ticked items off on the file. She was an attractive bird, if only she didn't hate me quite so much. This was the first time I had been in the office, though Tinker had been so favoured almost every visit. Galling. I suspected the old devil of trying to con her into lending him a few quid for beer, this being his great trick. When I asked him what the hell they talked about he only gave his horrible gappy grin and said to mind my own business, even though I threatened to thump him. Once he even joked about it, asked if I was jealous, the cheeky old sod.

As she wrote, a wisp of her pale hair curled round her nape on to her collar. She looked exquisite in spite of that crummy uniform, especially so preoccupied sitting that way with her legs twisted round each other like women can. Good enough to eat. And as for that delectable glass on her desk, it really put her in a breathtaking setting. The loveliest thing on earth, to me it was like an oasis.

There are millions of differently shaped glasses, but this was a marvel. 'Plain Straight-stem' drinking glasses are often anything but that. Antique dealers call them 'Cylindrical', which is a laugh, because they are nothing of the kind. This was Irish, too, a pedestal-type glass with a thick base, having collars top and bottom, but pristinely simple and unadorned. You usually find them—if at all—engraved with names, monograms, or personalized florets rather than plain.

I gazed at the rare little gem enraptured. Sister Morrison or somebody had stuck a single rose in it, a stark reminder of all the boring countryside we have hereabouts in East Anglia. It says a lot for its quality that the glass's beauty was quite undimmed by a grotty rosebud.

She clipped the papers and passed them over.

'Ta. That it, Sister?'

'Outpatients at two o'clock. You're not to be late, Lovejoy.'

I looked at the office floor. 'What if I can't make it? The police . . .' Ledger had told the hospital to phone Culver Street police station about my progress. She coloured slightly, which showed me she had already done the deed. A man's cough sounded from somewhere above my head.

'They will see you make the clinic,' she said, looking away.

'Thank you.' I meant it but she flared.

'Lovejoy. Isn't it time you mended your ways, went straight?'

'I am straight.'

Her face was suddenly pink with vehemence. 'You are hooked on vengence. I know what you'll do—go after Sam Veston and . . . and this Clarkie person. And I know why. You'll get into still more trouble over this church silver. And all because of that horrid woman. There's simply no *point*. It's all so stupid. Can't you see?'

I stared. How the hell did she know so much? Admittedly, she must have heard a little when I'd made that first phone call, but . . . I thought of Tinker's cosy little teatimes with her in this very office and my good hand flexed in anticipation. I'd cripple the gabby old sod.

Again that rasping cough from over my head. I glanced up. There was a small row of receivers on the wall. One was lit by a small red pilot bulb. Light dawned in my thick skull. I leaned forward and peered through her window down the rows of beds. The bloke in that transparent tent moved slightly with a cough. It sounded over my head. My heart sank.

'You heard everything?'

She nodded, correcting me. '*Over*heard.'

That explained her taking my part like she had. And she'd heard the Sal bit, for God's sake. And the true story of the cloth job. And my threats. And on top of that, she was clever enough to have got all the rest of my sordid history out of Tinker. What she hadn't overheard she'd wheedled. That's women for you.

'Are you going to tell?'

'No — as long as you promise not to fight these two people.'

The age-old dilemma of falsehood or truth confronted me. As always, perfidy won. I looked straight into her grey-blue eyes, and swore I'd not lay a finger on Sam and Clarkie.

'I promise, Sister,' I told her. 'Thanks for trusting me.'

'I'm aware,' she went on, 'from my conversations with Mr Dill of the everyday violence of your business, but there's no reason for you to be so shabby morally or physically.' Mentally I promised Tinker hell. I'd teach the silly burke to blab about our sordid game to a do-gooding cherub like her.

I grovelled uncomfortably and nodded, pulled my forelock and swore I'd be honest and true. Anything to get away from those earnest eyes and that high moral tone. As it happened, Ledger saved me just as I was feeling suicidally holy.

He came in smiling. 'On your feet, lad. G'day, Sister.'

A uniformed constable hovered outside, partly to catch

me if I made a run for it and partly to ogle the nurses' legs. Ledger was full of beans. Sister Morrison abruptly became her old frosty self while they signed me over like parcel post.

'You won't handcuff him or anything, will you?' she asked, a last brave try to lessen my burden. Ledger said no and boomed a hearty laugh. I rose to go.

As it happened it was the last laugh he probably had for years, because at that moment the most gorgeous creature I had ever seen in my life stepped into the office. Lustrous dark hair, overwhelming perfume, attired in furs and material that obviously cost a fortune, she wore so much gold and jewellery every step she took made her chime like a Buddhist temple in a gale. For an instant she stood there while we all gaped, then she stepped forward with a little cry and enveloped me in a suffocating embrace while I tried to keep my swathed arm from being crushed.

'Lovejoy, darling!' she cried softly. 'I've come at last! To stand by you! To . . . *own up!*'

There were tears in her dark amber eyes. I swear I'd never seen such remorse.

'Eh?' I nearly asked who the hell she was but her eyes said *not yet, not yet*. I shut up.

'It's no good, darling,' she sniffed. 'I tried to stay away, but I couldn't bear to read what they were doing to you. Day after day of absolute agony!'

'Lovejoy's been well cared for!' Sister Morrison said in her bandsaw voice.

The bird ignored her and sailed straight on into the big scene. 'And now, *arrest!* Oh, dearest darling! I'll tell the truth, reveal all to protect you!'

I'd never been in a Victorian melodrama before so I was stuck there, dumbfounded, under this exotic creature's armpit. The gimlet-eyed Ledger was quicker-thinking.

'Truth?' he ground out ominously. 'Own up to what?'

She dropped me and swung theatrically in obvious torment. I nearly fell over. Sister Morrison saved me as the woman rounded on Ledger, her bosom heaving, all Lilian Gish in dazzling colour.

'Own up to what, Corporal?' she said soulfully, gloved hands clasped together and eyes welling with tears.

'Detective-Sergeant.'

She ignored him too and appealed to the heavens. 'Own up to what? To what happened the night of the crime! Proving poor Lovejoy's complete innocence! Own up to his nobility in sacrificing his own reputation to save mine!'

There was a lot of hate around. Ledger turned puce, and Sister Morrison, having enjoyed herself preaching sweetness and light at me a moment ago, now looked as peaceful as a panther. I was lapping it up, sensing rescue.

'Don't, darling,' I said brokenly, right on cue but guessing a script quicker even than Ingrid Bergman ever did.

Tearfully she wrung her hands, though the size of her superb Edwardian double garnet rings (once so fashionable worn on ladies' gloved fingers) caused her some difficulty. With a clang of precious metal she turned to me, a sob in her voice.

'It's no good, darling! How could I go on?'

'Madam. What is your connection with this man?'

She blotted her eyes with a lace handkerchief so beautiful it dried my throat. You just don't get lace more exquisite than the lace the Sisters made at the Youghal Presentation Convent in County Cork before 1913. It's flat-point lace, and some find it too indiscrete on edgings, but to me it's perfection. When I came to she was raising her eyes adoringly.

'Lovejoy was in the church with me, Lieutenant—'

'Detective-Sergeant.'

She was terribly brave, Mary Queen of Scots on the scaffold. She reeled slightly. I thought that was a bit much, but I steadied her manfully. 'I'm — I'm married, you see. Lovejoy knew that, didn't you, darling?'

'Please, love,' I muttered, all heroic.

'We met in the church. Yes.' She raised her head so the light from the window stencilled her profile really well. 'Yes! I admit it! We were . . .' her voice sank to a piteous whisper . . . '*lovers*!' She said klov-erz.

'I deny it!' I cried, clearly heartbroken. Sister Morrison's eyes lasered into me. She didn't believe a word of it, the suspicious bitch. Women are like that. No trust. I often wonder why that is.

'My card, Major.' The woman passed him a card and a bulky envelope.

'Detective-Sergeant.'

'My statement is inside, witnessed by a notary public. You'll recognize his signature, Constable.' She fluttered her eyelashes. 'Lovejoy and I were . . . being klov-erz in the church when we saw these four men trying the inner door. Lovejoy sent me away while he tried to stop them.' She sobbed quite effectively for a quick incidental moment. 'I saw him run out, holding his arm. The candlestick, that terrible journey to the organist's cottage . . .'

'And where were you?'

'Too terrified,' she swept on. 'Too *selfish* to help! I was in my car down the lane.'

Ledger's gaze locked on mine. 'Is this true, Lovejoy?'

I faced him nobly. 'I cannot compromise a lady.'

Pure hate shone from him. 'And you, lady. How do I know *your* story's true?'

'Oh. Didn't I tell you? My chauffeur was with us all the time. Keeping watch. He saw the men, too. His statement's in the envelope as well.' She eyed Ledger shyly. 'Properly witnessed, of course, Colonel.'

'Darling,' I reproached her, thinking it was Christmas.

'You'd do this for me?'

She took my arm briskly, now quite matter-of-fact. 'Are you ready, darling?'

'Lovejoy.' Ledger had ripped the envelope and was scanning the four typewritten pages. He looked up quickly. 'What's this lady's name?'

I said, 'Erm . . .' but she was too quick for us both, simpering, 'Lena Heindrick. But Lovejoy always calls me Cherub, don't you, darling?'

'Yes, Cherub.'

Ledger was now an unhealthy purple and his breathing was funny. Still, if he infarcted now he was in the right place. He'd have ten doctors competing for his remains in a trice. He gave a despairing flap of his arms.

'All right,' he growled. 'But one day, Lovejoy. One day . . .'

'Thank you, Corporal,' I said innocently and drew Lena close. 'Let's go, er, Cherub.'

Had I known it all then, I'd have gone with Ledger like a lamb, and counted myself lucky. Instead I went proud and smiling, like the nerk I am.

Going down to the car park I asked in a whisper who she was, but she only kept up that determinedly fond smile and whispered, 'Not yet, Lovejoy. Not yet.'

CHAPTER 4

'What's the game, missus?'

We were in the back of this Rolls the size of a tram. She just smiled and lit a cigarette with a cube of bullion shaped like a lighter.

'Game, Lovejoy? No game. I'm deadly serious.'

'Drop me here, please.' We were passing the antiques Arcade. 'Ta for the rescue.'

'You're going to your home with us, Lovejoy.'

'Who sez?'

'Kurak says.' She pointed with her fag at the chauffeur. He had a neck like a tree-trunk. 'And Kurak is a good obedient man.'

'Yooorr serffint fur life, modom,' the bloke said. He didn't even turn.

'Get him from Goldfinger?' I joked, but was thinking, funny accent. Keats had once written 'sea-spry' for spray, but Keats was sort of Cockney. Funny name too, but us Lovejoys of this world don't joke about names. She too had a slightly foreign accent. Lovely bird, but older than I'd thought at first. Luscious, though. Edible.

'My husband Kurt is waiting in your cottage, Lovejoy.'

I started to ask how he'd managed to get in without a key, but remembered the silver patten in my cistern and shut up.

My cottage stands on the side of a little wooded vale on the outskirts of a village a few miles out of town. It is truly rural, as house agents say, meaning cheap and gungey, but I was glad to see the old heap in its tangle of weeds. The village council told me off last autumn for having a garden that always looks back-combed. I'd lost us the Best-Kept-Village-in-East-Anglia Competition by my display of 'horticultural negligence', and unreasonable hatreds had smouldered against me ever since because that cardboard cut-out toytown near Melford won again. They polish the pavement.

I stepped out, grinning like an ape and taking a deep breath. Your own smog's always best for breathing, isn't it? A giant Bentley on the gravel path dwarfed my thatched dwelling.

'Lovejoy, I presume.' This elegant stoutish man was in my porch (get the point? *My* bloody porch). He was smoking a cigar, his waistcoat chained in with baubled gold. Maybe ten years older than Lena, he wore that sleek

air of affluence you only see on politicians and butchers'
dogs. I'd never seen a cleaner bloke. His teeth looked dry-
cleaned, his shirt a façade of polished marble. You could
tell my grubbiness unnerved him. To preserve the sterility
of his podgy-bacon hands, he carefully avoided shaking.
'I'm Mr Heindrick."

Good old Kurt waved me in, bloody cheek. I heard him
say to his bird, 'Lena, my dear. The interior is rather . . .
unappealing. Perhaps you would care to wait in the
Rolls?'

'I'm curious, Kurt,' her bored voice cut in as she swept
past.

'As you wish, my dear.'

The Heindricks were making me feel like a specimen in
a jar. I admit the place is always a bit untidy and they had
got me off Ledger's hook, but I can get very nasty when
I'm narked, and they were narking me at a worrying
speed.

The cavalcade followed me into the main room, Kurak
with them.

'Sit down, please, Lovejoy.'.

Kurt seemed to change as I looked around the familiar
interior. The police must have done a thorough search, in
their own inimitable style. Like customs men, by law the
Old Bill don't have to tidy up after shambling your
things. My kitchen alcove was strewn with crockery and
pans. I only have one set of curtains and they were in a
heap. The place was a wreck.

Mrs Heindrick stood gazing round in awe. I swept some
old newspapers off a chair for her. She sank gracefully on
to it, not losing poise.

'Why do you cut them up, Lovejoy?' She meant the
papers.

'Important bits about antiques.'

'So this is where it all happens!'

'All what?'

Kurt posed before my cold fireplace like a Victorian father about to pronounce. 'Mrs Heindrick means your nefarious dealings, Lovejoy.'

Being up so long was taking it out of me, but I wasn't having that. 'Look, mate,' I said tiredly. 'Nobody calls me neffie and gets off without a limp. I'm no better and no worse than the rest. Okay, so you sprung me. I appreciate it. But I don't take kindly to being sneered at.'

Good old Kurt looked interested. He smiled and apologized with grace. 'You will forgive, I hope. An older man sometimes finds difficulty recognizing the values of a . . . a person so much younger than himself.'

He nearly said 'scruff'. I'd have scruffed *him*. Instead I nodded. 'Accepted. Well, folks. Thanks for the rescue and all that. Now I suppose you'll be going.'

Nobody moved. Kurt said, 'You're wrong, Lovejoy.' I looked round. Kurak stood by the door. The woman was half-smiling, observing me with her head tilted. Nobody was going anywhere yet.

'Wrong?' I guessed.

'Your description of yourself is completely false.'

'What are you on about?'

'Saying you're no better and no worse than the rest.' He smiled quizzically round at me. 'You are exactly both, Lovejoy. There's no need to pretend. Not with us. We're your friends.'

'Explain, Kurt,' Mrs Heindrick said.

'Explain what?' I asked innocently, thinking: These bastards know about me.

Heindrick deliberately dropped ash on my threadbare carpet. 'You are a financial wreck, Lovejoy. Your antiques business, *Lovejoy Antiques, Inc.*, is a deplorable front for this derelict hole. You have no fewer than eleven sets of impressive calling cards claiming—quite fraudulently—you belong respectively to Sotheby's,

Christie's or Glendinning's of London. Your liaisons with women—'

'Now look,' I said weakly.

Mrs Heindrick leaned over and pressed my arm. 'Shhh. You're interesting.'

Kurt sailed glibly on. 'Your liaisons with women cross all known marital boundaries. Currently you consort with Mrs Sally E. Dayson, a magistrate's wife of Dragonsdale village.' He twinkled a mischievous smile, the swine. 'And with Mrs Margaret Dainty, antique dealer of the town Arcade. And with Miss Lydia—'

'Look,' I snapped. 'Where's this leading?'

'And sundry others,' he cruised on, 'as far as your perennial poverty permits. You own one jacket and two frayed shirts. You live and look like a filthy tramp on the bread line. Apart from the . . . shall we say *donations* given you by these undoubtedly generous women, you shun affluence. Your one associate is Tinker Dill, a senile drunkard who sleeps in the town doss-house, on the rare occasions he is not destitute, and cinema doorways and pub yards when he is.'

I said defensively, 'That's not my fault. I give him what I can.'

'Curiously true,' Heindrick said. 'You are the only antique dealer who we could find who pays his barker fairly. Yet you live in squalor. And it gets worse. Your police record covers dozens of shady—'

'The police are biased.'

'Of course,' he said politely. 'But your record includes an alarming number of fights, thefts, disturbances, wholesale robberies, and several deaths.'

'Those were accidental.'

'Naturally. We know that most sincerely. Don't we, my dear?'

'Most sincerely, Kurt.'

You couldn't help looking from him to her. Sincerity

was very, very lacking.

Heindrick's voice hardened as he continued. 'It all adds up to a shady, penniless antique dealer scrounging a meagre living off any woman who wants ravishing by an unshaven shabby down-and-out crook.' He nodded with sadness. 'Oh yes, Lovejoy. You're worse than the rest of us. Much, much worse.'

The silence lasted a fortnight while I mopped my forehead with the sleeve of my good hand. The bare bones of Heindrick's tale were true, but I'm not as bad as that. And none of anything's really been my fault, not when you look at things honestly. Events get distorted in the telling. Everybody knows that.

Mrs Heindrick pressed my knee. 'It's a matter of record, Lovejoy.' The hypocritical bitch had the gall to sound sympathetic — most sincerely, of course. Irritably I pushed her hand away.

Kurt crossed to stand before me, a curiously threatening picture of affluence. 'On the other hand, Lovejoy, you're better than the rest of us.'

I cleared my throat. 'Better how? You've just proved the opposite.'

'Because you're a divvie, Lovejoy.'

I should have guessed. They knew all the bloody time.

'Divvie' or 'div' means different things to different people. To teenagers the word divvie means a numbskull, a stupid nerk. To a housewife it's a shopper's discounted dividend. But to antique dealers a divvie is somebody almost magical. I can't even explain it myself.

The nearest I can get is saying that something happens inside you when you come into the presence of a real antique. Maybe its love reaches out to touch you, that secret recognition each of us carries inside.

You ought to know first that most antique dealers, in addition to supreme and unadulterated ignorance, possess a blind spot for antiques. The tale of Sid Greenshaw will help to explain:

Sid is our local faker. He paints 'priceless' early English watercolour paintings. One day he was commissioned by a Paris gallery for ten copies of an eighteenth-century painting by an artist called Cozens. This sad genius isn't heard much of nowadays, but the mighty Constable, the immortal Turner and that bobby-dazzler Tom Girtin thought him the greatest genius 'that ever touched landscape'. And he very nearly was that good. Check for yourself — his stuff's in the galleries.

Anyhow, so far so good for Sid Greenshaw. Faithfully he set to work copying from an actual original which the Paris gallery thoughtfully sent over. Sid is painfully slow doing Cozens fakes because, right up to the moment that John Robert Cozens died insane, he used a strange monochrome underpainting technique as if painting in oils. It takes an inordinate length of time to fake a Cozens, not like a Samuel Palmer or a Constable, which have to be done at speed.

So Sid contentedly worked on between other jobs in his attic, leaving partially completed 'Cozens' for the monochrome underpaint to 'fix', as we say, and doing a cracking job on the phoney frames. He's a real craftsman is Sid, one we're really proud of along the estuaries of East Anglia. Anybody will tell you where he lives — and usually how he's getting along with his latest creation. He's no secret except to the poor buyers.

Well, the time came when, after months of skilled labour, Sid began to send off his fakes to Paris. (We ship them crated up as unsigned 'Reproductions', the signatures usually being done by specialist forgers on arrival.) Now this French lot decided to get Sid to do them because of his famed ability, which was a mistake because naturally, while the money was coming in, Sid did what every other forger does: he made a 'foreigner'—one fake just for himself. In time he dutifully sent off the ten fakes, plus the Cozens original, and sold his extra fake to a pal in Lavenham for a few quid. There was one slight snag: the stupid goon *had sold the original Cozens painting to his pal by mistake*. He'd sent eleven fakes to Paris.

It was a real laugh, especially for Sid's pal in Lavenham who made a fortune once the truth dawned. You can imagine. The Montmartre gallery did its nut because they now had eleven fakes instead of ten plus their priceless original. Sid's name was mud. He eventually bought off their heavy mob by giving them three years' free hard labour making fakes—under close supervision. That way, he kept his hands and feet. Which for such a daft mistake was a bonus.

I tell you this amusing story to explain what a divvie is. A divvie could never make a mistake like Sid had, because a genuine Cozens—a genuine *anything*—shrieks and clangs and hums like a chime of cathedral bells. A fake just hangs there, a splatter of paint on paper rimmed by strips of wood. A zero. A dud. No sound, no magic melodious clamour. The odd thing is that a divvie like me quivers with these mystic emanations just by being in the same room as a genuine antique. You hardly need bother to look. God knows how it works. Just as a water-diviner doesn't need actually to see the water before his twig writhes with the magic vibes of the subterranean river, so it is with me. Had Sid called me in, the siren song of the genuine Cozens would have been unmistakable. Needless to say, a divvie is worth his weight in gold—to anybody with enough money to buy genuine antiques, that is.

Like, it seemed, the Heindricks.

'Yes. I'm a divvie.'

They exhaled simultaneously, exchanging a glance. Kurak stirred. Quite honestly, that was the first time I felt

queasy in their presence, and was not pleased. Others call
it worry, but to me it's fear. Lena Heindrick was looking
at me with undisguised interest now. Kurt's attitude was
one of curious relief. I tried to suss out Kurak but by the
time my eyes swivelled he had arranged his expression
accordingly and revealed nothing. Where had I seen him
before?

'Then you are the one we . . . desire, Lovejoy.'

That ambiguous line from Lena. I said, 'Me? What
for?'

'A little trip. To find something old and valuable in the
ground.'

'Lena, my dear,' Kurt warned.

'Trip? Where to?'

'You will be told as soon as you are fit.' She smiled.
'Foreign, but you need no passport.'

'I'm going nowhere, luv.'

That smile moved its wet mouth and I heard, 'Then I'll
phone Detective-Sergeant Ledger and tell him you
blackmailed me into providing your alibi.'

'Blackmailed how?'

'I'll think of something, Lovejoy. A woman's always
believed when she makes an accusation concerning sex or
money.' We all paused, considering. Hardly a proposition
from Wittgenstein, but still food for thought.

She collected her gloves, saying, 'That will be all so far,
I think. Kurt?'

There was something curiously displeasing in the way
she had taken over. Kurt stood there exhaling smoke and
smiling most sincerely. She rose to go and we all moved
obediently. I knew from the way we were avoiding each
other's eyes that she knew my sudden hunger. The trouble
is, women always end up the boss. She pressed my arm,
smiling into the middle distance.

'Do get better soon, Lovejoy. We have *so* much to do.'
Kurt patted my good shoulder as he passed.

It was just then that the phone rang and everybody else froze. I jumped a mile. Kurt gave me the nod. I went to answer it, Kurak balefully letting me pass by twisting his gigantic torso.

'Wotcher, Lovejoy!' Tinker, phoning in the hubbub from some pub orgy, clearly delighted with himself and three parts sloshed as usual. 'I found Clarkie and Sam! They're in the A12 caff.'

'Good evening,' I said politely. 'Thank you for your enquiry.'

'Eh?'

'I'll try to arrange matters accordingly,' I said smoothly. Kurak loomed at my elbow to listen.

Tinker got all peeved at my apparent disinterest. 'You told me to find the bleeders, Lovejoy!'

'Excellent, sir,' I warbled. 'I'll attend to it.' Quickly I replaced the receiver. Kurt was behind me, suspicion creasing his brow.

'Who was that, Lovejoy?'

'Tinker Dill, ringing from the boozer.' I pushed past him back into my room. 'He's found an antique I was looking for.'

'Business as normal, then?' Kurt said pleasantly.

'Almost.'

Lena Heindrick gave a woman's careful riotous non-smile at my bitter reply, and cruised calmly past out of the cottage. Kurak smouldered his way to the Rolls, vibing pure hate in my direction. The end of a riotous party. Kurt strolled behind the wheel of the Bentley.

As the Rolls crunched away Lena Heindrick's window wound down.

'Make it soon, Lovejoy,' she said, still not looking directly at me. 'We're in a hurry.' Kurt just smiled.

I said nothing, watched them off and did not wave.

Then I tore back to the phone. Ted, the White Hart

barman, fished Tinker from the maelstrom of the taproom.

'Tinker? Lovejoy. Get me a lift, sharpish.'

'Here, Lovejoy,' he croaked tipsily, peeved. 'What were all that?'

'Never mind. Hurry. Try Helen or Maud or Margaret. Anybody but Patrick.' He would scream the house down at the first sign of aggro. 'I'm going to bend Clarkie and Sam.'

'Oh Gawd—'

I said, 'You heard,' and went to brew up while waiting, but my tea bags had been nicked. Bloody police. Nobody thieves like them. If it wasn't for them there wouldn't be all this crime about.

CHAPTER 5

It was getting dark by the time we reached the nosh bar on the A12 road. Clarkie's motor was among the cars and lorries, so we settled down in the car park for a long wait. Rain tapped on the roof and fugged the windows.

'Can't I go in for a pint, Lovejoy?' Tinker asked hopefully. He'd gone almost an hour without.

'No.'

'The boozers will be closed soon,' he grumbled.

'For heaven's sake, what are we *doing* here, Lovejoy? It's *pouring*.'

Janet Erskine had been the only lift Tinker could get me. Approaching her forties, she was even more scatterbrained than the rest of us antique dealers. She says she specializes in 'All kinds of antiques and things', which reveals all you need to know about her brain power. Be careful with Janet, though. Her ignorance of antiques is mindbending. Oddly enough, her good humour and her luck were a legend. I had often wondered if, beneath that frilly gear and blowsy exterior there didn't beat the soul of a secret divvie, but finally decided statistics were against that theory. She is always highly scented, very flouncy and feminine. I like her. We could have done worse. Her husband works in an ambulance depot somewhere in town, playing billiards and swilling tea.

'Waiting.'

'Frigging Clarkie's in there getting sloshed with Sam—'

'Tinker,' I said over my shoulder, 'give me your boot.'

'Eh?'

'Your boot.'

Mumbling indignantly, Tinker passed his old army boot over. I tilted to examine it in the light from the caff. It ponged to high heaven.

'What on *earth*!' Janet exclaimed.

I stopped her switching on the interior bulb to help, and chucked the boot behind me to Tinker. 'Cut the tongue out. And give me both your laces.'

Tinker knew better than ask daft questions like what for. 'I've only got one. But you can have me belt, Lovejoy.'

'What's going *on*, please!' Janet cried.

'I said laces, you stupid burke.'

'It's string.'

I nicked Janet's manicure set and made Tinker pierce four holes in the leather tongue with her nail scissors. Under my instruction he threaded the lace and the string through.

'You should be in bed, Lovejoy,' Janet accused, with the self-righteous anger of a woman fetched out in bad weather. 'You've only just left hospital.'

'Tie them in loops, Tinker.'

Cars and lorries came and went. We waited another sulky half-hour before the door flashed a slice of yellow light into the wet night and Clarkie and Sam showed. A third bloke with them turned to our right and went towards a big articulated lorry. It looked like Dickie Dirt, least reliable of our vannies, but in the darkness you couldn't be sure. Knowing Dickie, he would have some woman waiting snoozing in his cab. He never goes far without one.

'You want me wiv yer, Lovejoy?' Tinker's unconvincing quaver gave me a free grin.

'No. Stay here.'

Janet started up indignantly, 'But he has no *coat* . . . !' so I put the door gently to and floated through the rain among the saloons and road haulage wagons. The night air felt fresh after the boutique-riddled smog of Janet's car. I reached Clarkie's motor before they did, and stood in the shadow of a goods vehicle as the chatting villains approached.

The one good thing about East Anglia's countryside is its flint stone. Over the ages these decorative little round stones have provided temples for Rome, roads for the Early English, castles for the Normans, dazzlingly beautiful spired churches for the post-Conquest Christians, and sparks for the Brown Bess gunlocks of civilization's biggest — and last — empire. They are attractive and smooth, and come in sizes from giant cobbles to small pebbles. Best of all, they lie everywhere, in fields and lanes. Waiting for Tinker and Janet to arrive, I had collected a dozen walnut-sized flints. If there had been enough time, a couple of practice throws with my improvised sling would not have come amiss. A bit lopsided with only one good arm, I had to let them get almost too close before letting fly with my first shot. The stone caught Sam in the throat and he fell against a small Ford, choking.

Clarkie said, 'What the hell . . . ?'

I spat my next stone into the sling and held it against

my chest. The remaining ten stones were in my pocket on my good side.

'Only me, Clarkie.'

'Who's that?'

The poor goon was in oblique light from the caff while I was still in shadow. Sam looked in a hell of a state. For a minute I wondered if I'd done him some serious damage—after all, Goliath got done the same way—then suppressed the twinge. The sod had nearly killed me.

'Lovejoy!'

He yelped and backed away, leaving Sam to rot and trying to shield his eyes against the light. I whirled the sling and gave him the next stone in his midriff. He folded with a whoof and fell to his knees on the tarmac, groaning.

'Don't move, Clarkie.'

Loading the biggest stone I had, I stepped up to Sam and kicked him as insurance before carefully toeing his knife away under the Ford. He couldn't have been all that badly injured because he had been surreptitiously easing it into action, the pig.

'For Christ's *sake*, Lovejoy . . .'

I punted Sam again in his groin.

'Hands and knees,' I said into his scream. 'Both of you. Side by side.'

Most of the bigger trunk road cafés have a footbridge over the road, joining the two sections. I herded Sam and Clarkie through the teeming rain on their all fours on to the footbridge. Nobody could see us through the gloom—I hoped. They shuffled on all fours over the bridge. Occasional cars swept by underneath, putting a gruesome wash of light across the scene. I kicked them both hard occasionally to make sure they would be handicapped at least as much as me. Well, they had four arms to my one. Fair's fair.

'Whoa, lads,' I commanded, whirling my sling in what I hoped was a threatening manner. It went *whum-whum*. The world was beginning to oscillate unsteadily. I began to realize I hadn't eaten for some time. All this aggro was draining me, so I was pleased when Clarkie vomited from pain. I needn't worry so much if we were all ailing. Sam just lay there wheezing, clutching his groin.

'What do you want, Lovejoy?' Clarkie whispered. 'Honest, we meant no harm.'

'Clarkie.' I stepped closer, whirring my sling. 'You and this pillock nearly did for me. See this sling? If I let it go, it'll go through you like a dose of salts.'

They whimpered, scrabbling away from me along the footwalk while the cars swished wetly underneath. I edged after, still whumming my sling.

'I want you to do something, Clarkie.'

'Yes, yes, Lovejoy,' he babbled. 'Anything.'

'Throw Sam off the bridge. Now.'

'Christ!' Sam screeched. I punted him and he whooshed into silence.

'You can't . . .' Clarkie whispered.

'Or,' I said affably, 'he throws you off. When he recovers consciousness, that is. Be sharp.'

'Please, Lovejoy. For Christ's sake, it was all a mistake. I swear it.'

Whirring the sling was tiring me fast. 'Who made you rob the Fingringhoe church?'

'I don't . . . I can't . . .'

'Right.' I made a sinister show of being about to unleash the sling and Clarkie yelled up, 'I'll tell! I'll tell!'

'Who?'

'Joxer paid me. He set it up. He was there, signalled when we were to leave the Colchester road lay-by and pull the job.'

'Joxer? You telling the truth?' I didn't believe him.

'Honest, Lovejoy. Forty quid and he'd keep watch. He

had muscle, Lovejoy. A scarey great bleeder with him who said nowt. We didn't mean it, Lovejoy. Please.'

So there I was, torn between mercy and revenge. Sooner or later somebody has to chuck in the sponge on vengeance. Otherwise we're all at war for ever and ever, and life's nothing but one long holocaust. I thought angrily, why should that somebody be me?

'Right, Clarkie,' I said, and turned as if to go.

Next morning Janet woke me by rolling on to my sore arm. I shot into consciousness with a scream of pain and cursed, full of self-pity, while she rose blearily and brewed up.

I was still grousing when she came back with a tray, eggs and toast and bowls of those flaky bits with nuts for adding milk. The phone had rung while she was up but I refused to go and fiddled with my dud radio instead. She answered it.

I asked, 'Where did you get all this grub, love?'

'Called in at home taking Tinker back to town. Remember?'

'No.' I'd slept all the way, dozy as an angler's cat. 'I remember some stupid bird giving me a blanket bath before she let me rest. And feeding me some rotten broth.' With Janet's broth knocking about no wonder there's all this malnutrition.

'Broth's good for invalids.' We started breakfast in a peeved silence.

It was quite ten minutes before she told me it had been Ledger on the phone.

'Mmmh?' I asked innocently. 'How is he?'

'He wanted to know where you were last night.'

'Nosey sod.'

'I said you were resting here. Tinker and I were with you.'

'Great,' I said. 'I'll see your honesty is duly rewarded.'

Janet was slightly pale about the gills as she told me Ledger's bad news. Poor Clarkie and his partner Sam Veston appeared to have fallen from a footbridge on to the A12 near the Washbrook turn-off. Both were in hospital, with severe internal injuries. Poor Sam was very dicey. And, would you believe it, in the very same ward I'd just left, Sister Morrison's ward in the male surgical block.

'What a coincidence!' I exclaimed, meeting her stare with all the frankness and innocence of which I am capable, which is virtually unlimited. 'Fancy—'

'Lovejoy.' She gazed at me. 'When you went to talk to Clarkie and Sam, nothing happened, did it? I mean to say—'

I chuckled. At least I tried to, never knowing quite what chuckling sounds like. 'You mean, did I beat them up and throw them off the bridge?'

'Well, yes.'

'With one arm? Just out of hospital? And them two big tough men, armed with knives?' I went all noble and quiet. 'I see, Janet. So you believe like the rest, that anything bad around here is my fault, even when I'm obviously still weak—' If I'd been upright I would have put on a convincing limp.

She put her arms round me, nearly tipping the tray. 'No, darling. I'm sorry. It's my stupid imagination.'

'That's all right,' I said brokenly, being all forgiving. 'Is there any more egg?'

'Yes, darling.' She scrambled out of bed. 'Half a minute.'

I shouted after her, 'Love. Throw my robin some cheese, if there is any. It's tapping on the window. And when Tinker rings ask him to suss out Joxer Casey for me, sharpish.'

Janet's patch was warmer than mine so I edged across the divan to pinch it. My nineteenth-century walnut carriage clock showed a disgraceful ten o'clock. Another hour and the pubs would open, bringing Tinker staggering into the world again. One hour after that and I'd have Joxer by the throat.

Remembering Lena Heindrick's words, Ireland's the only place that could be described as 'foreign, but you don't need a passport'. And Irish Joxer's a boisterous Dun Laoghaire man who works in a shed near Priory Street in town. I felt quite perky. It was the first link I had.

The only trouble with confidence is that it never lasts. I was to learn this elementary lesson the hard way.

CHAPTER 6

Janet had to go at eleven-thirty. She made yet another breathless phone call home to explain her absence, drenched herself in gallons of scent from an array of misshapen bottles out of her handbag, and we hit the road just as the rain stopped. She dropped me near the old priory ruins in the town centre and gave me a couple of quid to be going on with.

'Eat, darling,' she commanded. 'See you tonight.' Smiling, I watched her go. She'd told me, 'I'll *have* to call in. We have this Ming celery vase on offer.' She meant celadon, not celery. Knowing Janet, it could be anything from the Portland Vase to a plant pot, though with her fantastic luck . . . She shares a stall with Sandra Mesham, a lovely girl. Sandra's pretty good at early Islamic ceramics and calligraphy, and did Arabic, Sanskrit and art at college. She has a lovely figure. Janet hates her.

Saturday morning turns any town centre into hell. With the crowds and the traffic I was too preoccupied to give Helen more than a passing wave. She's the only really breathtaker we've got among the dealers, and was beckoning me from Jason's window. Probably she wanted my say-so on that terracotta portrait bust of the Florentine Benivieni, supposedly a genuine article made about 1530 when the great philosopher was getting on for eighty. Tinker had told me the tale during one of his hospital visits, now Helen was keen to buy but uncertain. I knew what was worrying her — the world's greatest-ever terracotta faker, Giovanni Bastianini, had done brilliant fakes which went for fortunes in the 1860s. I'd sent a message to Helen through Tinker to buy the damn thing outright because, like the famous Billie and Charlie medallion forgeries, Bastianini fakes are now more famous than the originals. And, by that incomprehensible quirk of the public, often more pricey. Helen had obviously got cold feet and wanted me to divvie it for her.

Full of the comradeship for which antique dealers are famed, I quickly looked away from Helen's alluring beckon — not easy, this — and ducked into the alley between the music shop and the grocer's. In a dozen strides you leave the heaving street behind and enter a different world.

This is the amazing thing about these East Anglian market towns. Their main streets could be mistaken for part of the busiest city in the world. Step a few paces to one side, and you recede centuries.

The tranquil ruins of St Botolph's Priory are fairly immense as ruins go. They stand between the huge nineteenth-century brick reconstructed priory and the old churchyard. Several figures were standing among the gravestones talking. Others moved carefully about on the trimmed wet grass. I recognized most of the local dramatic society, including Marcia. Their next open-air production was due soon. They looked perished.

' 'Morning, Lovejoy.'

'Wotcher.'

'Want a part, handsome?'

There was a roar at Marcia's crack. I smiled weakly and edged past the rehearsal. She meant the time when I stood in to read three announcer lines to start a Melville skit and nearly fainted from fright. I'd been going out with Marcia at the time.

'Never again,' I said fervently.

'We stop in an hour, Lovejoy. Free lunch?'

'Don't trust you actresses. You'll give me a part again.' I tried to keep it light and made the path safely. Marcia was smiling far too brightly. A few of the others shuffled and looked at the grass as Jimmy Day the producer quickly took it up.

'Go again, people. Page thirty of your Fourth Folios . . .'

A relieved laugh broke the embarrassment and they went easily back into Big Bill's *The Winter's Tale*, saving Marcia from her brief lapse so I didn't mind Jimmy's dig at me.

Joxer's shed is a converted chicken coop, and is situated among the nettles and brambles which overgrow tall fencing rimming the churchyard. Some lone heroine was busy scraping lichens from a nearby headstone to record the inscription as I opened the creaky door.

'Top of the morning, Joxer.'

'Hello, Lovejoy.' He looked up from his workbench. 'Watch that bleeding draught.' He is our plate man, and was busy French-plating across a damaged Sheffield plate. He had the silver leaves still in block, thank God, or they would have gone everywhere at a breath, and his agate-stone burnisher all ready with the plastic comb and toothpicks handy on the shelf. He's a good workman, is Joxer, so it was all the more upsetting for him when I reached across and took hold of his bunsen fan-burner and ran it gently up his arm.

'Be careful, you frigging lunatic? You burned me!
What—'

He dropped everything and tumbled off his stool.

I leaned on his workbench. 'You never *do* get these
seams right, Joxer,' I lectured sadly. 'Genuine Sheffield
plate has seams. Electroplated stuff is uniformly coated
pure silver. How many times do I have to tell you to follow
the seams when you do *cuivre argenté?*'

'What's up, Lovejoy?' He was scared, which was fine by
me, because I was in a temper.

'People say French plating's only good enough to repair
Sheffield plate worn down to the copper, Joxer.' I snuffed
the bunsen and slung a hammer into the plank wall
beside his head. He yelped and jumped. 'About a certain
church at Fingringhoe, Joxer.'

He licked his lips, looking at the door. 'What about it,
Lovejoy?'

'Poor Clarkie and poor Sam. Make sure you send
flowers.'

His shoulders sagged in surrender. He's not daft. 'I
knowed it was you did them over, Lovejoy. Only you
could be that cruel.'

'*Me?*' I'm honestly astonished by this kind of
accusation. No other antique dealer contributes to the
Lifeboats Appeal like I do. And it's always other people
force me into violence. If only everybody would leave me
alone I'd be an angel.

'Yes, you.' He righted the stool and lit a rolled fag. 'I
told them to look for somebody else, only they were
hooked on this Kilfinney thing.' He gave a wry wink at
me. 'A Dun Laoghaire man helping those Limerick
people's a terrible thing, Lovejoy.'

'Really?' I said politely. For me these places might as
well be on Saturn.

'It was a woman and a man. Rich, Rolls motor, the lot.
She's boss, I think. Called him Kurt, talked like Froggies

in some language to each other. Hardly any accent.' He blew smoke. 'It had to be Fingringhoe, that church, that day, that hour. They wouldn't say why. I'm no cloth-job man. You know that, Lovejoy. Clarkie jumped at it for forty quid.'

Which sounded like the Heindricks all right. The top silver leaf lifted gently on the bench beside me, which meant that somebody with the strength to lift the creaky door into silence as it opened was coming in behind me. I saw Joxer hide a smile in his glance at me, and smiled openly back, which meant he knew I knew he knew about that somebody.

'Wotcher, Kurak,' I said without turning round. 'You touch me and so help me I'll do the opposite of what you want. Otherwise, I'll come quietly.'

'He means it, sor,' Joxer said quietly towards the door.

The door groaned as the giant bloke let it go. 'Then come,' he growled.

'Say please,' I said, still not looking. My spine felt crinkled.

After a silence, 'Please,' landed across my shoulder like a cross.

'Certainly,' I said. 'Cheers, Joxer.'

I was to remember what happened next for a long, long time.

Suddenly Joxer said, 'Lovejoy. Can't you watch a minute with me?' He'd gone quite pale, as if realizing something horrible.

'No,' I told him. I was in enough trouble, and he'd done me no favours. His expression was abruptly that of a man looking at the end of the world.

'Cheers, boyo,' Joxer said. His voice was fatalistic but quite level.

If I were not so thick I'd have expected trouble of the very worst kind. But I *am* so thick. So cheerfully I walked with Kurak up to the street, waved to Marcia among

Jimmy Day's acting crowd, and was driven off in grand style.

That's how wars begin, by not thinking. My kind, that is.

CHAPTER 7

The Heindricks' house was even more imposing than their motors. It stood overlooking the Blackwater estuary. The gardens had that scrubbed look which only a battalion of dedicated gardeners can give, and the drawing-room where we sat had that radiance which unlimited wealth imparts.

'You travel in four days, Lovejoy.' Kurt could have been one of his own antiques, he was that polished. He was clearly monarch of all he surveyed, and possibly of everything else as well. Standing before his log fire and issuing directives, he caused a weary sinking feeling in my belly. All my life these bloody people have been giving me orders with complete disregard of the consequences — for me.

'Will I?' I said sourly.

'You will.' He smiled with benevolence. 'Mrs Heindrick will meet you at the destination.'

His missus clapped her hands — and I do mean actually clapped them, as they once did for slaves. Instantly a rather surly bird appeared with a tray of those small cakes. She had already done one circuit but I'd had all the savouries. I was still famished and tried to be casual reaching for the fresh plate. God knows who invented manners. Whoever it was had never felt hunger, that's for sure. It's desperately hard taking less than you want in other people's posh mansion houses — and everybody, honest and dishonest, knows that's the truth.

'The terms will be excellent, Lovejoy,' Lena said. She had spotted my glance at the retreating bird's shape, which is typical of women's sly behaviour, but I was only interested because I'd never seen another slave before. Mrs Heindrick's lips thinned with displeasure. She must have detected the same kind of lust when I glanced at the oil painting, but she wasn't as narked at that. 'Beautiful, isn't it?' she said. 'It's—'

'A copy.' I wasn't really glad, but it was one in their eye. The pair of them exchanged significant looks.

'But laboratory tests show it to be an original early eighteenth-century oil of a seafarer, Lovejoy.' That from connoisseur Kurt, whose untold wealth had always gained perfect grovelling agreement to any banal utterance he chose to make. Until now.

'Oh, John Tradescant was a seafarer all right.' I rose, touched the oil's surface reverently and found myself smiling as the warmth vibrated in my fingers. 'And it's old. But a famous building off Trafalgar Square'll be very cross if you go about telling fibs, mate. *They've* got the original.'

'John who?'

I was enjoying myself. 'Tradescant only sailed about to nick seeds, bulbs, plants, anything that grew. His dad was as bad. He even raided the Mediterranean pirates to get a bush or two. Between them they introduced a load of stuff—apricots, Persian lilac, Michaelmas daisies, the larch. They did Russia, the American colonies, North Africa. Tradescant's collection became the Ashmolean at Oxford.' The old copyist had got Tradescant's wryly wicked smile just right, but the date of 1612 was a shade earlyish.

'A *copy*?' Lena Heindrick spat out a vulgar curse, which made me blink.

'Don't knock copyists. Turner himself started out as one.' It's a daft joke we play on ourselves, really. Find a genuine flower painting by Palice and it's not worth a fiftieth of the price of a Turner copy. 'Copy and original are linked by greed, Mrs Heindrick.'

'Don't be so bitter, Lovejoy.' She was smiling again and the thought crossed my mind that she had only been goading me. 'Let's get back to that subject, then, shall we? Money.'

'A good daily rate, all expenses paid, and a share of the profits.'

I weakened at the thought of money—which meant antiques and food, in that order. 'Four days? Why so soon? You said I could get better first.'

'Because if you stay here you will be in even more trouble.' Kurt exposed his pearly teeth. I just couldn't imagine him ever growing stubble. The hair follicles just wouldn't dare.

'I'm not in any trouble.'

'Oh, but you are. Detective-Sergeant Ledger's phone call to your . . . consort Janet this morning was quite explicit.'

The mansion was plushily furnished with a skilled admix of antiques old and new. I couldn't help feeling sad, having been at the original auction some years ago. The old East Anglian manorial family had sat there in pained dignity while us dealers and auctioneers had robbed and fiddled them blind. Here's a free lesson: promise me you'll never, never, *never* sell up by means of an in-house on-site auction. This or any other doorstep selling is ruinously wrong. You might as well just throw the stuff outside to the rag-and-bone man. At least he'll give you an honest donkey stone for it. A shoal of antique dealers and auctioneers won't.

'More blackmail?'

'Yes.' He smiled and decanted sherry—the Kurts of this world do not simply pour—while Lena pressed the cakes on me. She was watching me nosh with a kind of appalled awe, but it was all right for her. Women don't get hungry, only peckish. 'It has become a matter of urgency. If you will go about throwing people off footbridges and talking to the careless Joxer . . .'

'Have you had me followed?' There was even a peacock on the lawn, radiantly displaying its fan. Lena Heindrick saw me looking and smiled.

'Of course.'

'Okay. Where do I go?'

'You'll find out when you arrive.'

'Why can't whatever's there be fetched here for me to suss out?'

'Why do you suppose it's only *one* thing, Lovejoy?'

'Mrs Heindrick hinted,' I said, wondering if that was true.

'Very lax of us all, my dear,' Kurt said without admonition. 'But especially Joxer.'

Lena shrugged, an attractive business. She had dressed for the interview in a neat black dress with only a late Georgian alexandrite brooch for ornamentation. Plain matching belts go in and out of fashion, but she wore one, the right touch of disdain towards those birds who need to conform to prevailing styles. I could have eaten her. Kurt was as clinical as ever, stencilled in a Savile Row jacket and city trousers. It was as Joxer said. Clearly she was in control, Kurt the mere business end of the team.

'You will be given your ticket and an allowance on the journey, Lovejoy.' Kurt came near to cracking a joke by adding, 'Performing our task will keep you out of mischief, no?'

'Only possibly, Kurt,' Lena smiled.

Kurt chuckled at that, his flabby jowl undulating. I watched, fascinated. Why didn't his starched collar sever his jugular? But I got the joke. 'Only possibly' meant a rip, a scam, a lift, something illegal anyway. *And I knew it was in Kilfinney*, wherever that was. My one concealed trump card.

Then Lena shook me by catching my hand as I reached the nth time for the proffered plate. It had one cake left, but that was Lena's fault. Posh cakes are only little and don't fill you.

She said, 'One thing, Lovejoy. Sister Morrison?'

'You mean outpatients?' It was a good thought. That sombre-eyed lass would go berserk if I failed to make the appointment.

'No. Your relationship with her.'

'Nothing I can do about that. It wasn't my fault she ballocked me most of the time. Why?'

She smiled then and let me reach the grub. 'Only that she has called twice at your cottage.'

'She did?' I said blankly. 'Probably to confirm my clinic appointment, something like that.'

Kurt interposed, on cue. 'The fewer encumbrances the better, Lovejoy, while you're working for us.'

I stood then but kept my temper out of respect for the delectable antiques all around. Nobody tells me who can call at my cottage and who not.

'Who says I'm working for you?'

Kurt chuckled. Lena looked me up and down with amused insolence. 'Me,' she said softly. 'Kurak will call for you at midnight, four days from now.'

'Not me, mate,' I told her, and left.

They saw me crunch down the avenued drive. Kurt must have given some signal because Kurak stayed leaning against the Rolls and watched me go.

I got a lift from a school football bus, coming back from a match. They'd lost six-nil. If I'd half the sense I was born with I'd have recognized the omen, but not this numbskull. Within seconds of being dropped on North Hill I was in the Marquis of Granby pub phoning the hospital to bleep Sister Morrison and claiming it was an emergency.

CHAPTER 8

Sister Morrison was not keen on coming off duty straight into a pub so we met by the post office. She came driving up in grand style, and I darted across the pavement once I was sure she was the woman at the wheel. The town's traffic always builds up a little in the early evening but she coped calmly. All that surgical training, I supposed. She didn't even tut as the rain started again before we made the road out to my village.

'Did I get you in trouble, Sister?'

'I was just coming off duty anyway.'

It had been an awkward phone conversation nevertheless, with me stuttering that I was only phoning to check my next appointment and her saying it was all right and she would explain the details while giving me a lift. I looked at her as she drove, profile in repose and coat collar turned up to catch the tendrils of hair as they came beneath her knitted hat.

'Sorry I wasn't in, erm, when you called.'

'That's all right. I only called on the offchance.'

That couldn't be true. She must have got my address from the records and actually asked the way to my cottage once she reached the village. We have no real road signs, and numbers are unknown. Some offchance.

She was making me nervous. I'm not used to serenity, never having experienced that condition myself.

'Which part of Ireland are you from, Sister?'

'Sinead.' Only she almost pronounced it Shin-neighed.

'Where's that?'

She fell about laughing, with momentary difficulty controlling the wheel. 'Stupid man. It's my name. I mean stop calling me Sister. You're not in hospital any more.'

'Gaelic?'

'Ten out of ten.'

'I've always wanted to visit Dublin. A bookseller-printer there owes me.'

'Don't go scrapping till your arm's mended.'

There's nothing you can do when a woman's got the upper hand, especially when that woman has washed your bum twice a day lately. I fell silent. Sisters clearly had more ways of shutting you up than mere nurses. She must have felt concerned because she resumed, 'In the west of Ireland we have traditional names. It's only recently easterners have moved into the market.'

She shot a glance at me and changed up for the long pull on the hill above the brook which marks our town boundary. Beam lights of an oncoming car lit her face and brought my reflection into the windscreen. Our reflected gazes met.

'Erm, we'll go to the White Hart, if that's okay.'

'Me in my old coat?'

Nursing staff aren't allowed in public houses wearing uniform. I knew that. Sinead had on a navy blue topcoat. I can't see these things matter much, but women find disadvantage in practically anything.

'Bear right at the fork.' My cottage had been abused enough lately by visitors. Anyway, as we ran together through the rain into the tavern porch I thought she looked bonny.

The pub crowd naturally gave her a cautious scan, when we pushed in, all except Patrick who let out a shrill whoop and trilled a roguish yoohoo. The usual weird mixture of dealers and barkers were busily slurping booze, pretending the antiques game was going just perfect. Tinker saw us and reeled across, ponging to high heaven and filthy as ever, greeting Sister Morrison with such familiarity everybody stared. He showed every sign of joining us till I gave him the bent eye and a quid.

'I thought we wuz broke, Lovejoy,' the stupid old soak croaked.

'Er, my reserve.'

'Mr Dill.' Sinead had her handbag open as we crammed into the nook furthest from the fire. 'Lovejoy can't carry the glasses. His arm. Would you please oblige?'

Tinker scarpered to the bar with her money while I tried to recover my poise, and still I went red. The hubbub battered our ears. Sister Morrison saw me sussing out the crowded, smoke-filled bar and leaned forward, her eyes glowing with interest.

'Who are they all? Everybody knows you.'

A faint scent wafted the smoke aside for an instant. 'Well. Yon, er, eccentric bloke with the silver gloves and red bolero's Patrick. He's a dealer, not as daft as he pretends.'

'And his lady-friend?'

'Lily. She's married, but loves Patrick. She deals in William IV furniture, when Patrick leaves her the odd farthing for herself.'

That set me off chatting about them all. The elegant Helen, raising her eyebrows at the sight of me bringing in a class bird. Old bowler-hatted Alfred, the Regency prints and mezzotint man, battling with his moustache to get to his pint ('His wife's too fierce for him ever to go home,' I explained). Brad the cheerful extrovert flintlock weapon specialist. Big Frank from Suffolk, currently half way through his second pint, his fifth wife and the latest Sotheby's silver catalogue. Poor Denny Havershall, desperately trying to sell a Cotman forgery to the morose Wilkie from Witham — hard going, because Wilkie had faked it in the first place. And Denny's wife Beth had just produced her second little girl last week. Then there was the blonde Marion (mostly Roman pottery and early Islam ware) suggesting to the wealthier

Jason from East Hill that they make a go of a partnership. Tarantulas make similar arrangements.

'He's a cold fish,' Sinead observed.

Which surprised me, so I had another look. Marion was working her eyes and cleavage overtime, ignoring the table's beer puddles despite her splendid Aran woollie. Jason's ex-army, and our one inherently wealthy dealer. He has a big place overlooking the Blackwater estuary. Telling Sinead that reminded me of the Heindricks, which reminded me of the spot that I was in, which reminded me I needed to know why Sinead had been seeking me.

Tinker came with the drinks, all agog with urgency. The goon had brought Sinead a pint as well, but in a handle-mug, this being his idea of gentility.

'Here, Lovejoy. The Old Bill's out for you.'

'George?' He's our village bobby. Whatever it was, I'd manage him.

'No. Ledger. But no paper.'

Thankfully, I nodded relief at this news that Ledger held no arrest warrant. 'Ta, Tinker.'

'And Harry's bought that collection of pot tennis balls from Dragonsdale.'

'Hell fire,' I cursed. Harry has a stall in the town antiques Arcade. I'd been hoping for them, a genuine mahogany-cased set of four.

'Pottery? But that's impossible.'

'He means carpet bowls,' I explained as Tinker dived back towards the bar. 'Queen Victoria's favourite indoor game. They fetch about fifteen quid apiece, but a cased set's damned hard to find. A full set is three lots of four, with a little white "jack" the size of a golf ball. You play like lawn bowls.'

'You're upset,' she interrupted in wonderment. 'Over a pottery ball?'

'They're very rare now, especially in mint condition.

These had a luscious blue circle-and-petal design.'

'You should buy things when you see them,' she was preaching, when my red face beaconed through to her and she dried. 'Sorry, Lovejoy. Are you really broke?'

'It's being in your lousy hospital,' I groused. 'I missed all sorts of chances.' Discomfiture gave me the courage to ask outright what was burning in my mind. 'Look. Why did you come to the cottage?'

'Not here,' she said quickly.

I drew breath to say why the hell not when our little party ended.

Marcia ruined everything by coming to aghast us all. She rushed in excited and dishevelled, choking on the news that there had been a fire. Joxer's work shed in the Priory ruins had burned down after a small explosion had occurred. People were saying it was one of Joxer's gas bottles, that kind of thing. Some of the amateur dramatics men in the Priory parish hall, painting new sets in a desperate race to meet their dress-rehearsal deadline, heard the sound and rushed out to investigate. They made heroic attempts to beat the flames down, but without much hope. Then the fire brigade had arrived and had a go. The Priory ruins were, well, ruined anyway and the new church hall was safe, so what? Marcia had looked everywhere for Joxer to tell him, but he was nowhere around.

Nobody seemed to have been hurt. Sinead relaxed at that. It was probably her nursing instinct which made her so tense at Marcia's babbled news. Talk resumed. We all made clucking noises and some kind soul gave her a port-and-lemon. Then we all forgot it. Except me.

I sat for a long time looking at the table as the taproom babble went on and on, over and over Marcia's account. Patrick dramatically fainted, with Lily, his accolyte, frantically trying to bring him round with smelling-salts from his mauve handbag. After a long time I realized –

Sinead had taken my hand. I wasn't scared, not really scared, but a hint is a hint is a hint. All Heindrick had said was, 'Very lax of us all,' and poor Joxer gets his old shed blammed. I could only think of my grotty little cottage. It looked like the Heindricks had a divvie after all.

Sinead shook me gently.

'Are you all right, Lovejoy?' she was asking, and I came to. Her grey-blue eyes were anxious. I looked into them, thinking, well, all living is risk, isn't it?

'Yes, fine, thanks,' I said. 'Look, Shinny. About Ireland . . .'

CHAPTER 9

Things went from bad to evil that night. It seemed to end on an increasingly worse note every few minutes. First, Sister Morrison dropped me off outside my cottage about an hour afterwards. We talked in her car, mainly about Mrs Heindrick, even though I was dog-tired.

'That's what I wanted to tell you, Lovejoy. She's up to no good. She's been on the phone asking about your condition.'

That narked me. 'She could have asked me.'

'Don't worry. I disclosed nothing, and the doctors won't.'

One thing struck me. 'Why were you reluctant to tell me this in the tavern?'

'That cold fish.'

'Jason?'

'Yes. Mrs Heindrick's friend.'

Again that disturbing chill touched my neck. 'Friend? Are you sure?'

'I saw them both leaving my cousin's place together the

day after you were discharged from my ward.'

'Cousin? Er . . .'

'Joe. Joe Casey. He's like you, an antique dealer.'

Odd, that. I'd always thought I knew everybody in East Anglia. Now there were all these unexpected cousins and friends of friends. Worse, friends of enemies.

Sinead went on, 'Joe doesn't trust her, that's for sure. He did a few small jobs for the Heindricks. They were so bitchy about his work, checked every little detail.'

Well, if they were paying a workman they would naturally want good value. But I was thinking, Casey? Joe Casey? The name sounded oddly familiar.

'Recently?'

'Yes. Now. He even had to start work for them twice when it was dark. I ask you. He told me about it and we had a good laugh.'

And *still* it seemed unimportant, though I was to learn different before the night was through. I said thanks for the warning, and we made our rather stilted goodnights. Puzzled, I watched the red tail-lights flicker as she drove off along the hedged lane. Too many problems and too knackered a brain to cope for the minute, so I went in thinking it was time I had a quiet night. Things would seem clearer in the dawn.

He came for me about two, keeping on knocking even though I was yelling I was coming, for heaven's sake. There were headlights outside from a car reversing to face the lane slope.

'Who is it?' I called, pulling the bolt.

'Police.'

'Come off it, George.' I peered blearily into the gloom. Our village bobby stood there, at least as embarrassed as I was. 'You're not proper police.'

He drew himself up at that insult. 'You're to help us with our enquiries, Lovejoy. Get dressed.'

'I've just come out of dock, George. How the hell could I have pinched, forged or stolen any antiques? And you've Mrs Heindrick's alibi for that cloth job.'

'Murder investigation,' he said.

That shook me. 'Eh?'

'Get him out here,' another copper called wearily from the car, stationary now. 'Ledger'll be going, berserk.'

George wouldn't say any more so I dressed awkwardly and was whisked in town by a dozily irritable constable in a posh police saloon. So many things about the whole business had bewildered me that it was only one more mind-duller when the motor cruised the wrong way down Priory Street and pulled up at the narrow iron gate leading to the ruins. The bobby parked illegally and led me through the old graveyard with the aid of his torch. Ever been in that state of mind where you can fully understand everything that's going on, yet you know you're not really taking any of it in or even believing what you see with your very eyes? Well, that was me when up ahead through the spectral yew trees we heard voices and caught sight of the great ruined arches washed by shifting torchlights. I *knew*, but didn't gather quite what everybody was on about.

'This way, sir. Mind your head.'

The lights blended into a brilliant glow as we came into the main flooring opposite the sanctuary area. A generator whirred, steadied, and floodlights hit from three directions. I'd never seen so many of the Old Bill not in a procession. Ledger was talking with two other plainclothes blokes and jerked his chin at me to follow among the mounds and gravestones.

'You took your time, Smethurst,' he grumbled to the constable.

'My fault,' I said, more to nark Ledger than from pleasantry.

'Know what, Derby? Every bloody thing's Lovejoy's

fault. Torch.' One of his tame nerks snickered, and beamed his flash. Ledger led us through the nettles towards another island of floodlight where Joxer's shed had once stood. Now the scene was a shambles of charred bricks and stench. An angry uniformed copper approached. He was covered in ash. Sweat glistened on his stained face.

'Sir. These fire-johnnies are buggering us about.'

'Stop them, Lynley.'

A yellow-helmeted fireman came up, sweatier and even angrier. The six others at the scene wore white helmets. Presumably he was the gaffer.

'Sergeant Ledger! My duty is to excavate and neutralize all fire—'

Ledger spat on an innocent floodlit nettle. 'Your duty is to make it safe here for my men.'

'Then that means—'

'Standing by until we tell you.'

The furious fireman tried to overbear but Ledger wouldn't give way, and stepped down to where Joxer's floor once was. I had difficulty seeing even where the bench had been. Ledger scuffed the debris and balanced on a piece of corrugated metal, part of Joxer's fallen roofing. Ash clouded in the beams up to our knees. The white glare and the abruptly stencilled shadows made it a mad lunar picture.

'Tell him, Derby.'

Derby intoned, 'Antique dealer and fabricator known locally as Joxer, height—'

'Yeah, yeah.'

Derby shrugged, skipped some. 'Found dead in his burning workshop. Cause of death yet to be reported, but—'

'Skull fracture,' Ledger cut in. 'Our quack says it *might* have been falling brick.'

Joxer was dead. So somebody had been hurt in the fire

after all. I remembered Sinead's sudden tension at Marcia's news.

'Might means might not, Ledger.'

'True, Lovejoy.' He kept balancing on the debris, hands in his pockets, looking at me. 'You accuse Clarke and Sam, and they inexplicably leap off a motorway bridge. You visit Joxer, and he gets stove in and stoved.'

'And you're arresting me for coincidences?'

'Don't be silly, Lovejoy. Last time that rich tart unhooked you. Same thing'd happen.'

'Would it?'

'Lovejoy.' He came and stood by me. If I didn't know better I'd have said he was feeling sad. 'You're in something deep with that pair of crooks—'

'Which pair, exactly?' Things were stupifying me.

'The Heindricks. And I want you to know something.' Derby was standing close by. 'This old town of ours saw the Roman Empire out, saw the back of the Saxons, Normans, and withstood the Black Death. It's going to survive the Heindricks. Understood?'

'Yes.'

'Even if the Heindricks team up with a wriggler like you, Lovejoy.'

'Okay. But what do you think happened to Joxer?'

'I believe the Heindricks—or you on their orders— foully murdered Joxer and tried to burn his corpse.'

'What makes you think—?'

Ledger lost patience. 'Piss off, Lovejoy. Sign him out, Derby.'

Derby produced a clipboard and asked me to sign a form stating I had been interviewed at the site of a crime or accident. He gave me a pen. I started to sign, then tilted the board to catch that garish light and read it several times till Ledger asked what was up.

'Ledger, who's Joseph Xavier Casey?'

'Joxer. His real name.'

A piece of gnarled twisted iron the size of a small horseshoe lifted from the ash as I moved my foot. Burning anything gives off a terrible stink. My breath was slow coming, but the sound it made caused Ledger to look harder. I signed his stupid form quickly, thinking of Sinead's cousin Joe Casey who did clever special nocturnal work for the Heindricks. I'd been so wrapped up in my own plight I hadn't even thought. Sinead had told me about her cousin Joe Casey soon after we heard Marcia's news in the pub. She must have thought I'd realized they were one and the same person.

'May I have a lift home now?'

His hesitation made me mad, but I maintained my sorrowful visage. He's a cyncial sod. Not one ounce of trust.

'Lovejoy. If I once find you —'

'I don't feel so good.'

He agreed, with yet more mistrust, which was how I thankfully found myself in Constable Smethurst's car bombing back to my cottage. Near the brewery I conned a coin from the lad to ring my doctor urgently, or so I told him. Anyway he could afford it. The Old Bill pay themselves enough. I tried the hospital, saying it was an urgent message for Sister Morrison. The beleaguered Night Sister frostily told me that personal calls were forbidden on internal lines, and anyway Sister Morrison didn't live in the nurses' home. That was the end of my day. About three-thirty I waved so-long to the copper and went indoors, not even a respectable failure.

The rest of that night was a bad one for me. The trouble is, when you are so utterly tired it sometimes works the opposite way and you can't drop off no matter how hard you try. I'm one of these people who never cares whether I sleep or not, which is okay as long as you aren't grieving. And I was.

My divan bed unfolds in my cottage living-room. I've

no upstairs, except for a crummy bat-riddled space under the thatch, which you climb into like Tarzan of the Apes. I hate those ceiling lights which always dangle glare in your eyes, so my two electrics are controllable table things. Tonight, though, I was in a familiar morose mood and fetched out my old brass oil lamp to shed a more human glow on the interior. Then I drew the curtains and lay in bed, thinking of Joxer and the state I was in.

Folk come and go in your mind at the best of times, always in and out of your life. Because of all this movement, it's a sad mistake to try to keep things just as they are, though God knows enough people desperately keep on struggling to. Okay. That's life, and I have sense to accept it. But Joxer had been killed, and I wasn't going to accept that one little bit.

The Heindricks wanted a divvie — me. They'd given me four days to recover. Then they were sending me somewhere, a place overseas where I wouldn't need a passport. Lena Heindrick had said that. And Joxer had said Kilfinney. As a warning, as a tip-off? I'd never know now he was dead, but you don't need a passport to Eire and Joxer was Irish and Kilfinney sounded vaguely that way on . . .

To my astonishment I woke with my robin tapping like hell on the window, greedy little swine. I'd slept into daylight, which was just as well. I was in a hurry.

Four days' start on the Heindricks.

Just a word here about antiques, because nowadays there's more villainy over antiques than oil, sex, and foreign currency put together. And antiques are my only skill.

There's the legit kind — honestly made way back in history (or 50-plus years ago, if you choose to believe the recent British Customs and Excise ruling) and honestly bought and sold, with dated receipts and all. Then there's the phoney, usually a forgery made with ignorance and clumsiness and instantly detectable at a range of miles in a London peasouper. Then there's the 'tom', which once meant newly nicked jewellery of any kind but now means anything precious but stolen. Naturally, we lowlifes use the term to include antiques because antiques are the most common items of burglary nowadays. Which brings me round to the subject of *your* own valuables, and the noble art of stealing. If you own anything old, learn this next bit by heart.

Once upon a time, valuables were stolen by stealth. Skilled burglars did Murph-the-Surf scams à la Topkapi. You know the scene: teams of ex-service SAS types dangled from ropes or did the hang-glider bit between skyscrapers. You remember the screaming newspaper headlines and the Hollywood films that followed. Well, all that excitement was great while it lasted — thrills, spills, and the sequelæ of the Great Train Robbery meant good news copy, became a real industry in fact. Not any more. Things are different now. Times are modern. Above all, times are *new*. And the newest thing of all nowadays isn't bad manners, idle teenagers, or hysterical marching on Parliament. The newest thing now is theft, plain old simple stealing, by sleight-of-hand. And you don't use a team or a league or a twilight army. You do it on your tod, on your little own. And usually you get away scot free.

Think back over the latest rips. Notice anything special? They were casual and quiet. No, the main feature of modern robbery is it's a walk-in. In other words, the thief is legit and law-abiding *until the rip's pulled*. Don't believe me? Then you just keep an eye on the papers for a month or so (preferably July or August, peak months for nicking antiques). The famous Van Dyck portrait of Queen Henrietta Maria wasn't ripped from Nostell Priory by helicopter squads with flamethrowers and gasbombs. Somebody paid a quid admission fee, cool as you please, and sussed the place out first. And he had time to nick nine other paintings and four precious miniatures as well.

You'll notice something else while you're thinking about it. Antiques aren't merely ripped from private mansions. I mean, I sometimes think I'm the only bloke on earth who hasn't nicked Rembrandt's 1632 portrait of Jacob de Gheyn III from the Dulwich Picture Gallery in London. (It's small and painted on wood rather than canvas, so that helps.) It gets lifted regular as clockwork, and the last two times were walk-ins through the guarded entrance in broad daylight. One bloke simply popped the Rembrandt in a plastic shopping bag and pedalled off on his bloody bicycle. I ask you.

See what I mean? No banzai-parachute-grenade-Jaguar-jet-to-Morocco jobs nowadays. Museums and art galleries expect those. It's the 'oncer', as antique dealers call it, the legitimate art-lover who strolls in, and strolls out. And anybody can stroll, right? The big question stuck in my mind. Now that it's easy as all that, what the hell did they need a divvie for? And Kurak crisped old Joxer for being too chatty about their little enterprise, so it wasn't a simple walk-in. And it wasn't going to be any easy cloth job, either.

CHAPTER 10

Sunshine slammed into the cottage as soon as I pulled the curtain back. I'm not keen on a lot of fine weather, though birds seem to brighten up in it. Needless to say, my horde of garden scroungers were glaring in at me. Shakily I diced a grotty piece of cheddar and went outside to sprinkle it on the decorative little half-completed wall near by backdoor. I'll finish it when I get a minute. The blue tits have to manage with nuts in a net string on the apple tree but the robin's daft on cheese. Ten minutes later I had made myself more or less presentable and was entering Lyn's little garden down the lane carrying my egg wheel. The back door was open.

'Am I allowed?'

'Lovejoy!' She was at the table with her twins. They let out a shriek and hurrayed me into the kitchen. They were having breakfast, so I'd guessed right. 'Come and sit *down*! Just *look* at you, with your arm all *bandaged*! We heard such *awful* things about you, in the paper and *every*thing!' Lyn gave me a quick buss, and the girls sploshed milky lips on my cheek. Lyn and me had been quite close before she went and married a decent, reliable wage-earner. Which only goes to show you can't really depend on women. It was honestly coincidence which brought Lyn and her family into the same lane as me. Honestly.

She bustled about to get coffee, all pretty and pastel colours and yapping platitudes like they do. It was quite a hero's welcome. I was quite moved. It could easily have been the sailor's elbow even though I sometimes baby-sat for Lyn and David.

Little Rebecca asked, 'Did you have your dinner in prison, Lovejoy?'

'Shush, Becky!' Lyn reddened and said could I stay for breakfast because it was only eight o'clock and she was just going to do some for herself.

'Er, thanks, love.'

Alison, Rebecca's twin, was painstakingly dipping egg soldiers. She confided to me in a whisper, 'We haven't to say you're in prison, Lovejoy. Not to *anyone*.'

'Shush, Lally!'

'It's true!' Alison retorted. 'Daddy said!'

Rebecca joined in. 'We've to tell everybody you're

staying at your Auntie Lydia's.'

'Just listen to the pair of you little sillies!' Lyn's face was scarlet with embarrassment. She skated toast on to a plate for me but avoided my eye. I hadn't realized everybody down our lane knew about Lydia, my one-time learner assistant. She was not quite my auntie. Which accounted for Lyn's moods lately. Hey ho.

Alison had five egged soldiers now. With the deliberate actions of a child deciding to feed someone else, she directed one into my mouth, frowning with concentration. Rebecca was undeterred.

'Daddy said—'

'Becky! Eat your breakfast!'

'Daddy said you didn't really steal the church's kettle,' Becky explained.

Allies in unexpected quarters always warm your heart. I smiled at the kettle bit. 'Tell him ta.'

'Daddy said *you'd* not have got caught, Lovejoy.'

'Becky! One more word out of you!' Lyn cracked an egg on the edge of the pan. Women do that great. I've tried it but the shell always clings tight at the rim and the egg slides on to the floor.

Alison took up the refrain. 'Mummy said—'

'Both of you! Not another word!' Lyn dithered furiously between the stove and the table, threatening with a spoon. 'Absolute silence until you get down, or no playschool! Do you hear?'

The twins' faces turned mutinous but it must have been some threat because they went quiet. On my last baby-sitting visit they hadn't been speaking, some ferocious dispute over who had the right to move Lally's pot pig from its place on the windowsill. Lally had on her hooped red hairband, only plastic or something. I resolved to try to find her an antique one of woven glass—blue and white plaited, soft and pliable as silk. They are expensive, but one might turn up as a 'balancer', as we call the small antiques thrown in to make up a price. The shape of Lally's hairband made me think of something vitally important, but it escaped my consciousness as Lyn asked, not looking, how I was managing.

While she got the grub I told her all about my arrest, but omitted the Heindricks' part in my release. I made it out to have been a mistake. Naturally I said nothing about Sal, or Joxer for that matter.

'Lyn, love. Selling houses.' Her husband David is a chartered surveyor.

'Lovejoy! You're not thinking of—?'

' 'Course not. It's, er, this house somebody's selling in Sudbury. A dealer I'm friendly with might put a deposit down.'

Lyn smiled and tipped the fat over the edges of the eggs. She'd stir it all into a mess soon, knowing I can't stand looking into those reproachful orange egg eyes on the plate. 'And we thought Lovejoy came to see us, didn't we?' she said almost playfully to the twins.

'I did, love. If somebody puts a deposit down on a house, but doesn't sign anything, is it a legal sale?'

She looked doubtful and began to stir the yolks in. 'I don't believe it is. Not till the written contract is exchanged. I'll ask David.'

I thought for a minute. 'Could you?'

'He won't mind. He'll phone me about ten o'clock.'

'Lyn, love, I'll be away a day or two. Can you do my wheel?' I'd put it on the kitchen floor.

'That old thing? What is it?'

I explained. It is only a wooden wheel suspended on a crank. You lodge fresh eggs in holes in the rim. 'Give it a quarter turn dawn and dusk, and the eggs don't go bad. Victorian.'

'Oh, Victorian,' she said, voicing an age's criticism.

'You're jealous. Just because the Victorians invented everything and conquered the world on foot—'

'You need a fridge to store eggs.'

'Whatever you say.' Women are like this.

'We'll turn your wheel, Lovejoy.' Lally and Rebecca chorused. They were so keen to get started I knew my eggs would be spin-dried as soon as my back was turned.

'I'll do it, Lovejoy,' Lyn corrected, glaring them down. 'Where are you going? Somewhere nice?'

'Maybe,' I said, swallowing a sudden twinge of apprehension.

Then Becky said in her penetrating whisper, 'Don't be frightened, Lovejoy.'

'Frightened? Of what? Who's frightened?' I demanded coldly, but that shook me. Kids say some bloody wrong things at odd times when they should shut up.

'I told you to be quiet, miss,' Lyn said, placing my food and looking at me carefully now.

'Yes. Eat your breakfast,' I added sternly.

The twins said together, watching, 'You eat yours.' So I did.

Then I went to sell my cottage shakily and a bit scared, because I wasn't sure if they'd try to kill me here first or wait till I reached Ireland.

Patrick had only just risen when I arrived on East Hill. By a curious blunder, our village bus had arrived on time so I was in town by nine-thirty and waiting for Lily to come to the door. The antiques shop had started out as Lily's, but it is Patrick's now, for obvious reasons. I often wonder if Lily's husband will ever ask for his deeds. Lily came to the door and let me in. She looks an absolute wreck in daylight. I closed the door and followed her down the narrow hallway into her living-room. Someone screamed. It was Patrick, all dramatic on the couch with his eyes padded.

' 'Morning, Patrick.'

'Lovejoy,' he moaned. 'I might have known. You

thundering great *clumsy*, you. You deliberately *slammed* that door.'

Lily tugged anxiously at my arm. 'Shhh, Lovejoy. He's got one of his heads.'

But I was in too much of a hurry for suchlike gunge and said, 'That's a rotten dressing-gown, Patrick. Can't you afford better?'

He sat bolt upright, glaring and spitting venom. 'Vermilion and sepia are natural *partners*, you cretin!'

'It's the scarlet belt, Patrick. Doesn't go.'

He rose and rushed apprehensively to a full-length wall mirror and paraded a minute, tying and untying his belt. 'Oh, Lovejoy, don't you think so? Are you sure?'

He looked ridiculous, but you daren't tell him so outright. 'It's a problem,' I murmured, my stock phrase when I haven't a clue.

Patrick rounded on Lily. 'Why didn't you say, silly cow!' he shrilled.

'Well, dear, you were so certain . . .'

I cut in. 'You want my cottage, Patrick?'

'*What?*'

He'd been after buying it for years. 'You want to make an offer? I'm trying to raise some gelt to build up my stock.'

'You're going to sell, Lovejoy?' Lily breathed. 'Oh, Patrick, darling—'

'Shut up, silly cow,' he commanded. 'How much, Lovejoy?'

'Well, I'm having it valued today. Naturally I'd want at least the market value . . .'

His eyes narrowed for business. 'You'll give me an option?'

Innocently I shrugged, smiling. 'I don't mind much. Just thought I'd drop round and let you know because—'

'*Please*, Lovejoy,' Lily exclaimed. 'Patrick's always loved that spot.'

'Well . . .' I dithered, really quite convincing.

'*Please*. We'll put down a deposit, to be first.'

'Look, Lily, it's not even been listed for sale—'

'Then we'll be at the head of the queue, decide terms later.' She rummaged in her handbag and fetched out a lovely thick virgin cheque-book. It was beautiful. 'It need only be a token sum.' That sounded horrible. I needed more than token sums.

'I'm not sure . . .'

'Let's see,' she mused, finding a pen. 'The usual deposit's, say, ten per cent of the purchase price, so let's say half of that?'

'No.' Patrick was gauging me warily. As I said before, he's a shrewder nut than he makes out, the pest. 'Point five per cent's ample.'

'All right.' I put the best face on it I could manage and five minutes later was down their steps carrying a crossed cheque, not for as much as I had hoped, but stealers can't be choosers.

My luck was in that morning—or so I thought in my ignorance. The phone kiosk opposite the Ship tavern had not been vandalized, by some strange oversight. After listening to a brisk altercation between Rebecca and the operator, Lyn breathlessly managed to wrestle the receiver away from her offspring and accept reversed charges for the call. I asked if David had phoned in.

'Yes, Lovejoy. I asked him, like you said.'

'Were you right?' I meant about the house purchase law.

'Yes. David says the legal point of sale is the formal exchange of contracts. He says if you want to call in tonight he can explain in more detail—'

'Thanks, love. That's great. You've really helped me. So long.'

'Lovejoy?' That was Rebecca, penetrating the conversation by some bedroom extension. 'Are you in prison again?'

'Becky! Put that down at *once*!' Lyn's voice receded as she ran to the next room, her receiver clattering my earhole.

'Shhh, love,' I said furtively, doing my sinister act. 'I'm going to Ireland, but it's a secret, right?'

'Right,' Becky whispered.

Emerging from the kiosk I felt good about the information, but something was niggling. It was the kind of odd discomfort which comes when you remember passing a face in a crowd and only realize hours later it was a long-lost friend. Something was wrong, and I couldn't put my finger on it.

When I'm in one of these uncertain moods I gravitate towards antiques, but first I solved the innocent little Kilfinney mystery. The town library had opened by then. It consists of a modern hexagonal brown brick monstrosity with metal-and-glass doors which function like a nutcracker. I strongly believe they are a Malthusian solution for the population problem of our cripples and geriatrics, but no analyses have yet been done to count corpses. By a whisker I made it to the safety of the foyer, dishevelled and bruised.

'Hello, Marlene!'

The girl on the desk was frantically dialling on the emergency phone. 'Mr Scotchman! Mr Scotchman! Lovejoy's in! He's on the escalator!'

I gave a royal wave down to her as I was lifted among a throng of grannies and housewives up the moving staircase. More people than just myself have hated the new library, and not only because our lunatic town council demolished thirty sixteenth-century dwelling houses and Mr Wesley's chapel to erect it.

'Guard me, Auntie!' I said piteously to an old grey-haired lady as we cruised heavenward. 'They'll want to chuck me out.'

'The very idea!' she quavered. 'Stay close to me, young man!'

'And I only want to look up my grandad's birthday.'

'They're too bossy by far!' her mate warbled, grasping her umbrella with grim intent.

'Thank you, thank you.'

At the top the thin, belligerent form of our town librarian, Scotchman, was standing. He stepped forward, a fierce smile stencilling his lips. 'Out, Lovejoy. *Out!*'

Sad and humble, I murmured, 'I knew it. Poor old grandad . . .'

'Fiend!' my older protectress cried, prodding the librarian aside.

'Fascist!' Her mate buffeted him against the wall with her basket and I was past, trotting into the reference section. People lifted heads and tut-tutted, but I was at the famous 1837 Lewis *Topographical Ireland* in a flash and looking up K in Volume II.

There was a Kilfenny, a Kilfeighny, a Kilfinnane and Kilfinney in Limerick in 1837, so I supposed there still was. Keeping a wary eye on the main glass door, where Scotchman cruised in impotent fury and glared at me, I waved cheerfully once, then read, absorbed.

The ashes had cooled among the ruins.

Places look so different in daylight, don't they, quieter and more controllable. Standing there among the weeds and tombstones I felt my old discontent return. Here, at this precise spot in the Universe, poor Joxer had died. The silent malevolence of the Heindricks' Slav chauffeur, the almost jovial calm of Kurt's admonition, the sexy allure of the feline Lena — on the face of it they didn't add up to much, yet look here. Ash and charcoal. Restless, I scuffed the ashes and walked slowly along the wire mesh fence. Some white police marker tapes were still there. Lazy sods. The weeds in the corner of the Priory's ruins stood tall, but those in the vicinity of the crime were trampled down, presumably by the firemen and the Old Bill.

Over towards the church hall which the dramatic society uses there is a minuscule cobbled road leading to the town's main street. They used to fetch the horse-drawn hearses there at funerals. No car-tyre tracks traceable that way, and the street road that ran along the churchyard's top slope was free to anybody.

I walked back to Joxer's ashed workshed. The little redbrick factory on the other side of the tall wire mesh was functioning busily. Its nearside wall was smudged with black. Its narrow strip windows held only opaque glass, so no hope of finding some vigilant night-watchman garrulous with clues. Yet what was I doing hanging about here when I should be hitting the road to Limerick?

There's nothing quite so messy as a drenched fire. Black ash clung to my shoes and crept stickily on to my socks. My trouser edges were damp and flecked, and the uneven rubble made me wobble uncertainly. This odd restlessness, as if Joxer himself had returned to warn, had me jiggling nervously on the same corrugated iron where Ledger had uttered his ridiculous threats. I stepped off and the same bent piece of iron lifted out of the ash just as it had last night. It felt rough when I picked it up, not even warm. Maybe seven inches or so, it had been spindle-shaped, but now it was twisted along its length and curved into a crescent. Or, I wondered with quick interest, had old Joxer actually cast it in that shape? Holding it up, I turned for better light—and saw Sinead Morrison not ten feet away, standing watching me.

She was lovely, a picture. The sun falls through the great arches of the fawn-red ruins and pools the grass into green brilliance. Sinead was above me on the slope, a broad arrow of sunlight colouring her pale face and hair. The whole composition was breathtaking. I wanted to

love her then, because she was lovable in her long
swingback coat.

'Loot, Lovejoy?'

'Eh? Oh.' I dropped Joxer's old iron in the ash and
climbed the slope. 'Look, love. Sorry about your Joxer.'

'Sorrow, Lovejoy?' Her pale eyes blazed into me. 'You
don't know the meaning of the word.'

'Eh? Look, love, I did try—'

Her relentless voice was quiet but still shut me up. 'Last
night in the tavern you realized that there'd be a chance
of some loot, so you said nothing when that lady brought
the news of the fire. Your evil brain just filed the
information away, so you could come picking over the
ashes like the carrion crow you are—even though Joe's
hardly cold.'

I listened, aghast. 'No, love. Look, I honestly—'

'Honestly?' She stepped away to laser me with those
radiant eyes. 'You, Lovejoy? Honest? I really fell for your
flannelling at the hospital.'

This couldn't be happening, not to me. Not from her.
'But you don't understand—'

'Correct, Lovejoy. I don't understand you at all. But
everybody else does. The point is, they're right about you
and I was wrong.'

She left then, walking with grace along the slope's
contour between two lichen-covered stones, her coat
moving softly and her lifting heels shining among the
grasses. It nearly broke my heart. I tried to call after her
and couldn't.

It's really lucky for me that I'm used to bad luck, or I
would have been too cut up to do anything at all the rest
of that day. Anyhow, with my record I'm used to
heartbreak, so within an hour I'd been to the bank and
talked them into letting the cheque through. Ten minutes
later I'd found Tinker. He was waiting forlornly for
opening time on the step of the Three Cups near the old

Saxon church. I gave him a couple of notes and told him to get some tins of ale and meet me outside the Castle.

I went then to a travel agent's in Cross Wyre Street and booked a ticket to Ireland.

CHAPTER 11

Janet's car is a blue Morris, fairly easy to spot even in the usual tangle near our market. Tinker had cleared the contents of his tins by the time she came. She saw me, aloofly driving past and drumming her fingers on the steering-wheel, mad at something. I sighed at this hint of more trouble and gave Tinker one last reminder.

'Anybody asking after buying my cottage, you send them to Lyn and David's, okay? Down the lane.'

His rheumy eyes looked up quizzically from the bench. 'Here, Lovejoy. We really clearing out?'

'Are we hell, silly fool.' I ticked off on my fingers. 'Antiques: Liz over at Dragonsdale has a late Regency ostrich fan. Get her to hold it for me.'

'Christ,' he moaned. 'She'll want the Crown Jewels, Lovejoy. Where'll we get that kind of gelt?'

That is horribly true nowadays. You can buy a new car with less money. Still. 'And Margaret Dainty's got a collection of antique barbering instruments, combs, scissors, razors. Tell her I've a buyer—'

'Have we?'

Sometimes Tinker's thick. 'No. Try to find one before I get back. I should only be a day or two. And tell Big Frank from Suffolk I need a couple of George IV period stitch samplers, framed, dated and named if possible.'

'But we've a half-share in that pair of samplers Leggy Baldock's trying to sell.'

'Quite,' I said patiently, inwardly pleading God-give-me-strength. Tinker never learns. 'But Big Frank doesn't know that. So he'll go to Leggy's stall next Saturday and —'

Tinker's gnarled old face lit up. 'Hey, Lovejoy! That's great! But what happens when Big Frank buys them and fetches them to us?'

'We tell him we've already done the deal elsewhere, see?' Janet tooted her horn impatiently.

'He'll do his nut. Here. What you going to Limerick for, Lovejoy?'

'Holiday,' I said laconically. 'Ta-ra.'

'Go safe, mate.'

My train was at four, so I had time to invite Janet in for a cup of tea, as women euphemistically call it. I was glad about her willingness, because although she's quite a bit older than me I find more gratification in older women, and anyway they're better. It isn't just staying power, it's having more style or something. When she left at one o'clock to get some shopping done I had a sleep and was packing my small — actually my one-and-only — cardboard suitcase by two, and feeling fine. I remembered to put a three-foot length of hosepipe conspicuously in the centre of my garden. Cats think it's a snake and go elsewhere, so I'd find no dead birds about when I got back. Lyn and the twins would scatter bird cheese morning and afternoon for me.

There turned out to be only one snag when it came time to catch the train, and it was Jason at the station. I'd made Janet go, after borrowing some change for the phone, because I hate these farewells. I waved her off, then rang Helen, and Margaret Dainty, and Liz at Dragonsdale. Finally, thinking I was laying a false trail, I dialled Patricia Harvest, a money-mad investor who with her husband Pete ran a fruit farm down the Goldhanger estuary. Patricia's one of those rich women who dress like a scrapyard. She's always crying poverty, but then so do her three gardeners. I asked her what museum exhibitions were on at the moment. She can afford the posh antiques journals where they're advertised.

'Nobody else would know, not like you, Pat.' I awarded myself ten points on the creep chart for grovelling.

'Patricia,' she corrected mechanically. 'Where? National museums? Oh, Turner watercolours in the Brit Muzz—they're doing that sublime bit. Then there's Manchester . . .' She prattled on, visions of tax-free capital obviously warming her marble heart.

'And Dublin?'

'Yes. The Derrynaflan finds, with early exhibits from Armagh. And the Dublin Antiques Fair's on next week.' Her voice broke momentarily under the stress of listing so much wealth owned by somebody else. 'Ooooh, Lovejoy,' she moaned. 'Are you doing a sweep? Take me, and I'll see you right, darling. *Please.*' The thought made her frantic.

Weakness struck, but I remembered that lives were at stake—mainly mine. So I lied, 'See you in Dublin, sweetheart. That big hotel, the poshest one, right in the centre near that park.' I was smiling, because in any city there's always a big posh hotel in the centre near a park. 'I'll divvie for you. Next week, okay? You can pay me—in kind.'

Her voice went husky. 'You will, darling? I'll be there. You'll not regret it.' She's always trying to get me to divvie for her, and has heap big methods of persuasion.

Cheerfully I put the phone down and damned near scalped myself emerging from the idiotically-designed perspex hood—to realize a thin spread of waiting travellers had listened to every word. Of course they were carefully pretending, in the very best English manner, to be preoccupied with books and the middle distance. Even that crook in the ticket office was all agog. That would not have mattered much, but Jason mattered very much indeed after the warning Sinead had given me about him the other night.

He was buying a paper so very casually from the girl on the box stall. The local mental hospital sets it up to give the patients pin money. People mostly give more money than the newspapers cost. Like I say, folk are a rum lot. No good trying to work their motives out.

Jason saw me with a theatrical start of astonishment and took in my battered cardboard case.

'Hello, Lovejoy. Off on holiday?'

'No. Taking stuff up to Maggs on the Belly.' Even as I spoke I knew I'd made a mistake. It was too early in the week to be making deliveries to the Portobello Road antique market. And he could phone Maggs to check.

'Big dealer, eh?' He grinned, all even teeth and perfumed talc. 'Think you could wait a day or two and take a couple of things for me?'

'Due in today. There's this painting . . .'

'Ah.' He nodded wisely. 'I understand. Nothing I can say to persuade you to postpone your journey, Lovejoy?'

'Not really.' I grinned but without much conviction. What with Jason in his cavalry twills and his army-officer efficiency, the Heindricks and their murderous driver, and trouble with Ledger and his merrie men, I was really in the gunge now.

'You wouldn't be crossing to Ireland?'

'That *Paradise Lost* you got me to buy? No, Jason. Forgotten all about that.' That was the bookseller-printer I'd told Sinead about, who owed me.

'A natural mistake, Lovejoy.'

'Sure it was. See you, Jason.'

He said evenly, 'Soon, eh?'

Recognizing me, the ticket collector did not hold out his hand for my ticket, having once had his thumb clipped with his own clipper by a certain antique dealer to whom he had shown ferocious rudeness. I paused. He recoiled into his red booth, wincing at the memory, hands behind his back.

'Go straight through,' he said in a shaky falsetto.

'Go straight through . . . ?' I prompted.

'Go straight through . . . sir.'

The train was on time. Janet had made me some cheese and tomato butties, which lasted me almost till the station was out of sight. All I could think of was Pat Harvest, with annoyance. The British Museum Turner exhibition 'doing the sublime bit', indeed. That innocent exhibition of watercolours had suddenly informed everybody how important some ideas are — and promptly sent the price of first editions of Edmund Burke's book on the *Origin of our Ideas on the Sublime and the Beautiful* soaring five hundred per cent in three days among dealers and provincial antiquarians. A mint copy cost a few bob in 1757. It makes you sick.

Still, a few things stay the same in this murderous antiques game. Dear Patricia's idea of the sublime and the beautiful hadn't changed since she was born. Money. And at least I'd tried to lay a false trail by repeating those different locations to anyone who cared to listen. Like Jason.

On the plane they gave us those plastic dinners. I always get confused by so many little pots and get fed up halfway through. The hostess was bonny but their uniforms look so sterile they put me off. I dozed, worried about the mess I was in.

My mind goes funny when I'm sleeping yet not sleeping. Joxer had done some quiet jobs for the Heindricks, so quiet indeed he had been compelled to work in the night hours. Night, when there would be none of Marcia's amateur actors rehearsing on the greensward among the Priory ruins. Which meant stuff could be carried into Joxer's workshed and worked on without the chance of some stray actor witnessing Joxer's secret labours. I knew that Jimmy Day and Marcia and some of the others used Joxer's little loo, and occasionally persuaded him to brew up for them on his bunsen burner. He was usually pretty tolerant and pleased with company, though dramatics folk can't talk about anything else except drama.

As the plane banked, Joxer's last words came to me: *Can't you watch a minute with me?* Whether people ask for you to watch a minute or an hour with them, the answer's always no from goons the likes of me. Aren't people pathetic, I thought in my miserably fitful doze. And whatever I found in Kilfinney there'd be hell to pay when I zoomed home—Patrick would go berserk about being tricked out of my cottage, Lily would be demented about the money, the Heindricks would be decidedly upset when they found out I'd scarpered, and Kurak at having murdered Joxer for possibly nothing. But Jason was thick as thieves with Lena Heindrick, so Sinead said, and the bastard might have sussed me out at the station when I phoned Patricia Harvest. And Ledger distrusted everybody. I groaned inwardly, remembering I'd signed his bloody form the other night. Had its typescript included a promise not to leave the area without letting him know? What a mess.

The trouble is, I always feel like a chicken in a Western—under the pony's hooves, desperately at risk from stray bullets, unpaid, and never getting the girl. It's not much of a part.

The air hostess was shaking me then.

'Dublin,' she said, smiling nearly like Sinead. My heart turned over.

'Do we get off now?'

'Yes. Unless you want to go back.'

I thought a bit, then did what she said. Once a chicken, always a chicken.

CHAPTER 12

When you go to a new place I always find you have to adjust, but the adjustment isn't a matter of simple surprise or pleasure. You need a positive effort to rid yourself of preconceptions. Where the hell we get them from Heaven alone knows. If you're like me, you spend a time being astonished that it isn't at all like you'd somehow tricked yourself into thinking it would be. For a start, Dublin has no Tube. Why I'd ever assumed it would have, I've no idea. See what I mean? And Dublin's trains are noisy little diesels pulling orange-and-black coaches, another mind-blower. And their lads and lassies seem to smoke continually, everywhere. Like everywhere else, Dublin was showing signs of making living impossible in the interests of greater efficiency. And the traffic was at least as dangerous as everywhere. But I liked the way cars halting at traffic lights waited airily in the very middle of the crossing.

That evening I plodded round the darkening city looking for a place to lay my weary head, finding still more astonishments. Why no dots on the letter 'i' in names of streets and stations? And Dublin seems to do without those great office blocks most cities find indispensible, which is pleasing. The day was falling into its ember sky by the time I found a nosh bar near the Abbey Theatre and slammed a couple of pasties down in a sludge of tea. Time was getting on then, so I started blundering about a bit faster, trudging my cardboard suitcase along likely streets.

The River Liffey when I found it turned out to be as black as your hat, again a new fantastic fact. Guidebooks say Dubliners call it 'Anna', but I suspect they use the nickname as often as cockneys call their river Old Father Thames. Anyhow, I crossed by the Halfpenny Bridge feeling a bit lost and downhearted, wondering what on earth did I think I was doing here, miles from home, in search of more trouble than I had even back in East Anglia. But at least I was among people, though the city centre didn't have as many of those around as I'd have liked.

Dublin chimneypots are really great, genuine collectors' items. It's a wonder the whole lot haven't been whipped years ago. Believe it or not, but in one narrow street behind that big bookshop on the Liffey side I saw a good set of clay coloured Blashfield Hexagons, which are rare enough for those who collect London chimneypots, and a delectable group of eight Fareham Reds. Don't laugh. I honestly do believe the Fareham Red's pie-crust edging and its pretty white-painted rim band to be a work of art design. Anyway, why scorn a lovely piece of genuine eighteenth-century sculpture just because it's been stuck on a roof and become a bit sooty? You don't laugh at the Venetian crucifix on Giorgio Massari's reconstructed Church of the Pietà, same age. And across the road there was a triplet of tulip-shaped serrated crowntops, though mostly you see these 'Wee Macs' round Burton-on-Trent.

A fine drizzle started then. In despair, and not having pockets big enough to carry nicked chimneypots, I walked on and settled for a small terrace house with steps and nice but rusting Victorian iron railings, scrapers and door furniture. It advertised *Vacancies* and was not too far from the well-lit centre where the cinemas and pubs were still booming and buses tried to run you down at least as fast as I was used to. Inside, the house was a bit faded and peeling. Mrs Johnson the landlady was homely and chatty, gave me a room for an advance and promised to wait up to let me back in. 'You'll be off for a drink, I expect,' she said wisely. As I went forlornly off towards O'Connell Street I consoled myself that at least I was untraceable by practically everybody, friend or foe. Nobody knew I was here in Dublin, and tomorrow I could hire a car at first light and bomb off to Kilfinney. I'd still be ahead of the Heindricks' game.

Next morning the car hire looked quite a grand firm. It turned out to be the most complicated one on earth, what with phone calls to check my licence, a bloody test drive if you please, and a long wait while they did something to the mileometer. And I'd never seen so many forms in my life. Finally they said it was ready. I thanked them, and walked out to where the car stood at the kerb. I had this odd feeling as I went to open the driver's side door, telling myself not to get spooked in broad daylight.

' 'Morning, Lovejoy.'

Lena Heindrick was sitting in the passenger seat, giving me one of those non-smiling hilarities women emit when they see men squirm. She was as elegant and stylish as ever, diamond-stud earrings, a tight scroll hairdo, and a smart Donegal tweed suit. I didn't dare glance at her legs. The Edwardian silver-set sapphire brooch unnerved me enough as it was. She leaned across and gently pushed the door ajar. Her eyes were absurdly big.

I shrugged and sat. 'So that's why they took so long to hire me the car.'

'I had Kurak contact every firm, Lovejoy.' She smiled, her hand on my thigh.

'Then you just waited by the phone?'

'I did so want to . . . talk.' She traced with her fingers. 'It will be a great deal easier here, since Kurt has urgent manufacturing business to attend to in London.'

Finding somebody else, now Joxer was too dead to work for him? I swallowed. 'Where to?'

'That's better, Lovejoy. Drive out towards Sandymount. Don't be nervous. I'll direct.'

I always notice Daimlers, because they remind me of Daimler himself, who once prophesied that motor-cars hadn't much of a future—because there were only 1,000 chauffeurs in the whole of Europe. A large black Daimler pulled out behind us as I drove away. Lena hadn't come alone, it seemed.

The place at Sandymount was near a rugby ground. Over the flat sealands into which the duck-riddled river ran you could see the incongruous twin slender chimneys of the power station. It didn't look much like a pigeon-house to me—another nickname gone wrong. The area was largely terrace houses with oddly pleasant wide-arched doorways, and narrow, shaggily unkempt gardens.

'Left here, but park outside.'

The place was a walled garden surrounding a large house set back from the road. Nearby was a school noisy with playground squeals, and a little bridge over the river opposite. A couple of chatting women stirred their prams the way they do. Calm, quite nice really. Yet the feeling was tight in my throat. I switched off and met her eyes. I'd never known a woman smile as much as her.

'I needn't have come.' My defiant reminder only made her luscious red mouth smile wider.

'Of course you needn't, darling,' she said. 'Tell your conscience you were kidnapped.'

Women get me really narked. They always assume you have no bloody will of your own. Furiously I started up, 'Listen, you—'

She raised her hands to heaven in exasperation and broke in. 'Lovejoy,' she said wearily, 'for heaven's sake get me out of this car and up to Flat Five. Whatever you're going to do to me's not allowed in parked cars.'

There are some things you can be really proud of, like the times you help a person for nothing, or when you pull off a coup you never really expected. The trouble is, those events don't come along so often, and if they do it's accidental as far as I'm concerned. The rest of life is filled with occurrences you try to avoid remembering. Like Lena.

Lena's one of those women like Helen, who want a smoke after. And oddly it's then that they talk, when the man is dozing after that minor death which finally washes out the orgasmic rut of love. Women nark me like this. Sometimes they're thick. Not everybody has to be talkative the way women are. I'm not. When I was a kid I went silent days at a time, sometimes for devilment, as my old gran used to call it, but often because I just felt like some useful silence.

'Darling?' Lena must have asked me God-knows-what. The ceiling was a bit cracked. Her head of hair was lovely on the pillow. She's got that sheen into it which Margaret Dainty has. 'I said are you all right?'

'Ta.' Why are women's breasts always cold?

She half rolled and leant over me. 'What do you think of, Lovejoy? You are always miles away. A woman doesn't like to feel her man has slipped off into a world she doesn't know.'

'Brew up, chuckie.'

She stared in astonishment, then laughed and laughed. Her eyelashes were long and dark, her breasts full and smooth. Puzzled, I asked her what was up.

'You're impossible, Lovejoy!' Shaking her head disbelievingly, she rose and went through the corridor, draping a bath towel round her waist. She had to step over our clothes which were scattered over the floor. It had been a right scramble into bed.

I shouted after her, 'How did you know I'd gone to Dublin? Jason?'

'Yes.' She must have sensed me wondering about her and Jason. 'He does try so, poor boy, but he's hardly your rival, darling.'

There was a nasty sound of womanly permanence about all this. Better to keep it safely into matters of business, keep on playing dim. 'Lena. Why Dublin?'

A pause, a rattle of cups. 'You tell me.'

'You said that about not needing a passport but foreign. And Joxer is—was—Irish.'

If ever a mature living woman stepped straight out of one of those voluptuous Victorian engravings, it was Lena Heindrick when she came to the bedroom door and stood looking.

'The last time I waited on a man was ten years ago, Lovejoy.'

'Then you've been bloody idle. Get a move on.'

The kettle shrilled. She went out, laughing. I suppose Lena Heindrick seethed with breeding, because I'd never known a woman so sure of herself, so unbelievably positive. Oh, I admit every woman has this knack of somehow turning sexual supplication into a royal command, but never before had I encountered a woman who best-guessed like her.

'You brought your Slav gorilla over?' I called through, wondering if it wasn't overdoing the idiot bit.

'Have I?' she answered mischievously.

'The Daimler.'

'Well spotted. He was necessary—till now.'

Oho. I rose and padded about, looking for my trousers and my jacket. I could have sworn I'd shed them in the corridor between the living-room and the bedroom, but maybe Lena, in an epidemic of homeliness, had tidied. Women do that.

'Where are my clothes, love?'

'You don't need them yet, darling.' Her voice was smiling.

The window overlooked a stone-rimmed courtyard. Kurak, all million tons of him, was sitting on a decorative stone. He was in a bad humour, and staring malevolently up at our net curtains. He was cracking his knuckles, straight out of a bad supporting feature. My soul chilled. I'd seen that horrid habit before, in . . . in a bloke exactly like Kurak, three years ago. In . . . in Northampton? At an antiques function, where . . . where . . .

Lena returned carrying a tray with cups and all the gear, pleased with heself. There's nothing prettier than a well-loved woman just that little dishevelled. By then I was in bed, trying not to look worried sick but restless as a cat on hot bricks. She came in beside me without shaking the house down or spilling everything, another female knack.

'There! Well? Aren't you proud of me? Tea in bed?'

'I'll arrange the knighthood. Where's Kurt?'

She turned and put a finger on my mouth. 'Shhh. Kurt's a man whose only interest is antiques and art. He's not here, which suits me fine.'

Well, pretence is everything nowadays. 'Does he know?'

'Know, darling?' She stopped pouring, the spout dripping.

'About you and Kurak.'

For a split second her nostrils flared, almost too quick to notice, but it happened and should have warned me. My only excuse for what eventually occurred is that a woman in bed is a terrible distraction to common sense. She poured the tea, stirred and carefully passed mine.

'There's such a thing as change, Lovejoy. Kurak's served his purpose, now that . . .'

'Now I'm here?'

She lit a cigarette and jerked her head to show supreme irritation the way they do. 'Too pure, Lovejoy? Well, are you? I read your life story. Kurt had three agencies on you for weeks. Every tart, every shady deal, every forgery, those silly bored sluts of housewives pretending to be Sweet Little Alice in exchange for a good rut. It was all there, every detail.'

My life isn't the way she made it sound, really sordid. Anyway, Lyn's not a slut.

'Kurak had his uses, Lovejoy, just as Kurt had his.'

'Past tense?'

'Certainly.' Her brown eyes enveloped me. 'It's you now. Or are you too stupid to realize?' And, honestly, she smiled as she said the words, her lips widening and her cheeks dimpling. I swallowed tea to wet my throat, suddenly dry.

'Me for what?'

'Two things, darling. One, we find a fortune.'

'And two?'

She slid down, covering her shoulders with the sheet, and gave my belly a lick. 'Finish your tea, darling.'

I can't drink tea hot like women do, so I put it on the bedside table. The Duc de Charost actually read a book in the Terror's tumbril, and, when it came his turn for the scaffold, calmly turned down the page to mark his place. I wish I had panache like that. It would give you some control. Anyway, he'd still got the chop, poor sod, and I was trying not to.

A click fetched me conscious.

Lena was sleeping hunched, her back to me. We lay sideways across the disarranged bed. My leg was over her waist. In sleep my right hand had reached round to hold her breast. The pillows were anywhere. It was still daylight. I kept still and listened. No further sound. Kurak. It *had* been Northampton, that auction. Only he was no Slav then. I'd seen him across the crowd of bidders and dealers.

Without moving I estimated Lena's breathing. Regular. I stirred, moved my leg, freed my hand and rolled on my back. Lena didn't shift. Flat out. The click didn't come again. There was no movement in the other rooms that I could tell.

Her skin was flawless, full and smooth. It took an iron will slowly to reach the other way, and gently find the teacup. My finger touched the wet tea. Barely warm. Maybe an hour at the outside.

The edge of one sheet lay across my chest, but Lena had pulled a blanket over our legs and somehow got herself mostly burrowed under. Women do this in half-sleep, being naturally petrified of coldth.

One thing I'm a world expert in is leaving bed with great stealth. I've trained a lifetime. You don't do it inch by inch. You sigh, yawn, flop a bit, because those are the natural movements a woman's senses expect of a sleeping companion. Getting yourself vertical's the main problem. The best way is to sigh, then, making sure your limbs are free of all encumbrances, in one movement you smoothly swing your legs over the side, simultaneously bringing your torso erect. You stay sitting there, breathing regularly so the vibes of kipping lull any alerted senses back into oblivion. Then you slowly stand up, and you're off. Check first that your escape's not left her more uncovered than when you were *in situ*, so to speak, or chill will bring her to.

That should have been the end of it, except my jacket and trousers lay too neatly on the carpet of the living-room. Practically folded, as if the trouser crease was still traceable. Now, I didn't like this at all because I don't fold things. I liked it less when finding my wadge of money was gone. My gear had been cleaned out, down to the last Irish florin. No sign, though, of anybody—such as Kurak—in the flat.

Underpants, singlet, shirt (sleeves rolled up to conceal its button-free cuffs), trousers and jacket. A man feels better when dressed, probably because blokes look so daft in the nuddie. Socks were difficult, till I remembered I'd slung them off in the bedroom. Worse, Lena's handbag

was missing. And I knew it should have been by the telly
where she'd carelessly laid it as she lit a cigarette. I
padded over to the window. Kurak was still down in the
courtyard, now smoking a cigar and much less edgy. Just
as sullen, but no knuckle-cracking. Exactly like a bloke
who had just obeyed his mistress's command: nick
Lovejoy's gelt, don't let him get away, and wait outside
until you're told different. Well, I now knew how
persuasive Lena could be. I was hooked on her myself,
daft sod. Silently I floated into the bedroom, and found
my tatty socks near the dressing-table.

Lena had turned over. She now faced the corridor
door, and I was sure she was still sleeping . . . I think.
Suspiciously, I waited a few moments but there wasn't a
quiver from her eyelids. Her handbag wasn't in the
bedroom either. That took a minute, which was fatal.
The bed sounded, too sharply.

'Lovejoy? What are you . . . ?'

I'd clocked her one before I could think. She exhaled
and slumped on the bed, moving slowly, in a daze from
my blow. The recollection still makes me embarrassed,
but what else is new? Anyway what can you do when it's
courtesy or survival? Instinct takes over then. Nothing
actually to do with thinking or behaviour or conscience.
Another choice was on me now—keep on searching for
the odd groat, or scarper. I settled for escape in poverty
and hit the road.

The door had a simple lock. Kurak was a nerk to have
let it click—you pass any modern lock with a comb or a
few celluloid toothpicks. He ought to have known that.

The kitchen clock said two o'clock. There was part of
the day left, but it was now much less promising. I left by
the back door, climbed a wall and in an hour walked into
Dublin town.

CHAPTER 13

Not a farthing, no help, no car. I sat on a bench in draughty old Pheonix Park, thinking, unable to go home or reach Kilfinney two hundred miles away. Hunted by vengeful Heindricks, trapped into immobility by poverty. And you need money to finance the kind of war I was in.

The quickest way of course is roulette, though it's a mug's game. Mind you, there's an infallible system — or, rather, there used to be. Clever Victorian Joe Jagger spotted it in the Monte Carlo casino by hiring clerks to sit at each wheel and list the numbers, but then Joe was a meticulous engineer raised on a lifetime of Lancashire cotton-mill spindles, and he knew all about eccentricities of balance mechanisms. His relentless winning streak is the reason that the roulette wheels of the world are now perfectly balanced by gimlet-eyed serfs at half past seven every dawn. Reminiscing, I grimaced to myself. The famous Joseph had more sense than most. Evenually rumbled by the panic-stricken croupiers, the world's only infallible — and sensible — gambler simply packed his bags with his fortune and scarpered. The trouble is, gambling isn't like antiques. It's guessing. Look at that con artist Charlie Wells, the original Man Who Broke The Bank At Monte Carlo. Kept on gambling, finished broke. Well, I was broke to start with.

A sparrow came to my feet full of hope, and went on its way. Not daft. It was going to where it had prospects.

Prospects! Like being *owed* money? I remembered Jason's promise of a genuine first edition from, where was it, that printer's shop . . . near here. Fenner and something. I was owed! Therefore I too had prospects! At an antiquarian bookseller's, not far from the park.

Eagerly I rose and headed towards my own salvation.

The place when I found it was off the main road near Phoenix Park. I was glad about that. The nearest bus stop was quite a few hundred yards away and nobody waiting. A tatty printing shop front leading directly off the pavement, but with a grand new Rover parked outside and a smaller white Ford further along. Surprised at its dinginess, I went in. An old shop doorbell clunked above. There was a long counter and two blokes chatting away behind it. An aroma of fag smoke mingled with the bland bite of printer's ink. Untidy rows of books threatened a few desperate shelves. Founts of type were casually racked on trays all the way along the shop interior.

'Fenner and Storr? Antiquarian booksellers?'

'I'm one. He's the other. And you'll be . . . ?' The stockier, shabbier bloke broke off and came to lean across the counter as if it was a taproom bar. He seemed pleasant and bright. I was glad about that for his sake, because I find people like being happy, even if it's only for a short time.

'Lovejoy.'

'And from the sound of you you'll be a book dealer from over the water,' he chirruped. 'Now, what's your speciality?'

'*Paradise Lost*,' I said. The other bloke was nattier, county set in tweeds and twill with an elegant walking cane. He met my eye, nodded affably. I nodded back. No argument with him, only with this robber trying to flannel me across his flaky-paint counter.

'Ah. Blessed Milton, of the sweet tongue! Well, you're in luck there, sor!'

I let him rummage among the shelves a full minute before speaking. 'Two hundred and ten quid. Please.'

That caught him. He was in the act of turning towards me, blowing dust off a small ancient-looking volume, when the words arrived home.

'What's that you say?'

'Two ten. Please.'

The penny dropped with the other bloke first. 'Lovejoy,' he said softly. 'That name, Michael.'

'You're Lovejoy?' Michael the robber came slowly back, trying to judge my mood. 'East Anglia?' At my nod his jauntiness returned. 'Some mistake happened. You ordered *Paradise Lost*, first edition. We posted it, registered. Why, this is the very book.' He smiled and put it down between us. 'The parcel was returned-to-sender, wasn't it, Johno?'

'I returned it.'

'It hadn't even been opened.'

'But it had been paid for,' I said gently. 'Through Jason.'

'So now you've called for it in person,' Michael crooned. His stubble glinted in the sick light. 'And right welcome y'are—'

His voice choked off because my hand had his throat. I wedged the phoney book in his mouth and turned it till blood came.

'You sent me a shammer. I'd paid the price you asked, for a genuine first edition.'

'Hold your horses, Lovejoy.' The smartish geezer called Johno was tapping me with a sword. Honest to God, a sword in this day and age. I heard the cane sheath fall. A swordstick. Michael rasped breath in as I let him go.

'Glory be to God!' he croaked.

'Stand still, Lovejoy.' Johno Storr was calm, watchful. Risking his swordstick was too much of a chance. 'How do you know it was a shammer if you didn't undo the parcel?' His gaze cleared suddenly. 'Only divvies can do that. Well, well, well. We've a real find here, Michael.'

I said evenly, 'No, thanks,' slammed off out and went for a stroll.

A few minutes later I was back and placing two bricks into position in the gutter outside the bookshop. A Rover's a pretty wide motor so I had to measure it out with my feet. The car door wasn't locked, which pleased me because it saved quite fifteen seconds, and I was busily wiring the starter up and revving the engine before Johno Storr and his grubbier sidekick came to see what the hell was going on. Johno lost his cool then. He came banging on the motor's windows but I'd had the sense to lock all the doors and windows. Anyway, I was already moving, reversing across the street in the first bit of a three-point turn. Calmly I fastened the seat-belt while Johno yelled at Michael to phone the Gardai. He kept yanking at the handle my side. Michael Fenner had just gone in as I lined the big nose up with my two bricks and slipped the stick into first gear. Johno's expression changed from fury to incredulity as he realized my intention.

He screamed. 'Stop him! Stop him! For Christ's sake stop—!'

The run-up was hardly thirty feet, but the motor boomed into speed across the road, and I kept my foot down. My mouth was scared dry as the wheels bounced up on to the kerb.

The shop front abruptly filled the windscreen with a resounding slam. Glass shivered. Something thumped into my chest and the car burrowed into the shop in a hurtling nose-dive.

I suppose the impact dazed me a minute or two before I recovered my senses enough to look around. Through the dust I could see the front bumper was level with the top of the counter, and Johno was yelling blue murder while trying to unwedge his mate from the far corner. He was trapped by a printing press that had been crushed across the floor as my—well, Johno's—Rover stove the shop front in. I damned near sprained my ankle climbing out of a rear window, not realizing it would be so high off the floor. We were all three choking and spluttering in dust.

Fenner was whimpering, 'Help, for God's sweet sake—'

'Two hunded and ten, please.'

Rubble and glass seemed everywhere. Like being in a war movie. A couple of faces peered in, but I was past caring. I lobbed a brick fairly gently at Johno because Michael was in no fit state for more shocks. He was ashen and bleeding a bit. For the first time Johno looked scared. 'You're out of your mind, Lovejoy.'

Just in case, I broke his sword by swiping it on the edge of a press guillotine. Crummy modern crap. A genuine Georgian or William IV would have laughed at such treatment. Johno panicked then and fumbled out a wadge of notes a foot thick.

'Remember the rate of exchange.' That made him check and shakily restart his counting, but eventually the blissful feel of money warmed my digits.

Michael Fenner was fainting away when I left. Climbing across the shambles, I picked up a small booklet of gold leaf, as a kind of Lovejoy-tax on the two rogues, though what I could do with it I had no idea, and these booklets cost surprisingly little on account of the gold's thinness. A couple of elderly bystanders were outside admiring the unusual sight of a big Rover's bum sticking out of a shopfront window, its wheels a clear yard off the pavement. I hadn't realized till then how ugly cars are underneath. You'd think these car designers would at least try.

Somebody up the street was shouting so I broke into a trot, still coughing. I couldn't afford to get into trouble with the Gardai. The main road was fairly busy with cars. It was easy to slow to a brisk walk among the pedestrians—easy, that is, until Sinead stepped in front of me.

'Er, hello, Shinny,' I said brightly. 'Fancy seeing—'

'My car's here.' She had it parked by the kerb. For a

second I dithered, but here was suddenly a free way out. A lift from Sinead, and as long as she got me away from the district pretty fast, I could ditch her and be on my own.

'Why, thanks, mavourneen.'

'And you can stop that.' She was giving me the critical once-over as she slid into the driving seat. I must have looked as though I'd been in an accident, covered in dust with my knuckle skinned. 'Where to, Lovejoy?'

'Oh, anywhere. I'm in a hurry.'

We drove past the street where folk were beginning to congregate to goggle at those grotesque rear wheels. Shinny slowed, but I ahemed in annoyance and she accelerated past. I drew breath to make some cheerful crack about parking being such hell in Dublin, but thought better of it.

'We can't just drive anywhere, Lovejoy.'

'The National Museum, then.' That would be as good a place to ditch her as any. To show I honestly had no such intention in mind I said, 'If we get separated, meet at the Book of Kells, right? And I'll pay your entrance fee,' I finished grandly, remembering I owed her from the pub the night Joxer got done.

She shot me a mistrustful glance. 'Are you all right for money?'

'Thank you,' I replied gravely. 'Just been to the bank.'

CHAPTER 14

The museum didn't look much, but its displays were out of this world. A uniformed bloke sold me catalogues and let us in. 'Here, Shinny,' I whispered, 'did he get the prices right?' Some of the costlier-looking booklets were priced absurdly low. Sinead told me to keep quiet or the civil servants would put them up double. 'Got them here too, eh?' I was commiserating, when we hit the Derrynaflan display. It occupied almost the whole of the central recessed floor, case after case of the fabulous treasure with comparison pieces from earlier finds. I should have said it hit me, because my chest banged and quivered at the sudden impact and the floor sailed from under.

'Lovejoy!' Sinead had hold of me, grunting with strain under my weight. 'Thank you,' she was saying, 'thank you,' to an attendant who came helping. My legs went funny again as I tried to struggle away towards that dazzling display but she hissed abuse in my ear and obediently I sat on one of the benches. An arrangement of Irish glass impeded my vision of the cases, but the vibrations thrummed out into my whole being. I was shivering like a newborn foal and sweating cobs. 'He's not long from hospital,' Sinead was excusing to the attendants. 'He only needs a minute or two.'

'And not a drop in the place,' the senior uniform soulfully deplored, obviously burned up about a long-standing issue. People all about nodded understandingly.

'He'll be fine. A quiet sit.'

Heads shaking at this proof of an unmet need, they drifted and left us. While the museum resettled to torpor, Sinead delivered me a furious lecture in a suppressed hate-filled whisper. She called me callous, thoughtless, stupid, hopeless, bone-headed, selfish and ignorant. All I could do was sit there in the bliss-giving glow of that miraculous treasure find set in the glass cases.

'And furthermore, Lovejoy,' Sinead hissed into my poor old worn-out earhole, 'you haven't even asked how it is I'm here.'

'How is it you are here, alannah? I thought you'd written me off.'

'I'm sorry I called you all those things in the Priory

ruins. The night sister told me later you'd rung up asking for me and she had refused to give my location.'

'Then Tinker, I suppose?'

'Tinker sent me to Lyn. The twins told me.' She sounded close to tears.

'Gabby little sods.'

'And what's between you and Lyn, Lovejoy?'

'Help me up, love.'

She did, but crossly. 'You get five minutes gawping at this rubbish, then it's eating quietly you'll be for a while.'

Well, five minutes was better than none.

'It's thankful I am to you, mavourneen.'

'And you can just stop that.'

I said gravely, 'Would you be knowing where the other verbs are in Ireland?'

Sister Morrison at last revealed her true colours. 'Just shut up, Lovejoy,' she said.

Irish nosh bars are as grotty as ours any day. We found this side-street one full of guitar-laden posters and stained tables, just like home. Beans inedible, bread soaked to extinction. Lovely. Sinead had tried to insist on a posher place but I won by pleading queer legs so we slurped together in unison, trying for silence.

Then over a good cup of tea she asked me about the crowd in That Street, and wouldn't be deflected when I tried my beam of dumb innocence. 'That street with the car sticking out of the shop window,' she added pointedly.

'Really? Honestly, the sights these days.'

'Fenner and Storr,' she went quietly on. 'Printers and antiquarians, near the park. You mentioned they owed you.'

'I did? Ah well, I just dropped in.'

Her eyes were on her cup. 'You might have been killed.'

If she'd seen me do it, what the hell. I explained how I'd sent them the money for a genuine first edition of

Milton and been posted a shammer, a copy the two rogues had fake-printed themselves. The sheer absence of vibes had told me it was dud.

'And you didn't even need to *look*?'

'Right.'

She glanced out towards the museum and gave a shiver. 'So your performance in the museum . . . ?'

'Too many vibes all at once.'

'It's spooky.'

Angered, I grabbed her coat with my good hand. 'It's nothing of the kind, Shinny. It's detectable love, the love the craftsman had for his creation, the love instilled into an antique by its admirers over the centuries.'

Her hand reached up and held mine, locked on her lapel though it was. She seemed suddenly shy, not furious at all.

'Everybody else looks at antiques and sees only money, Lovejoy.'

'That's only their excuse. Money's respectable, love's embarrassing. So they say it's investment. Deep down, they all know it's love.'

She had my hand in hers now. 'Don't trust your belief too far, darling, will you?'

'Me? Trust? An antique dealer?' I was still laughing at her innocence when we rose to go. Honestly, the blind folly of women.

'I'll pay,' she said evenly. 'Then you can tell me all about the Derrynaflan hoard.'

Everybody must know of it by now. The real treasure, and the legends which have sprouted in so very short a time. Already there's a million versions of the story. Here's only one:

Once upon a time, this angler goes fishing in County Tipperary. His son has one of these metal detector things for his birthday and gets a bleep. Naturally he shouts his dad, who comes to look. They dig down to an inverted bronze dish, which covers an enormous decorated chalice, a strainer, a communion patten and a circular stand. Okay, maybe the clear stunning similarities with the great Ardagh find a century back escaped our intrepid angler, and maybe the shattering artistic evocations of the Tara Brooch did not spring instantly to his mind that day, but he clearly knew his duty. He rushed to report—and legend has him variously hawking his news about all Saturday and Sunday trying to find some authority to tell, or forlornly going back to the field to sit on guard till some bureaucrat sleepily came to.

Well, there's no stopping Irish storymakers with such a plum. You can imagine the hilarious accounts that have been invented or passed on—how at last the penny dropped, the message got through and teams of archeologists cavalcaded across Ireland to the monastic site of St Ruadhan of Lorrha and collared the lot. And how the Dublin papers grimly reminded everybody of recent notorious scandals where archeological treasures had been flogged to the highest (and in the antiques game that usually means the quickest) bidder.

Of course, the Derrynaflan hoard is almost beyond belief. Precious in its own right, it ranks high in the ranks of the discovered treasures anywhere.

'Look at Gallows Hill,' I enthused, my eyes misting at the thought of all thirty-three Roman silver spoons, the gold hinge-bow satyr buckle and the partially-completed eight-stone rings, the engraved gems and the precious-metal ring blanks, the emeralds, the silver strainers, the gold necklaces and bracelets, the garnets and amethysts. 'A Roman goldsmith's entire workstore.'

We were back in the museum by then, among the museum's crowd, me going on nineteen to the dozen about other finds even more weird and almost as wonderful. The little brass token in a box of rubbishy old buttons and scrap coins in North Yorkshire—which turned out to be a unique hammered gold Tudor Saint George noble of Henry VIII's reign, previously unknown except for a mention in a Flemish merchant's sixteenth-century handbook. Everybody finds the bloody things but me.

'You don't have to dig for Troy, love,' I said, husky from being in the vicinity of that breathtakingly lovely chalice, huge and embellished. 'I've seen a Gujerat medal from a button jar. A valuable group of *ojime*—a Japanese bead to hang on the end of a cord which suspends an *inro* carrying box for seals or medicines—sewn on a school kid's bean bag. And fortunes in old slung-out handbags on street barrows—a Saxon silver penny, a mint and valuable boxlet of ladies' cheek patches straight out of Beau Brummel's period, and gold buttons, gold necklets, gold toothpicks . . .'

A little girl tugged at my trouser leg, lifting her arms to be hiked. Still prattling to the amused Sinead—though why women laugh at me like they do I'll never know—I one-armed the infant up and let myself be steered through the press of crowds and cases. The little girl kicked her heels and imperiously pointed, one hand clutching my nape hair.

'. . . an ancient Egyptian votive scarab, and *not* a crummy plastic Brit Muzz repro . . .'

Actually, you have to smile. We wound up at one of the cases of Celtic gold torcs quite tastefully arranged, but they could have gone to a bit more trouble over the background.

I was going on, 'An Inca bead, two Benin dice—'

'There!' The little girl was triumphantly banging her tiny flat hand on the case glass. 'Like mine! See?'

'Like what, love?' I asked blankly. She tugged at her hair in exasperation and I saw she wore a hooped thing to keep her hair in place, like the twins. It was gilt plastic.

'You mean your headband?'

'Alice band,' she said with scorn.

'Beautiful, love. Really great.' I handed her over to her breathless mother, while Sinead was being all amused nearby. '. . . and a piece of an abacus, only seventeenth-century but not to be sneezed at, and . . .'

'Go on,' Sinead was saying. 'I'm loving all this.'

'. . . and . . .' I looked after the little girl. Then at the torc case. Then after the little girl. Then back.

'What is it, Lovejoy?'

'Nothing,' I said, third go, after a lot of throat clearing. But it was very definitely something. It's called knowledge. I knew why we were all here in Ireland, why Joxer had been crisped. And about that phoney Slav they called Kurak—no more Slav than me. And why the Heindricks wanted—*needed*—me. Nobody else would do. No wonder Lena Heindrick had pulled out all the stops. No wonder. The hooped Alice band. The hoop of iron in the ash of Joxer's shed. And the hoops of gold torcs in the cases around us.

'No bloody wonder what, Lovejoy?' Sinead was asking.

'Eh?' I must have spoken aloud. 'Oh, nothing, love. Look. Can you give me a lift?'

'Where to?'

'You drive. I'll direct,' I said, pushing through towards the exit and leaving her to hurry after.

But I meant Kilfinney.

CHAPTER 15

Sinead's car was gone. Nicked. I ask you.

Broad daylight, peaceful old Dublin town, people everywhere, and Sinead's car lifted by some drunken nerk. While Sinead rang the Gardai I perched on the wall outside and looked amiably about. Nobody I recognized, no big black Daimlers, and no sexy over-perfumed ladies with slightly foreign accents.

While Sinead marched out to confront the Garda who motored up and resignedly let himself be harangued repeatedly—women love saying the same thing; they think it's proof—I let my own mind drift back to the central problem of Kilfinney, poor dead Joxer, and now this business of Sinead's stolen car. We were stuck, stymied. With the car-hire firms under the eagle eye of Kurak the phoney Slav, and possibly with Jason's military brain ticking menacingly this side of the Irish Sea, a quick unperceived dash to Kilfinney was out of the question. The only good thing was that Lena and her strong-arm squad couldn't simply zoom on ahead and hang about till I came, because Lena had no way of guessing I knew that Kilfinney was the place she had rigged the scam. My main aim, now I'd rumbled her, was not to let on. Uneasily I wondered if it might be my one card.

Sinead was heatedly winding up her statement to the weary bobby. I felt sorry for him, but telling the truth would have made him wearier still so I said nothing. Sinead did a big finish, bleating about ruffians and Making Streets Safe For Ordinary Folk. Sundry aged birds nodded and tutted indignantly. One even joined in—exactly the same thing had happened three years ago to her sister's boy's motor over in Sligo, and what were the Gardai doing about *that* she wanted to know.

I just sat and thought about Kurak cracking his fingers down in that courtyard.

If I hadn't been so slow I'd have sussed him long before. What was it he'd answered, driving me home from hospital? 'Yooorr serffint fur life, modom.' Yes, Kurak was your actual dyed-in-the-wool grovelling serf—but he'd said lo-iff. Only Cockneys can make two syllables out of a miserable titch of a word like life. I'd even thought of Keats misspelling that sea-spray bit. The smile started on my face, gradually creeping into the corners of me, then splitting into a wide hundred-per-cent grin. And sweat started, trickling down my neck, but it was only relief. My whole body sagged. Suddenly I was on holiday, chirpy, restful and happy all at one go. Because I knew Kurak. He was that big knuckle-cracking Cockney bloke who now lived in the Midlands. And it *was* Northampton, that auction where he'd pulled the sleeper trick time after time. I remembered now.

More than that, I even remembered who he really was. Maybe not his name, but I knew him right enough. They call him the Sleeper Man. Let me explain about sleepers for a second.

Antiques are everywhere, bliss-giving and beautiful. Right? But like I was telling Sinead in the museum, not all see the light of day. Some do, like the poet John Donne's painting by Titian now in the undeserving Louvre, but some don't ever turn up. Others, such as the vast antique wealth of the *Mary Rose* warship and Jawa the lost city of Jordan's Black Desert, are still being discovered piecemeal. Still more get themselves mislaid, buried, hidden, nicked, pillaged, melted down, dismantled, lent, deposited in vaults, pawned, worn away, lost, horridly vandalized, horribly mended by bungling amateurs (or, worse, restored by alleged experts), purchased by city museums to lie in storerooms so nobody can enjoy them ever again, simply forgotten about, or sold to anonymous purchasers (such as our railways pension fund who secretly bought all that Regency English silver in 1979 as an inflation-proof investment, the callous sods). Or they get bank-vaulted as appreciating tax-free nest-eggs by stony-hearted cynics utterly incapable of love of any kind.

Or they 'go to sleep'. In the trade we call these antiques 'sleepers'.

Basically, a sleeper is an antique, usually of considerable value, which is not in general circulation among collectors and dealers. Oho, you say, immediately thinking of your Auntie Elsie's valuable George III commode which is about to shatter all Christie's records, oho. Your commode's a sleeper, and it's arrival will rock the London antiques world to its foundations. Well, not really. Your piece of furniture is really great, I'm sure, but it doesn't merit the appellation of 'sleeper'. There's one important characteristic which a sleeper has above all others: *it's existence is deliberately concealed*. In short, it is hidden from the cruel gazes and the jingling coins of the antique dealer fraternity. And your Auntie Elsie's commode is up for sale, remember? In fact, I'll bet you are screaming about it from the rooftops, pleading with the auctioneer to advertise it for all he is worth. No, it's no sleeper.

A sleeper is the treasure of the twilight zone. It is a legend in its lifetime, an ephemeral antique which slips out of sight and vanishes from public attention like Cinders at the Ball. One minute listed in the cold light of somebody's catalogue, and the next sinking into obscurity with only the odd rumour to mark its passing. Vague legends abound everywhere in the antiques game, of sleepers rare and priceless beyond measure. They exist in every country. A sleeper can be anything — coins, brooches, jewels, earrings, a valuable book, a miniature portrait. And there have been some notable near-priceless sleepers. But this hardly matters a damn unless you know where the sleeper is among the world's collections of ordinary run-of-the-mill antiques, junk copies, rubbish, forgeries, and laid-aside heaps of dross. And if you don't, then you're the same as the poor rest of us, living in hopes, right?

Yet one flaw remains in all this enduring ignorance. If you only *pretend* you know where a sleeper is, you have a very, very special kind of situation.

You have what people call the con trick.

I rose, mingled absently with the mob for a second, saw Shinny was still laying the law down, and slid across the road into a side street.

Then I ran like hell.

CHAPTER 16

She was a long time coming, but I didn't care. Women, basically unreliable, have one enduring characteristic: their conduct narks you endlessly, year after year. Irritating a bloke's their natural pastime. Yet a woman's a sort of necessary gout, especially if you're an itinerant antique dealer, temporarily broke in a strange country, and on the run from one — or was it two? — teams of rich homicidal fraudulent con-merchants. I had a headache.

The hall turned out to be a grand old place, everything I'd hoped. And a bonus, it was plonk in the middle of safe old Trinity College's grassy swards. The library was so worn and real that the coldest heart would have responded to the loving warmth of those emanations. Not just the walls and the books, but the flooring and the ceiling — and the Book of Kells.

One reason there's so much crap about nowadays masquerading as 'good' antiques is that most folk are too silly for words, too greedy, and bone idle. I mean, go and look at the blindingly clever artistry of the Book of Kells (it's actually in four 'books', but they put two on show usually) and you begin to appreciate the scale of the manuscript geniuses who created such illumination. Do the same with the British Museum's Lindisfarne Gospels.

Then try to copy a single inch of a single page of the complex decoration of either, and your education's under way. (If you can't afford the trip to see the real things, a postcard repro teaches you the same lesson.) That little try-out will only take ten minutes, but after it you will be ten—twenty—times harder to fool when some dealer offers you a 'genuine mediæval French page manuscript from a devotional Missal . . .' It's a very gratifying feeling to be able to look a fraud in the eye and say sweetly, 'Thank you. It's lovely. But do you have any *genuine* antiques, please . . . ?' See what I mean about being bone idle? A little effort, and you get the true feeling of an antique. That feeling is love, true love.

Apart from a couple of students reading on a central bench, an elderly geezer creaking among high shelves on a library ladder, and a pair of ladies blinking at such accumulated learning, the place was empty. I stood humbly before the open Book in its glass case, bathing in the unseen radiance of such a treasure.

You've seen some oafs pretending they're antique porcelain experts, by running a lead pencil round the rims of cups and saucers? Well, ask them why they do it and they'll have no idea. Oh, they'll say something like: 'If it leaves a pencil mark, it's genuine,' which sounds okay and deeply knowledgeable until you demand, 'Genuine what?' and they're stuck. As I say, too silly for words. The pencil-on-the-rim legend actually arose from the writings of a wise old Victorian character called Litchfield, who advocated this as a test for spotting Old Worcester porcelain, because its glaze often (*not* always!) shrank inside such rims leaving a faint crack. (Tip: let other people play at being experts. You just remember that a positive pencil test means only maybe; a negative pencil test does not necessarily mean no. It's only one poor test, after all.) Yet even genuine Old Worcester doesn't mean you should fumble for your cheque-book and pay through the nose. Much beautifully sparse Old Worcester was elaborately repainted and refired in Victorian days. The best scoundrel—and I therefore mean the worst—was Cavello, Italian chef to the Marquis d'Azeglio, Italy's London Minister. Nowadays dealers and collectors get taken in and pay highest prices, but don't you dare do anything so daft. Cavello's Worcester pieces give themselves away by thicker, clumsier decoration, and his colours are more opaque. All it takes is one careful look at one virgin piece and a suspicious mind. The price should be about a third of the un-repainted porcelain . . . Somebody touched my arm and I leapt a mile.

'What were you smiling at, Lovejoy?'

'Er, hello.' I clutched on to the glass casing to recover. My one and only helper had arrived, breathless, bonny and a bloody nuisance. 'Just thinking,' I croaked. 'Where the hell have you been?'

'You saw me, darling. That stupid Garda.' She linked my arm. 'Then I hunted for you high and low till I remembered you saying to meet here if we got separated. Why did you vanish?'

'They nicked your car so we'd be stuck, easier to follow. At least we've shaken them off now.'

She was pulling me briskly towards the exit. I tried to drag back. 'It's closing time, Lovejoy,' she pointed out. 'We have to go.'

Sure enough, the usher was edging people along the library. I hate women who're logical. Things are bad enough normally.

'Anyway,' she said, smiling. 'I got Gerald.'

'Erm, look, Shinny.' More help was the last thing I wanted. I still hadn't adjusted to her tagging along. She gave me a lovely beaming blast from her pale grey-blues.

'Gerald's different, Lovejoy.' Her voice had that quality.

I thought bitterly, oho, so we love this Gerald

character, do we? Great. That's what I needed. One more complication.

Gerald was different all right. I'd never seen anything like him. Thin as a lath, bespectacled, bad teeth, and the longest bloke you could imagine. Long as opposed to tall because he had all these unexpected joints. Even as we approached along the pavement he was folding and bending in odd places for nothing. He seemed all hinges. I couldn't help staring. He was my own age, and twice as shopworn as I felt.

'Ah, you'll be Sinead's feller,' he exclaimed, extending an arm like unfolding trelliswork.

'Lovejoy. Er, hello, Gerald.' We shook.

A bus honked, its way blocked. Somebody had dumped a derelict van outside the college's main gateway. Completely unconcerned, Gerald led the way to this decrepit horror and climbed into the driving seat, which was a wicker work laundry basket nailed in place. There was nowhere for me or Shinny except a small mound of wood and some sacks. Gerald folded behind the wheel like some fantastic stick insect, all limbs and angles.

'Will you be moving this wreck now?' The bus driver descended and yelled in at us through where our rear doors should have been. An interested crowd was assembling. Cars were queuing.

'Sure, how could I till I get the thing moving?' Gerald bawled over his shoulder. We pulled away, me and Shinny jerking and rattling like peas in a drum. The bus driver shouted something after us, probably as logical as Gerald.

'Don't look so worried, darling,' Shinny called into my ear above the din. 'Everything will be fine now Gerald's with us.'

I managed a weak grin. I'd been hoping to flit silently out of Dublin like a night-stealing Arab. Instead I was

leaving the city with all the stealth of a carnival, in the
loudest, most open-air, least unnoticeable and most
police-prone vehicle on the bloody island. Still, Shinny
always seemed to know what to do. Hopefully, I
wondered if Gerald was some secret Bond-type agent, but
the wretched man dashed my hopes. He bawled questions
to me over the van's incredible din, wanting to know all
about me, which was fair enough. The one that got me
was what I did for a living.

'Antique dealer,' I yelled, clinging to Sinead.

'Are you now! I'm a poet.' He swerved us illegally along
a one-way street, tutting irritably when two cars tried to
make it in the legitimate direction. One car panicked and
hit a wrought-iron railing on the pavement. 'Ah,' Gerald
enthused, unabashed, 'isn't haste the terrible modern
disease! Where to, Lovejoy?'

'North, please.' Great. We need the SAS and get a
lunatic bloody poet.

'Anywhere particular you'll be wantin'?'

'Not too far north, please.' Quickly reverting to my
earlier plan, I realized I'd need to be near a sizeable town
to ditch Gerald and Shinny. Until nightfall I was
lumbered.

'Ah. The old backtrack, is it!' He flailed the van in a
clumsy arc and bumped us across a traffic island while
tyres screeched all around.

Shinny cupped her hands and yelled, 'Gerald.
Somewhere nearby. Lovejoy's all in.'

'Caitlin's,' he called back. 'Yes, Drogheda's the place
right enough!'

My mouth into Shinny's hair for secrecy, I asked,
'What good's a poet?'

'You'll see, Lovejoy.' She turned and held me steady. It
seemed natural for my head to fall on her shoulder.

'Will you be marrying me this year, Sinead?' Gerald
bawled as the road straightened into the main N1.

'Oh, whist, you terrible man.'

'Poets pay no tax on the Auld Green Sod, Sinead.'

'Nor have two pennies to rub together!' Shinny gave back. My eyes had closed but I didn't care. It was all too complicated. With the rain coming on and trickling down the van's rusty interior, and Gerald's bald tyres slithering us uncertainly northward, there was no chance of us reaching anywhere so what the hell.

The world began to fade, taking that horrible cacophony of Gerald's van with it.

That night I slept a couple of hours with a strange lady called Eileen, after proper introduction of course. Or, rather, she slept with me. She was about eighteen months, and after nosh swarmed on to me as I dozed by the fire in Caitlin's little house. Her bare feet were perishing. Despite her lack of years, she had that female knack of winkling her coldest extremities on to your belly and murmuring gratification while you gasp at the shock. I should have expected it. I've had a lifetime of women and never met a warm one yet.

Caitlin was a vague relative of Gerald's and Sinead's and had that gorgeous Irish combination of gleaming jet hair and royal blue eyes. She looked me up and down candidly, saying to Sinead, 'Don't you feed the man, for God's sake?' but it was only women getting at each other and Sinead sharply told her chance'd be a fine thing. The two of them had a high old time while they got some grub, talking of families and exclaiming at who'd moved where. Caitlin's husband Donald, a pleasant grinning redheaded bloke who mended motors for a living, rigged up an outside lamp to have a crack at Gerald's uncontrollable van. Gerald spent a sad hour discovering I knew next to nothing about the Movement poets, but Shinny rescued my reputation.

'For heaven's sake say you like Milton,' she said sweetly,

'or Lovejoy throws a car in your window.'

'You did *that*?' Gerald said in awe. 'I saw it!' His face broke into smiles of delight. 'And no more than you'd deserve,' he cried, opening some bottles of that horrible black stout.

Caitlin and Shinny gave us one of those hyper-filling Irish meals with practically no veg, and tea strong enough to set. Then I joined the two old folk round the fire. Caitlin's dad was disappointed I'd not fought in his regiment at the Second El Alamein, though I wasn't, and Grandma was astonished I did not have the latest lowdown on our politicians' secret home lives. She made up for my ignorance by giving me intimate family details of the Taoiseach, their prime minister. Dozily, I kept asking how you spelled local words, but in the end gave it up. Ireland's the only place on earth with spelling worse than mine.

The whispering with my name in it woke me about nine that evening. Everybody was in the parlour, telly was on and little Eileen was snoring with her dewy head thrown back on my arm. Gerald and Donald were chatting competitively, Gerald about pararhyming techniques and Donald giving him a long tale of a dud carburettor. The old couple were reminiscing. Odd that a whisper in such family pandemonium can wake you. I suppose it's wavelength or something.

'Ask him,' Caitlin was urging.

'Not yet,' from Shinny.

'What?' I whispered, as if I didn't know.

'There! He's awake!' Caitlin ran upstairs to bring out the stuff.

Wherever a doctor goes, people automatically start hauling out their shirts or unhooking brassieres to show him their operation. Being an antique dealer's just the same—out come da Vincis and Gainsboroughs and the gunge. The big joke is that priceless antiques actually are there, sometimes and somewhere.

'Here!' Caitlin returned breathless, holding a small clipped leather case in the palm of her hand.

Grannie snorted. 'Them's old earrings.'

'Whist, Mam! Let him speak.'

Caitlin unclipped the case, only big as a Swan matchbox, and honestly it really gets to you. I'd never seen an original complete set before, though you come across singles. They lay in their velvet lining, two large thin gold rings and two genuine pearls on slender S-shaped stems with their stud loops. All four, perfect. Marvellous. I felt dizzy. Of course, women would never wear them nowadays.

'Breast rings. Those are breast jewels.'

'Glory be!' Caitlin cried. Grannie thought it was scandalous, though I expect the old devil had known all along.

Women of the 1890s had their nipples lacerated and perforated just like they have ears pierced nowadays. The gold rings were inserted through the nipple exactly like gold 'sleeper' rings for an earlobe. The jewels, most often diamonds, rubies or pearls (*never* baroque pearls, though, for obvious reasons) were mounted on either gold rings or on S-shaped gold stalks for passing through the nipple laceration site. The jewel either lies in the nipple's recessed tip, sits on the teat or is pendulated from the nipple's corona.

'But I've never come across any woman wearing them.'

'See, Mam! Told you they weren't earrings!'

If Caitlin and Shinny were fascinated, Donald was awed. 'Didn't it hurt, Lovejoy?' He prodded the gold rings with a large oily finger.

'Like hell, apparently, at first. The women's magazines of the last century are full of details—'

'Yes, well.' Shinny swept the case back into Caitlin's hands. 'There's such a thing as being too nosey.'

It's always like an outpatient clinic. They brought out a pewter dish next. You have to smile at some antiques. Pewter's a lovely metal, only now coming back into well-deserved popularity. If you were starting a collection of antique pewter, though, I'd go straight for 'pewter specials', as they're called in the trade, meaning pewter items a little different from the average. Caitlin's dish was essentially a plate, but nearly two inches thick. You can always tell these rare and highly-sought hotwater dishes because they are lightweight for their thickness, and they have two hinged pewter loops at the edge, the sort you pass straps through for carrying.

'For carrying,' I explained, 'though women used their apron ribbons often as not. The plate got hellish hot because . . .' I ran a finger slowly round the top edge, found the crack and flipped upwards. A tiny trapdoor popped up, revealing the dish's hollow interior. 'You pour scalding hot water in here.'

They hadn't realized about the hole. Caitlin asked about its value. I don't give valuations in money—however accurate you are, it's wrong tomorrow. Usually prices keep going on up and up, but you can go catastrophically wrong. Remember when the bottom fell out of the Old Master market in the London auction scene, July 1981? And the same happened to the mediæval silver coinage market all over the collecting world in the late 1970s following the discoveries of immense coin hoards on the Continent and in England? No, I give valuations in terms of time. The easiest way is to express an antique's money value as a proportion of the national average wage, because this tells whether your selling price gives a real or merely a numerical (and therefore false in inflation-riddled years) profit.

'Your cased nipple set's very rare. The pewter dish is about the same price actually at any local auction, but only because people don't recognize the nipple jewels for what they are.' I looked about for a point of reference for them. 'All your furniture could be bought new for what you should get from the two antiques.'

That set us all going for the rest of the evening. We talked into the early hours, the old folks bleating about things they'd used in youth which were now called 'antiques' and cost the earth in junkshops, and me waxing on household collectibles. It became quite a ceilidhe, a couple of neighbours joining us about midnight. They brought some bottled stout and two old pictures which had puzzled them for years. One was an English sandpainting done about 1837 or so, the heyday of that art (you arrange grains of sand of different colours into a picture, glueing them down to glass or fine-textured linen). The usual subjects are churches, landscapes and nature scenes. It's a vastly underrated art, highly skilled at best. An authentic picture, like Caitlin's neighbours', currently fetches only the average week's wage, or less. A gross underprice. The other picture was an aerophane—an early collage done by assembling fine silk-gauze colours into a scene, thread by painstaking thread. Nowadays, when embroidery and textile societies are all the rage, pictures such as these are at a peak price and a 'signed' one will buy you a good month's happy unemployment or even longer.

As the fire died and little Eileen snored, we nattered on. The rain pattered on the windows and the wind whistled, but we were cosy and safe and friendly. Everybody was smiling and talking. Nobody was daft enough to suggest banishing the little one, either. I was glad because it's always better for people to sleep on each other than on their lonesome, and that goes for infants too.

The reason I'm dwelling on this particular evening in Donald's house at Drogheda is that I began to feel I was trying to repay them in the only way I knew for poor

Joxer's loss. After all, he was from their family, distant relative or not. Also, it was peaceful.

The shambles and holocaust began the very next day.

CHAPTER 17

Next morning we really hit the road. North-west, away from the direction I wanted. The trouble with Ireland is the same as with England — for a townie like me there's just too much countryside. It's all green and boring and completely lacking in antique shops. I notched up another stray fact, though, under the stress of being torn from Donald's safe inglenook: Ireland's short on trees, really smoothish and bald. Weird fact, that.

I directed Gerald towards Ardee to make anybody following think we were hurtling for Ulster. Once through there, I'd simply nick the van, ditching Gerald and Shinny, and lam down the main N52 which transects Eire obliquely from Dundalk to the bottom of Lough Derg. A stone's throw to Limerick, and I'd be within an hour of my destination. Great. Better still, I'd be travelling light — by which I mean without help, which is always an advantage.

Caitlin had given Shinny two cushions and some blankets. 'Isn't it the world's worst deathtrap!' Caitlin exclaimed as we emerged that morning.

'It is,' I said, eyeing the van. 'Hey, Gerald. What's that glass thing on the roof?' There was this glass cockpit-like dome up there, partly concealed by lashed tarpaulins. I'd not noticed it before.

'That's my other motor-car, Lovejoy.'

Well, if he didn't want to tell me it was his own sarcastic business. I shrugged and entered the van. You don't kiss so-long in Eire like you do in England so I just said be seeing you and thanks and all that through the holes in the van wall. Caitlin said whist man and little Eileen clenched a hand in farewell. Donald strapped a long thin case to the van's roofing, probably Gerald's fishing tackle. Maybe it would lend the van some support, like a truss. Gerald folded a million or so joints in his anglepoise limbs, and we were off in a lessening drizzle.

'What was all that whirring, Lovejoy?' Shinny asked as the van trundled precariously down the slope towards the main road.

'Eh?'

'Early this morning.'

'Mind your own business,' I said sharpish, but suspected she knew all right from the way she was smiling in that irritating way.

I'd been up early. Donald had an outhouse-cum-workshop with a giant metalworker lathe, easy to somebody like me used to a homemade treadle. Unable to find any other wooden dowelling, I'd raided Caitlin's parlour curtains and nicked the curtain rod, replacing it with wool from Grannie's knitting to keep the curtain droopily in place. I'd slept downstairs on the couch so there was nobody to see as I slipped across to the outhouse and cut the dowel into four-inch sections. The electric lathe was unbelievably fast. My eight-foot length of dowel just made 24 lace bobbins of rather reduced Buckinghamshire style, with a three-quarter-inch recess for winding thread. Naturally, I'd have liked to make up the lot with a quartet of Devonshire dump bobbins, but they would have to wait. I like using walnut or proper fruitwood for these thicker ones and for doing the Midland ringed bobbins, but it wasn't my fault Caitlin's curtain rods were punk. As well, Eileen should have had a little apron of black sateen or velveteen (*never* white for lacework) and maybe an easel and lace-worker's cushion. Those too I would have to send over, once I made it safely home. Lace is definitely in since that hot 1981 August sun went to the bidders' heads and Sotheby's great lace auction started the stampede. The year before you couldn't give Honiton lace berthas away. Now, a tatty quartet of Victorian Bedfordshire lace cushion covers will bring a Troy ounce of pure gold. It's a mad world. I gave the set of lace bobbins to Grandad, swearing him on the honour of the regiment to give them to Caitlin for Eileen only when Gerald's lunatic van made it out of sight.

Caitlan had given us a good fat-riddled breakfast, a detail Sinead pointed out when I suggested we might stop for a look round Ardee. These places look grand cities on a map, but are hardly even towns.

'Coffee, then?'

'I've got a flask,' she said calmly.

'Ah,' Gerald sang out. 'If it's thinking to escape this terrible woman in the streets of Ardee y'are, Lovejoy, you're a terrible dreamer.'

'Nothing of the kind,' I lied, mad as hell that he'd spotted my plan. Where's all the trustfulness of the shores of Erin? Sinead was giving me one of her sweetest smiles, getting me madder still.

'Left, Gerald.'

Gerald swung us round a bewildered milkman's float on to the N52. 'But what can you expect when she's never once accepted my proposal, the heartless creature!'

Clinging on for dear life as we slid sideways into the thin traffic of the main road's south-westerly flow, I glanced at Sinead. She was still smiling and winked at me.

'We're sort of cousins, Lovejoy,' she yelled in the din. 'Proposal's his game.'

'She says we'll only have runts in our litter.' Gerald bawled the confidence, ignoring the road and turning completely round to enter the discussion.

'The road!' I screamed.

Horns sounded, tyres screeched. A white Ford saloon

rocked past on the outside, the driver fighting the wheel. I lost sight of it as we swung on a vaguely straighter course. More horns, a shout, then an ugly crunch of metal on stonework. We'd actually caused some poor sod to crash. Gerald, the bloody maniac, was expounding his virtues in a howled litany.

'I may not have many punts in the bank, Lovejoy,' he was going on, 'but I'm a born survivor. And once I get going, ah, what lovely poetry I'll be writing! I'll be on a pedestal like Billie Shakespeare, God rest the sainted man's sweet soul.'

I was trying to see back to where the white Ford was angled into somebody's wall but the road bent the ghastly scene from view.

Sinead reached across and patted my hand. 'It's perfectly safe,' she said. 'Gerald has his own way.'

'Never mind us. We might have just killed somebody.' My face felt prickly and drained.

'Is it the white saloon you're meaning, Lovejoy?' Gerald shouted. 'You mustn't be troubled about him, for heaven's sake. Sure now, he shouldn't have been hiding the night away down the hillside outside Donald's like a black-hearted heathen.'

I thought this over for a second or two while the van swayed hectically on down the main N52, drew breath to speak and thought better of it. Sinead leaned over.

'We're nearing Kells,' she yelled. 'Where your old picture-book comes from.'

'Ignore the silly bitch!' Gerald screeched over his shoulder. 'She's a vicious tongue in her head. Tell me, Lovejoy. Is it Milton's attitude to blank verse that grabs you, or his rationalized deism? I've been dying to ask.'

I thought, Christ, but Shinny saved me. 'Lovejoy doesn't subscribe to the notion of generative discourse, dear,' she pronounced.

'Ah, I quite understand!' Gerald howled. 'I'm a silent

man misself! Y'know I stand on Milton somewhere outside Professor Milner's sociological meritocracy ideas, though it's not at all a bad effort for a Yank from America.' He turned round and nodded seriously as though I'd disagreed. 'I know what you're thinking, Lovejoy: how does Goldmann's genetic structuralism fit in . . .'

I closed my eyes and ears to the racket and the yelling. Sinead said we would do a roadside stop for coffee beyond Delvin and work out the route. Gerald kept on bawling theories of Milton. The van bucketed on south-west down the road. Thinking back, the bloke fighting so desperately for control of the white Ford had looked very like that Johno Storr bloke, but I couldn't be sure.

'. . . And what of Hill's Third Culture theory?' Gerald was demanding of the world at the roadside. 'How far can you construct poetic analyses on a synthesis of that kind? Considering Saurat's repetitive Miltonic study in 1924 . . .'

We had stopped in a lay-by for Caitlin's coffee. Gerald had a couple of bottles of that black stout but I can't touch it to save my life. Shinny pored over the map with me. I kept trying to smile and nod politely at Gerald, who kept rabbitting on about poetry, but I'd have cheerfully throttled the noisy burke. At the back of my mind was that episode with the crashed white Ford. It *had* been an accident, due to Gerald's stupid carelessness . . . hadn't it?

'Excuse us, Gerald,' Shinny interrupted. 'Lovejoy's working out the route.'

'On the map!' He nodded like a pot Mandarin. 'That's a wise move, sure it is. I'd have brought my book of maps if I'd known we were going somewhere.' He unfolded himself and gazed at the clearing sky. 'First dry day since

St Patrick banished the snakes! I'll trot over the bog for an instant.'

I watched him stride out across the hillside. He travelled over the uneven rising round at a deceptively fast speed. He really did resemble an enormous malnourished scarecrow, his trousers flapping at half mast and his forearms protruding from his threadbare jacket. He was in a worse state than me.

Shinny was gazing fondly after him. 'Isn't he a darlin'! Always was the clever one of the family.'

'I can't make him out.' I nicked the dregs from the flask. 'Is he always like this?'

'Sure who'd want to change him?'

'Shinny.' I wanted to get a few things straight. 'Exactly what's he doing with us?'

'To help me protect you, Lovejoy,' she said evenly. 'Any other questions?'

Planning a trans-Ireland route isn't easy without revealing the destination, especially when a co-planner sits close to you and links your arm and doesn't pay much attention. We took some time. I must have become preoccupied because suddenly there was Gerald, theatrically distressed with hands spread on his chest.

'Ah, isn't it the bitter pill?' he exclaimed melodramatically.

'Eh?'

'Pay no attention, Lovejoy.' Shinny pointed at the yellow line of the N52 on the map. 'If it's Limerick you're wanting, we should keep on through Mullingar and Tullamore.'

'I turn me back and find you unfaithful! Marry me, Sinead. Get rid of Lovejoy! You'll have to sooner or later. The banns can be called—'

'*Gerald*!' Shinny tried her bandsaw voice but didn't quite make it. Gerald clearly had the knack of bringing out a bird's dimples.

'Very well!' He put on a show of inexpressible grief and collapsed his limbs behind the wheel. The engine wheezed into life. He bawled, 'Then, avaunt! I go!' The van jerked away, sending Shinny and me tumbling aside. We'd been sitting on the running-board.

'You silly—' I cursed after the goon.

Shinny was helpless with laughter as we got up. 'That Gerald!' she said.

I looked after Gerald's erratic hulk as it rocked on to the Dundalk road and headed back the way we had just come. An irritated saloon hooted at its sudden obstruction but Gerald's long thin arm only emerged to give it and the world a royal wave.

'I don't believe this. What the hell do we do now?' We had a dated map, now wet through from where it had fallen in a puddle, and an empty flask. I'd be surprised if that wasn't broken.

Shinny was still laughing. 'It's just his way, darling. He'll be wanting us to wait here.'

The recess was only thirty yards long. Another car swished by to Dundalk, and a container lorry pulled on southwards. It was a pretty lonely stretch of road. If we started walking we would be utterly exposed, caught in the open by any passing car. We were trapped.

'I'd strangle the lunatic. If I could reach his larynx.'

Shinny was astonished. 'Gerald? You *can't* be annoyed at *Gerald*!'

'He couldn't have left us in a worse place.'

'Can't you see? He's only looking after us!'

'Bring the flask and that map.'

The roadside was bare of cover, but the ground dipped from the road one side. I pulled Sinead's hand. We climbed over on to rather spongy ground. From there the slope undulated soggily up to a line of moderate hills. Walking across these fells would be murder, though Gerald had made it look easy somehow. Apart from a

plastic bag or two, nothing. Another car hummed past
heading for Mullingar. Another was coming from the
south. Asking for a lift would be risky. What if it turned
out to be Kurak?

'Here.' With some effort I dragged a longish stone
astraddle two others. As long as we sat there we could not
be seen from the road. Shinny came beside me, her arm
through mine. She was still enjoying herself. I said sourly,
'Lunacy run in the family, does it?'

'Silly!'

'Is this bog?' I nodded at the damp brown-green
countryside. We were leaning back. I'd never seen such a
smooth fellside in all my life.

'Sure what else could it be, you stupid man!'

That surprised me. 'I thought it was a joke.'

'Some joke.' She told me there were several sorts of bog.
'I guess this is red bog. It came about 4000 years BC. Just
grew, so they say, covering everything. People are always
studying it for interesting plants and digging up bones.'

'Whose bones?'

'The Giant Deer. Lived here, poor things, before they
died out. Red bog's ten yards deep.'

'Down to what?'

'Silly old stone, of course.' She snapped the words and
savagely turned on me. 'Lovejoy. What *am* I doing here,
wet through, talking about sphagnum moss when I could
be warm and cosy miles away doing something useful? I
must be off my head!'

Women get like this. I said helpfully, 'If you like,
Gerald can drop me off at Mullingar—'

'*Lovejoy*.' She managed the bandsaw voice this time
without effort. 'You think you can hide from everybody
for ever. All your crazy tricks, all your pretending—'

There was more of this rubbish. On and on she went,
yapping about my unnatural furtiveness and resentments
of people's perfectly human willingness to become

involved. I sat meekly by, nodding attentively as if I really was listening.

While she talked, though, my eyes were roaming the countryside and my mind was on the real surface of Ireland, ten yards down.

I'd imagined hearing that familiar clattering engine a dozen times and almost given up hope when Gerald returned, an hour later.

'Stay down, love,' I told Shinny. We listened as the van creaked to a halt.

'Repent, ye sinners!' Gerald's voice called. 'Do not think that you can hide your fornication—'

'It's him!' Shinny was delighted.

We climbed up sheepishly and got in. Gerald wagged a finger at us.

'Before we proceed onward,' he intoned, 'you'll be pleased to know I forgive you both!'

'For what?' I growled.

'Sinead for refusing to give me her wifely duty—'

'Whist, you terrible man!' Shinny was rolling in the aisles.

'And you, Lovejoy, for lack of trust.'

I wasn't having that. 'You left us stranded.'

'There's a petrol strike at the garages,' he announced inconsequentially. 'We're in terrible difficulty.'

The gauge had never moved off Empty since he had met us outside Trinity College. I was near to taking a swing at the silly burke. Sinead's hand fell restrainingly on my arm.

'Gerald,' she said, 'why did you go off like that?'

He looked suddenly shy and reamed an ear out with a little finger. Sinead reached for his hand.

'Please, Gerald. Say. Lovejoy's worried. He doesn't understand.'

Sheepishly he cleared his throat. 'While we were having

coffee and a chat, thirty-five motors passed us. One passed us twice, an old black Talbot. The second time, it was going back to Dundalk.' He jerked his head at the slope. 'Up there you can see quite far. The Talbot was parked a mile off. They followed me back into Kells. They're locked in a garage.' I drew breath to ask how come but thought better of it. 'To delay them,' he ended.

'There, Lovejoy!' Shinny's eyes were shining. She pulled herself forward and kissed him. 'Isn't he clever?'

'Then marry me, you stupid woman!' Instantly the old Gerald was back, and Shinny had to fight herself clear of his frantic leching.

'Get away with you!'

I was thinking, good old Lovejoy. Dim as a charity lamp. 'Look,' I said. 'Gerald, mate. Sorry. I'm just a bit thicker than usual these days . . .'

'Is apology needed between those who love the divinest poet — ?' He rolled the van out ahead of a demented two-tonner.

'Er,' I said, trying to make amends, 'er, what sort of poetry do you write, Gerald?'

'He hasn't done any yet,' Shinny explained.

'Ah! But what lovely words they'll be when they're spoken!' Gerald bawled, his limbs all on the go. 'I've thought of first using an overly-simplistic sonnet format . . .'

I subsided, Shinny holding my hand in consolation.

At Mullingar I told him to follow the N52 straight ahead to Tullamore and Birr. He cried out that sure it was a darlin' road, one to warm the cockles of your heart, and immediately swung us right on the N4 heading north-west for Longford. Shinny smiled at me. I swallowed, said not a word, smiled my best Sunday smile, and didn't raise a finger.

CHAPTER 18

That journey to Limerick was weird. It sticks in my mind.
Partly of course because of Gerald's demented driving, his
endless yap about poetry and thinking up daft schemes to
get Sinead to marry him, and partly because of the route
we took. On the map the N52 road does it all, running
slap into the N7 Dublin-Limerick trunk only a few miles
out of Limerick's safe haven. Instead, we travelled over
300 miles that lunatic day, all of it through bland, endless
countryside. I never thought I'd long for the sight of a
copse or a forest.

Gerald, spouting incomprehensible poetry, drove us all
that day, through Longford and across the Shannon, to
Roscommon where we might have turned safely south, on
westward over the River Suck, then doubling back into
Ballinasloe. There we had some fast grub and went to the
loo, then clattering on south through Portumna and
Scarriff into Limerick. It was getting dark by then, and
we had to find a hotel with a restaurant. Even then
Gerald couldn't stay still a minute, fidgeting and standing
up and walking about while Sinead and I ate. She saw
nothing odd in his behaviour. ('Oh, he's a born glassbum,
Lovejoy. Take no notice.') Weirdest of all, nobody else in
the hotel seemed to think him odd, either. They quite
took to him, all prattling away over that black stout stuff.

'Does he never stop talking?' I asked.

'Gerald?' The question puzzled her. 'Sure why would he
want to stay silent, a man like him?'

I gave up, still perished from that crazy journey.
Shinny had been cold in the van's uncontrollable gales,
but not spiritually like me. I felt like clinging to the stone
walls of real houses, streets, shops. I knew from the map

that luscious docks, post offices, libraries and churches abounded—an oasis of Mankind in all those miles of rivers, flat green-brown turf and low hills.

'Is it the chill in your soul you have, darling?' she said softly. We were in a hotel dining-room, me wading through the main course second time round.

'Just hungry.'

She smiled. 'Don't think about those horrible people if it frightens you—'

'Me? Scared?' I emitted a harsh laugh. The twins had thought the same. Women really nark you, forever reckoning they understand how you're feeling, the stupid burkes. 'Ice-cream was the third course at Henry the Fifth's coronation banquet,' I told her. 'Eat it up and be quiet.'

'Full, thanks. What happens tomorrow, Lovejoy?'

'We do the sights. Misericords in St Mary's Cathedral, antique shops.' Her eyes narrowed disbelievingly at this innocence. 'Is the Hunt collection still at that Education Institute? I've heard those Bronze Age gold torcs are local . . .'

I left Shinny and got through to Tinker in a phone booth a few minutes later. He was at the White Hart, and still only partly sloshed but delighted to hear me.

'Tinker,' I shouted into the hubbub of the taproom. 'That furniture auction, Northampton, three years back. Remember? You, me and Margaret?'

'Aye. That bloody escritoire.'

'Tinker, that big bloke on his own. Bid for a lot of Regency silver and got none—'

'You mean Big Joe Bassington? The sleeper man?' Tinker's emphysematous laugh ripped my eardrum. 'Never bought a thing at an auction in his life, thieving Cockney bastard.'

'Good lad, Tinker.'

'First met him pulling the old sleeper game down in

Bethnal Green with an early David Quare barometer—'

With a quick cheerio I hung up. Tinker's endless reminiscences were famous and intolerable. Besides, I had what I wanted. Big Joe Bassington was the sleeper man. So why all this Kurak-the-Slav business?

After supper Gerald was still flitting about somewhere like a talkative cranefly so we left him and went for a stroll. There's something about a town that no amount of picturesque rurality can convey, isn't there, bustle and contact and human endeavour. They say the Irish love a good gossip, and as far as I'd seen it's true, but Shinny told me that people living out in the remote countryside hardly ever spoke from one month's end to the next. Anyway, all that rusticity was past. In the safe confines of Newton Pery—the posh commercial bit—we wandered and looked at the shops and peered at the other hotels. We went to the bus terminus and the railway station. I began to feel quite warm again. Near there was an antique shop where I bought a dumb violin for the price of a box of fags. Shinny thought me off my head.

'What would we be wanting with that piece of rubbish?' she demanded. 'It's not even got proper strings.'

'We've just passed a music shop. Hurry, before they close.'

We made it with five minutes to spare, and I got a complete set of four new strings, including a good steel E.

I was delighted with it. 'It's a find, love. A really rare find.'

'Is it something for the stage?'

Dumb violins were made for practice, mostly in Victorian or late Georgian days. They are completely solid, not soundboxed like proper ones. This had rather faded sound holes painted on its table, and it's wooden bridge was tied round its fingerboard with a piece of old cord, thank God. The purfling was beautifully carved. Most exciting of all, the line between the bridge feet was a straight horizontal, not a modern curve. The bow had gone, but you can't have everything.

'No. Doesn't play at all — well, a sound like a trapped gnat. Only the player can hear, so you can practice to your heart's content. Even with other people living or sleeping in the same room.'

'Would you credit that!'

'When we've time I'll put the strings on and give you a silent tune —' I was quite serious, but she fell about.

'And you heathens think we are quaint! You'll serenade me with no tune at all?'

Her incredulity made me laugh and we returned slowly to the hotel calmer and happier than I'd felt for days. We looked in the bar but there was no sign of Gerald — or of Johno Storr, Jason, Kurak, the Heindricks, which was even better — so we settled down for a drink in the fug.

We laughed and chatted a good deal. Some time during that evening she took my hand to look at it for a minute and asked me to promise we would all stay together, Gerald, her and me.

'Promise,' I said, still in good humour. We'd got away from our pursuers, hadn't we?

'You'll keep your word, Lovejoy? It's important. Gerald's worried about something. I can tell. And I know you're on edge.'

'Hand on my heart,' I swore. 'Here. Keep my dumb violin as security.'

Pleased, she took the thing and put it on the seat between us, me ordering more drinks and thinking Lovejoy and my big mouth. That would probably be the last I'd see of it.

'Thank you, darling,' she said mistily. 'Now your money.'

'Eh?'

She said sweetly, 'I'll create a disturbance and get the Gardai called unless you do. As a token of your trust, darling.' I heard this in silence, was thinking, the mistrustful bitch. She leant over and bussed me, a cynical creature of no illusions. 'You can have it back at breakfast.' In silence I handed my gelt over. She bought the next round, which was big-hearted. That's women for you.

Gerald did not return before the bar shut.

The hotel gradually quietened, which meant Gerald must be miles off. I lay back and watched the ceiling.

Funny old place, Ireland. I mean, who'd guess that hotels organize the nation's babysitters? Or that the townships were all straight out of the old North Riding design of Yorkshire—a wide straight street of terraced stone houses? Or that obviously new graves were in evidence in practically every ruined abbey we'd seen, an indication of locals maintaining their familial right to monastic burial? Or that nobody much spoke Gaelic in everyday life? Or that you got money for actually living and working in the Gaelteacht, the Gaelic-speaking parts? Or that the museums and churches had such wealths of antiquities that set your breathing wrong even as you drove past? Or that there was so little noise?

Times like this, waiting for people to simply get out of the way, I wish I still smoked. Something to do. It was getting on for midnight. A few people used the stairs, one couple making me smile by talking loudly with the impervious good cheer of the tipsy. After that it got very quiet. I dozed a little, went over in my mind the possible antiques good old Tinker was hoovering up in East Anglia. I'd given him no money to slap deposits down on things, but locally they knew I was good for debts—useless with gelt, I thought wrily. If only I'd had a bit of credit. If I came this way again I'd bring every groat I could scrape up.

In a closed antique shop window Shinny and I had seen

a folding ivory fan. Closed, it was made exactly like a miniature 1780 musket, the unmistakable Short Land Pattern weapon. Only last year, such a mint treasure was an average weekly wage or less. Now it fetches half a year's salary in anybody's money. Look out for ivory fans in their original box if they're Cantonese, because that doubles the value, and remember that the fashion for Chinese stuff which followed MacCartney's embassy to the Court of the Imperial Dragon did much to stimulate copying Chinese art, but not much for imports. The almighty boom came around the time of the Opium Wars when Chinese (mainly Cantonese) bowls, carvings, screens, porcelains, statuettes, jewellery, clothes—much of it made in Kwantung mimicking Western fashions, to order—poured into England. I've yet to see an auction in any English town without a genuine piece of such date (1820-1850, give or take an hour) and origin.

Japanese influence, on the other hand, came . . .

My mind froze. 'Who is it?'

I could have sworn somebody scratched at the door of my room. Nervously I got off the bed and padded slowly across, wanting something handy to use as a truncheon. Nothing, of course, just when you want it. My throat felt funny.

The hotel corridor was empty when I managed to screw up courage to open the door and peer out. But that quiet sound had been very definite. An envelope lay on the carpet just inside the door.

Familiar scent and addressed to me in a woman's handwriting. Worse, the note was on hotel notepaper.

Dearest Lovejoy,

How very keen you are to get started! And wasn't that an absolutely lovely journey? *Such* pretty countryside! My husband has formed the strong belief that the fishing will be absolutely superb here this year, and is already talking of the salmon. He *so* hopes you will join

him. We have a delightful place away from that
dreadful new trading estate. Kurt would value your
opinion on our recent acquisitions. They include a
splendid sugar castor, Lamerie I am told. You'll love it.
We will expect you in the morning for breakfast — say,
nine o'clock? Our country house is on the old Ennis
road, twenty minutes away. Kurak will call for you in
good time. Please feel free to bring that scrawny female
and her strange young man.

Love,

Lena.

My overworked sweat glands panicked into action.

That leaf-on-a-flood nervousness returned. Everybody
else stirred up tides. Good old Lovejoy just drifted
helpless. Lena's message was clear and manyfold:
Limerick is home territory to us Heindricks; we are big in
the land with many mansions and even our sugar
sprinklers could buy and sell all the Lovejoys of this world
put together. Not only that; the Heindricks' scam was so
big that even zillionaires were keen on its successful
execution. That last worried me. I dwelled wistfully on
Paul de Lamerie, and knew that there had been one such
1719 piece of his up in a recent Dublin antiques fair for a
mere 29,700 quid. Lena said I'd love it — as a bribe?

The phone rang.

Once I'd subsided and got my heart back I said, 'Yes?'
A bloke said, 'Ah, just to check you're still there, sor. I'm
to say if you want anything urgent the two of us will be
down in reception.'

'Is this from Mr Heindrick?' I asked.

'His compliments.'

That did it. I slammed the receiver down. Enough's
enough, even for pathetic creeps like me. I switched the
light off, saw I had everything — in fact not a farthing, not
a weapon — and looked out.

Nobody in the corridor. Terror lends wings to others,

but stealth to me. I floated towards the stairs past Sinead's room—two along from mine. The passageway lights were still on, and stair wall-lamps so artistic you could hardly see a bloody thing. But in the well-lit lounge two tweedy blokes were swilling that black foamy drink in comfortable armchairs. The desk bloke was with them and the talk was all horses. No way past them, that was for sure, but I was past caring. The floor above had an end window and a fire escape, which squeaked from disuse when I trod on the fenestrated metal steps. Well if they heard me all that could happen would be they'd send me back to my room till 'Kurak' zoomed up.

Gerald's van was in the tiny carpark. A single neon lamp gave shadows everywhere. Its light showed that Gerald's weird glass bubble had gone from the van's roof. As I climbed in and groped for the wiring I saw his long thin case had vanished, too. The rope lashings and the old tarpaulin had been chucked in a heap. The silly sod had probably gone fishing, at this time of night. Or maybe he and Sinead were, erm, upstairs and . . . A bloke like him is really beyond me. I shrugged off the irritating image of him and Sinead and got the engine going. In the quiet night of Limerick City it sounded like a spaceprobe blasting off. Naturally I couldn't guess reverse and had to climb out and push the bloody crate myself to get room to turn. As I did so I noticed a white Ford saloon, about three cars off. Its front offside wing was badly damaged, as though it had run into a wall somewhere. I went and had a peer at it. Maybe it really was the one which had been parked next to Michael Fenner's grand posh Rover outside his bookseller's place. So it hadn't been Jason driving after all. Well, birds of a feather and all that.

Mulgrave Street was the direction I wanted out of town, parallel to the railway and heading for Tipperary. Only one headlamp worked so I was fortunate to see the turn-off. Within minutes the lovely safe city had ended, and horrible countryside was all around. Rain made it more difficult, speckling the windscreen. The wipers didn't work, and I couldn't get top gear. The fuel gauge showed empty. The wind whistled in through the holes in the bodywork. Wrestling with the wheel, I bungled the lunatic vehicle through the worsening weather, peering blearily out for the signs I knew would be there.

The dawn came up on the lake shining right into my eyes and the surface glittering. An entire picture of innocence with blandness all around.

The rain had packed it up about three hours before dawn, thank God. It was quite picturesque, really, if you weren't drenched, shivering under a filthy old wet tarpaulin and hungry. A fish plopped somewhere and a bird chirped happily, bloody fool. Time to look around and see precisely where Lena's merry mob were going to hide the repro gold torcs and pull their miraculous 'find'. There couldn't be many places, not here in all this remoteness. So I thought, though a duckegg like me can be wrong without even trying.

Walking ploshily down to the lake from the roadside was not as easy as it sounds. For a start, you can hardly ever tell where these lakes begin and end. Not like lakes anywhere else, which have definite edges. This had a sort of longish brown grass fringe. You go towards the lake and the ground just gets wetter and this brackeny stuff more prolific, until finally you realize you are up to your calves in water and are actually awash. It's a rum business. From my position in the van reaching the crannog looked easy, but proved hopeless. A crannog's a small fortified island — sometimes artificially constructed as a kind of little waterbound citadel. They were made in the distant past and proved highly effective — after all, the powerful Republic of Venice began as nothing more than a kind of posh multiple crannog. I stared across, ankle-

deep in water. The little crannog was out of reach on foot
and there were no signs of any regular disturbances of the
terrain between the road and the lakeshore nearest the
crannog. It could have been the obvious place to plant a
considerable number of gold torcs even if they had been
manufactured by poor old Joxer in his workshed back in
the grounds of St Botolph's Priory last month.

Squelching to drier ground, I went left and began to
work round the lake. The size deceived me. From the
road it had looked small, coming into the growing
daylight from the amorphous slopes of brownish green.
Now I realized it was over a mile across, and was indented
on the opposite side into large smooth bays, to north and
south-west of a fairly considerable hill. There was nothing
for it but to go the whole way round.

Our library had pinpointed the known archaeology of
the place quite well, though construction diagrams were
not available. Still, I could tick off on my mental list the
antiquities as I found them. The village of Kilfinney had
been even smaller than I'd learned to expect, a mere
thirty or so terraced houses asplay a single unlit street,
with one shop, a couple of narrow tracks leading off to
nearby crofts, and a diminutive chapel. The lake was a
handful of miles off. Remoter farms were shown on the
map far over the western side of the lake but nothing
immediately in view. One stroke of luck was that the main
Limerick-Cork road ran over to the east, and you
wouldn't want to reach Mallow or Tipperary by this
route. No car had passed once I'd found the lake in the
small hours. I was clearly ahead, in a narrowing race.

It took two hours. Between road and lake were two
stone circles, nothing like Stonehenge but still the real
thing, and a ring fort. If you've never seen one of these,
they are merely earthworks thrown up in a circle.
Archaeologists and other wastrels burn air exchanging
theories about ring forts (they were probably nothing

more than cattlepens easily defended against pilferers from neighbouring tribes). They have always disappointed treasure seekers. Stone circles, whatever they were actually for, were certainly too sacrosanct for the ancients to go digging and burying many trinkets.

The ground outcropped stonily when I reached the north-west corner where the foundations of old dwellings stood, maybe nine or ten. Each was double, like spectacles, linked by a narrow strip—maybe cottages with adjacent storehouses. For me they'd be too recent by at least a thousand years. In any case, ruined houses were places people were always robbing in the Middle Ages and later for building material. Moral: too unbelievable that a whole hoard might have remained unviolated. I went on, south now on the sheltered side of the lake. I could see Gerald's tatty van waiting like a faithful friend in the weak sunshine.

A lane ran a couple of miles east, ducking round Kicknadun, the lake's hill. The remains here were far more likely candidates for Lena's sleeper trick. Ring ramparts were only to be expected on a hillside. What interested me more were the Stone Age house, and the lone burial tumulus. The self-effacing mounds are all over the British Isles. They are smooth, sometimes longbarrows, shaped like inverted boats. This one showed no signs of having been tinkered with. I walked a couple of furlongs towards the Stone Age house site, over the rough tussocky hillside, then paused. A horseman was moving along the distant lane, making as if to skirt the eastern side of Kicknadun Hill. He was riding casually, not looking.

The ground was undisturbed round the site. Genuine, though, from the strong inner vibes its lopsided stone mounds emitted. The question was whether Heindrick had the nerve to use a place like this—not quite in the right period, obviously partly excavated. I scanned to the south-west where the two stone fort ruins showed. Well, the hotel's guide book had explained they'd been occupied till the tenth century at least. No, Heindrick. The forts were out. There was no movement on the hillside. That horse had looked useful rather than racey. A crofter? A riding-school leader sussing out the day's route? The rider had been carrying a stick.

Going round the southern extremity, the lake's terrain included a castle ruin, pretty prominent on a small mound. It was infused by legends of the White Knights. It looked lovely, good enough to eat, but I was becoming edgy. A saloon car came along the road, slowed near the van, then droned on towards Kilmallock. Not quite Lena's style, however, and too far off for me to spot any occupants.

A horseman showed beyond the castle mound as I walked on. Now I was heading for the van, which came in sight in another few furlongs. Different horse, different bloke. He too held a stick-shaped thing, carrying it lance-like, the way Red Indians do in Westerns. He remained motionless, just facing the road.

That left only one archaeological site. The hotel's local guide marked as a wedge, calling it 'ancient grave'. These things are small, but as I came on to it I guessed it would be a gallery grave. Vibes began shivering through me as I approached. Gallery graves date from about 3000 BC for half a millennium. They consisted of a long wedge-shaped gallery made of big stones arranged to form compartments. At the mouth was a space indicated by standing stones. Of course it was now only revealed by mounds and the odd projecting stone, but you could easily guess where the grave's entrance might be. Big medicine, I decided, but which of all these places was the likely one? And still no sign of disturbance by busy little Heindrick-motivated diggers, except for a recent pile of dark brown peat a hundred yards off, probably drying and waiting collection for the fire.

Was the scam therefore going to be pulled somewhere in that tiny hamlet of Kilfinney, then? If so, how? It was bright day now. The horseman by the castle ruins was moving slowly parallel. In another few minutes he would reach the road a mile or so off. I stood on the nearest stone and looked back across the Lough. The first horseman was silhouetted on the skyline, moving along the crest by the ring rampart. Great. In the distance a shrill engine whined, maybe from that lane beyond Kicknadun Hill, too far off to be any help. Well, they were both behind me if I headed for the van. I hungered for streets and traffic, but keep to a steady walk, Lovejoy. In this state I'd never make it running. I struck out north, converging on the road along the western edge of the lake, hurrying and covering the uneven ground really well.

Apart from an ugly reedy patch near where I'd gazed at the crannog, I made fast if rather breathless time. The horsemen showed no intention to hurry, moving steadily behind me at a distance, one heading for the road, the other following me round the lough. I was almost past my first two stone circles and in hailing distance of Gerald's van when it dawned on me. They were merely herding me back. I was *supposed* to come this way.

Stumbling across the tussocks I kept an eye out northwards. Sure enough, there was another rider on that bend of the lake. He must have just watched from there all the time as I'd been shepherded nearer and nearer. The trap was closed.

Wearily I plodded slowly towards the van. Of course I could have sprinted to it and tried a dashing Brands Hatch start, but I'm not that daft. Nor were the Heindricks loony enough to send their cavalry to herd me into a getaway vehicle.

I made it and climbed in, utterly panned out. A big

hand clamped on my shoulder though I'd made no move to start the engine.

'Look,' I said over my shoulder. 'If you're trying to frighten me to death, yahboo doesn't work after puberty, okay?' And continued into the disappointed silence, 'Joe Bassington, isn't it? The sleeper king? Dropped off from that car, and hiding under the sacks as I got in, right?'

'Okay, mate,' Kurak said. He looked close to tears I'd not run screaming. 'Don't start yet.' We waited till the three riders clumped up. Their sticks were shotguns, only crummy modern gunge but still superior armament of a kind I did not possess. Two of the blokes were the boozers from the hotel reception area.

'Top of the morning,' I said.

'All right, is it, Mr Kurak?' one said, eyeing me with curiosity.

'Eeess agutt,' Joe Bassington said, narked off that I was there to witness his phoney Slav act.

I fell about laughing to get him madder. One of the riders held up a warning hand. We all listened obediently. The shrill whine of an engine came quite clearly to all five of us.

'Not a car,' the horseman from the castle mound said.

The second nodded, said something in Gaelic. All three riders looked over the lake.

'Sure, from the lane.'

'Lambretta?'

It actually did sound like one of those motorized scooters.

'Who'll be having one of them things?' the north horseman said. He stood up in his stirrups to see further. They were quite at home on their bloody great animals. One stuck its nose in the van and frisked me for sugar with its snuffler. I've always found horses real chisellers.

'Sod off, mate,' I told it. Now I'd been rumbled I wanted my own breakfast. Besides, the selfish creature had helped to catch me.

'That teacher down in Rath Luirc, and the O'Donnells in Croom.'

'Not them.'

We all listened as the tinny little sound buzzed into a fade-out. Fed up, I started the van's engine. One horse started but settled down at a word.

'Cheers,' I said.

'We'll be saying so-long to you,' the hillside rider said courteously. I felt I'd been knighted and gave them an arm-wag to show there were no hard feelings. They even waved back. I ask you. It's a frigging rum world right enough.

I trundled the van northwards.

'Don't tell me, Joe,' I said to Kurak. 'Through Limerick on to the old Ennis road, eh?'

'Eeess arite.' He shrugged with embarrassment when I turned to stare disbelievingly. 'Well, Lovejoy. Heindrick'll do his nut if you've sussed me out.'

'Okay, okay, mate,' I said. 'I'll keep pretending you're Kurak. Let's hope Lena's got the kettle on. Here, Joe. That sleeper job you pulled in Northampton that time, with those rectangular folding card tables. You remember, copied from Stalker and Parker in walnut? How did it go? I never did hear the finish of it . . .'

I drove on, into captivity.

CHAPTER 19

Coming down the wide staircase, I felt like Noel Coward, a right lemon. The dressing-gown was all I had on, dragon patterns and those flame-shaped clouds copied from Ming Period stuff. A maid—in this day and age—had knocked about the bedroom while I bathed.

She'd taken my clothes, leaving one penny and a coil of four violin strings on the dressing-table, all I possessed, thanks to Shinny's mistrust. The girl was pretty but wanted to do my nails with a sandpaper spatula. I said no thanks, and she opened the door indicating I was wanted downstairs. The point is, you can't escape attired in only a dressing-gown.

The house was magnificent, antique furniture and trappings everywhere. If it could be faulted at all, it was in the mixture of styles. The Heindricks had accumulated paintings of different character and periods and simply put them wherever they had the next bit of space. On the stair wall, for example. You've never seen such a jumble: a Rembrandt etching, a swirly modern Henry Moore drawing, a Dante Gabriel Rossetti watercolour of the wife of William Morris (DGR reckoned he loved her, but I think he only ever loved his own wife, Lizzie Siddall, who died so soon). This hotchpotch gallery went on through a modern John Nash, a Rowlandson (I hate those) and ended in a painting of a Shakespeare scene labelled 'H. Fuseli, 1741-1825,' which gave me a laugh. I moved on down the last three stairs because Joe's big fist grabbed me and pulled me across the marble-floored hall and into a vast plush room.

'Here, Joe,' I whispered, annoyed, 'stow it, mate.'

'Eessa Lovejoyee, modom,' Joe said.

'How pleased we are that you could come.' Lena Heindrick, Heindrick, and Jason. In that order, I think, though I'm still not certain.

'How do,' I said, making sure my dragon gown was arranged right. 'Hiyer, Jason.'

Lena rose, placed a hand on my arm and led the way smiling through double doors. We followed, dithering about who went first. Give Jason his due, he was not in the least put out when I gave him one of my special glances, just nodded back. Mixed oak panel-and-plush breakfast-room. We were helped to the grub — arranged buffet-style like in rep theatre — by another maid, as if the kidneys and bacon and eggs were heavy as lead.

That breakfast was really great, plenty of grub, and chat about antiques. Some chat is more innocent than ours was.

'Mind if I ask,' I started up, thinking no time like the present, 'if that *Christ Conversing With Law Doctors* is the one nicked from Lausanne?' The thieves had done a simple switch, with copies made from an art book. The curators said the stolen originals were so famous they would be unsaleable, which is a laugh. The antiques game is in a right state, but you still don't have to give Rembrandts away.

Heindrick was amused, sipping a minuscule glug of juice at the head of the table. 'The *Musée de L'Elysée* got them both back, did they not?' So he didn't mind if the maid heard about the odd antique rip. I'd hoped a quick seduction of an honest Limerick lassie would spring me from all this, and now quickly abandoned that impromptu plan.

'Oh.' I was a picture of innocence. 'Were there two?'

'*Touché!*'

'You admired our collection of paintings, Lovejoy.' Lena nodded for the toast to keep coming.

'Well, in a way. I like genuine paintings, one of the most satisfying artistic —'

'Genuine?' Heindrick's voice sharpened. 'Are you implying — ?'

'Your Fuseli's duff.'

'You mean . . . a fake?'

Jason was eating breakfast like the true ex-military officer he was, scrambled egg patted into squares and precise kidney slivers doing a flanker. His knife and fork paused.

I nodded. 'The goon who sold you it didn't get the

surname right, either.' I spelled it for them, having a high
old time. 'Henry Füssli, though everybody else spelled it
Fuseli. I've a soft spot for him because he too was a right
robber.'

'In what way, Lovejoy?' I could have sworn Lena was
enjoying the consternation my patter was creating.

'Füssli was Zürich Swiss. Not much imagination but
great technique.' I cleared a mouthful to explain. 'And a
real talent-spotter. Admitted that William Blake was the
most superb source for the art copier.' I gave a benign
grin. 'Though *he* used the word steal. Naturally, he made
it into London society — wealth, position, status, the lot.
Blake didn't.'

'That painting is genuine, Lovejoy.' Jason's edible army
hadn't moved.

'Sure.' I gave him an ostentatious wink. Divide and
conquer, somebody once said. Heindrick had gone quiet.
Either Jason had charged them the earth for the Füssli or
Heindrick was thinking of other possible fakes in his
possession. Lena was smiling, full of hidden mirth, but
then she'd learned how to divide and conquer many
moons ago.

'Lovejoy might be joking,' she announced, patting her
hubby's hand consolingly.

'Watch him, Mrs Heindrick,' Jason said quietly. 'I've
seen him do worse than joke.'

'Got the torcs here?' I asked, to keep the serve. 'Or are
they down near the — ?'

Quickly Lena called to the serf, gazing distantly over
my head, 'You can go now, Mary. Thank you.'

' — Because time's getting on and I've an appointment . . .'

The door closed. Lena was observing me. I was the only
one noshing now. Heindrick was pale and uptight, Jason
silent with his military mind on the go.

'Torcs, Lovejoy? What do you know about torcs?'

'That mean I can't have any more, please?'

'As much as you wish.' Lena gestured me over to the bureau where I refilled my plate. I really hate to see class furniture used wrong. The coffee tray was placed on a mahogany tripod table next the bureau. It was 1750-ish, with lovely 'piecrust' edging. Underneath, it was supported on a 'birdcage movement' through a single pillar of three carved clawfeet. The birdcage arrangement means its top can be folded down. Rotten luck to be used for a grotty coffee tray, especially as it antedated the bureau and silver by a century.

Lena ahemed. 'Lovejoy, please.' I returned, smouldering about the the antiques. 'Lovejoy. *What* torcs?'

Apologetically I edged the toast nearer and started on the grub. Eating alone in company's embarrassing, but it's their fault they stopped. I've noticed that self-starvation is becoming pretty common these days.

'The ones you had made.' I offered Jason the butter but he refused without moving a muscle. 'Joxer, remember? The one who died by accident, in a workshop fire. Once he'd made the repro torcs for you, that is.'

'Who revealed more than was advisable,' Heindrick added.

'How, Lovejoy?' Trust Lena to stay on course. 'You're not psychic too?'

'One of Joxer's rough casts in base metal was left in the ash. I stood on it by accident while the police searched.'

'Did you—?' Jason began, but Heindrick silenced him.

'Lovejoy said nothing or none of us would have got this far.'

'Then I saw the museum exhibits in Dublin.' My continued story had blammed Jason's appetite. I wondered if he'd mind if I asked him if I could finish his grub for him. 'A lovely exhibition. Seen it?' Heindrick's head moved an inch in negation. 'You should,' I enthused with poisonous heartiness. 'It's in the same central display.'

'In the same central display as what?' Lena was worth ten of the rest of them.

I smiled. 'As the Derrynaflan Hoard.'

The silence was broken only by the sound of me finishing everything in reach. I went red because your mouth and jaws and teeth make a hell of a din when you're last to finish. Even a single swallow sounds like a sink emptying however hard you try.

'What's that particular treasure to us?' Lena again. Like I said, a real woman, boots and all.

'It's your blueprint.'

Jason rose abruptly and went to stand by the door. I nearly choked laughing. Big Joe, well, yes, especially if assisted by that cavalry. But Jason couldn't stop me in a million years.

Lena snapped, 'Sit *down*,' then turned to her hubby, smiling. 'Show them to Lovejoy, Kurt.'

Old Joxer, God rest him, had done a superb job, for all his habitual tipsiness. The weight of gold's difficult to judge—I mean, who'd think that a whole ton of the stuff makes a block only twenty-five inches long by ten by twelve? It's just so damned heavy.

Heindrick carried a case to a Pembroke table by the window and placed the torcs on a velvet cloth. There were fourteen, great twists of gold made into crescents to be worn by chieftans before the coming of Rome. Except they had been made over the last few months. They were exquisitely done, finished to a degree and gleaming with the love that the craftsman had put into them. My eyes blurred. That Joxer.

'One's genuine, Lovejoy.' Lena had approached.

'Balls—I mean they're all fakes, love.' There wasn't a vibe among the lot of them. I touched them to make sure.

'Well done. Show him now, darling.'

And Heindrick brought out a fifteenth. Well, I mean. If you've ever seen a diamond beside a burnt match—identical substance, but a world of difference. The ancient ages beat out of this pre-Roman Celtic torc with stunning impact. When my fingers lay reverently on its radiant surface all I could feel were the bell-like tremors in my chest. Genuine is genuine, and a real antique is nothing but pure solid love.

'What's the plan?' somebody said dully, and I thought with horror: *that's my voice saying that*. Whose side was I on for God's sake, theirs or mine?

'This way, darling.'

I don't know how, but the next thing Lena was walking me in the grounds, Heindrick and Jason presumably still mesmerized by all that gold.

The trouble is that women like Lena start life miles ahead of the rest. She was one of those birds who make your breathing funny soon as they're in reach. Attired in a loose high-collared knitted dress that could have given me security all year, and embellished with jewellery that made me moan, she was blindingly attractive. The fact that she pulled Heindrick's strings and therefore would effectively decide where the scam's profits went only weakened me further. Don't misunderstand: I really was honestly still bitter about Joxer's death, and being manœuvred into joining the Heindricks was particularly shameful. In any case it should be obvious to anybody by now that in spite of not having much in a material sense I'm consistent and pretty honest. But I've always found that women tend to deflect you from the right course. I mean, I'd have been light years off by now but for Shinny, and if it wasn't for Lena I'd be hiding on Kicknadun watching her men plant the sleepers and readying myself to happen by with a spade in the dark hours . . . We held hands like lovers do. I thought she was carrying an apple till I looked: it was only the enormous velvety Muzo emerald (the world's best, if you've a spare fortune to spend) in her ring. She led me towards a summerhouse in the landscaped greenery.

'Time to be utterly frank, darling.'

'I always am.'

'You and I have a kind of duty, Lovejoy.'

'To . . . ?'

'Each other, no?'

'And the torcs?'

'Let's think of those as—' she hesitated, all girlish charm—'the ties that bind two hearts that beat as one, shall we?'

'That's a hell of a way to put it.'

A couple of gardeners grovelled and melted among shrubbery in a practised drill. Clearly other companions had strolled this way before me. By the tall garden wall was a low brick structure. I sniffed the air—somebody was running a paraffin-burning kiln without its door sealed.

I felt a right daffodil in my dragon-covered gown, very conscious of the fact that men's legs always look a scream.

'Do come in, darling.' She led ahead into the circular summerhouse. It consisted of one large room. I'd never seen so many curves, bed, furniture, rugs, the vast disc-shaped carpet, mirrors, the lot. The curtains began to hiss closed. Lena had touched a wall thing. 'Do you like it?' The curtains stopped, all but drawn to.

'Are we going round?' The sun was ducking slowly from one drape to another.

'Of course. The summerhouse can turn with the sunlight.'

'Oh. Right, then,' I said lamely and perched on the bed. 'You can't mean pull the old violin gig on your husband, Jason, Kurak—'

'Let me explain, darling.' Lena undid the belt of her

dress. 'Money of itself has very little attraction for me.'

'Mmmh?' I said politely.

'That's God's own truth, darling.' She sounded quite earnest, really convincing. Her arms lifted, the way they undo zips. 'I want more than changing numbers on a bank statement.'

'Everybody's a collector, Lena. Of money, sensations, porcelain, vintage cars, experiences. If money's not your thing, what is it you collect?'

'I collect people, darling.'

Her dress fell. She did not immediately step out of the heap like other women do, just stood there turning slightly and slipping her rings off, one by one and watching herself in one of the oval mirrors. A lesser woman would have crossed to the dressing-table and immediately done something to her hair. Lena simply continued undressing where she stood, smoothing her petticoat away from her hips. The faience necklace was Egyptian, as old as some pyramids, and its eighty or so pieces were splayed across her breast exactly as the pharaohs' wives had worn them. Faience jewellery is only glazed earthenware or early pottery done in small palmates, fruits, dates and figs thread-linked between tiny cylinders, but worn right it is breathtaking.

'Are people collectable?' I said.

'Certainly.' All her clothes were about her ankles. She turned and walked in one motion.

'In bottles of fluid, like the Royal College of Surgeons do?'

'Not quite.' She stood against me. My face pressed itself into her of its own accord. 'I collect them for what they do.'

She raised a knee to the bed and pushed my gown from my shoulders, slowly with introspective care.

'And what do they do?' I asked, muffled.

'Everything I say, darling. From being exquisite bores,

like your Jason, to those who will commit savage, awful things.' She was breathing quicker, but not as fast as me.

'You mean . . .'

'Even killing? Yes.'

'Like Kurak?'

'Yes, darling. Like Kurak killed Joxer. And like you.'

'Me? You're off your head. I've never killed anybody in my life.' Except when it was accidental or somebody else's fault.

'Including you, darling.' We were on the bed now, hands and breathing anywhere and any old how.

'Why collect us—me?'

'Because you'll respond against your will. To me, darling. For me. It's thrilling.' The luscious faience motifs from Ancient Egypt fell over my face as she murmured, 'Power, darling. I crave it like you crave me.'

'Am I for sale?'

'Everybody's for sale, Lovejoy.'

I had to ask what my price was for joining her collection of serfs, each one of us blindly obedient to her whims.

'You?' She leant up on an elbow, smiling down. 'Your payment is a choice of the torcs once the scam is pulled—plus a permanent salary. Plus me.'

I started to say I would consider her offer but didn't quite make it.

In that little death which follows after, I became aware that the curtains had somehow accidentally hissed apart all round, letting in sunlight upon us. Anybody could have seen us, even from the house. We were like tomatoes in a greenhouse. I should have been anxiously working out what bargain Lena and I had sealed, but sleep wouldn't let me go.

Dozing on some time later I heard a whining mini-engine start up in the distance and dwindle to silence. Lot of scooters about in Western Ireland, my mind registered. I rolled over into oblivion.

CHAPTER 20

The crime-briefing conference opened with Cockburn's white sherry and dry biscuits. Kurt was at his preening best. I was afraid Lena's mood of creamy elegance would give us away but need not have feared. Kurt was full of the forthcoming scam. Only Kurak smouldered. Maybe he had taken a forbidden peek into the summerhouse, an unpleasing thought. Jason had gone, presumably taking the gold torc sleepers with him. Lena wore a new dress with a low waist, almost 1920 flapper style. On any other woman her age it would have been called too young. She wore a single sapphire pendant on a gold S-linked chain. Your mouth waters of its own accord when you see something that delectable. I'd only ever seen one bigger— the 393-carat Blue Star sapphire from Ceylon at the Commonwealth place in London, and they'd guarded that with a four-foot Sinhalese monocled cobra. I caught Lena's look and smiled innocently into her dark eyes.

Believe it or not, we received the lecture in the library, Kurt enunciating with characteristic precision.

'The plan is simple,' Heindrick said. 'No fewer than fifteen gold torcs of genuine Celtic design are discovered in a well-known archaeological site on open land. A miraculous accidental find. They are authenticated by a divvie who happens to be visiting the finder.'

'Erm, the discoverer, erm, sir?' I said humbly.

'Ah. That will be myself.' Kurt gestured eloquently at Lena. 'Out walking tomorrow, we pause. A small cave-in, a prod of my walking-stick, and I glimpse gold. Before adequate witnesses. The authorities are summoned.'

'That fast, eh?'

He shrugged expansively. 'Naturally. I am obviously wealthy and will use all my resources to exhort them to speed.'

'And what is a society crowd doing wandering out in sloppy countryside?'

'Looking at a private exercise session of my horses.'

'Is that plausible?' It didn't sound so, to me.

'Several million punters will find it so. Especially if two of those horses are running in the big race six weeks hence.'

'Fair enough. But who examines this archaeological site?'

'A famous archaeological department, the coroner — and you.'

'What if they refuse to accept me?'

He tutted at such disbelief. 'I'm your host. I *know* your particular gift of detecting genuine antiques from fakes. I will encourage them to make any test of your knack. You will convince them, as always.'

'Exactly where's this site?' I asked, 'Please, sir? Kilfinney's riddled with a score of genuine archaeological remains. There are more Bronze Age places around than the parson preached about.'

'That needn't concern you, Lovejoy.' Lena's sharpness dispelled the calm. Lena getting edgy over something? Carefully I avoided staring in her direction.

'Which of the gold torcs will be first out?'

'You already know. It will be the genuine one, naturally. In fact, I will lift it from the ground. To—'

'—To establish your claim as legally binding.'

Kurt was smiling. 'Had you any other idea, Lovejoy?'

'With your armed outriders on the skyline? Hardly. But one thing's troubling me.'

'The archaeological site, I take it?'

'You've done your homework. As far as I can see there's no way round the fact that to get the torcs into an underground Bronze Age crypt, burial site, foundation, or cave, we've got to dig deep.'

'So?'

'So archaeologists are well aware that the commonest con trick is to fake an antique item and bury the bloody thing, then miraculously "discover" it *in situ*. The trouble is, you leave slight traces of penetration, such as great mounds of rubble, bulldozers and the cranes you need to lift the Old People's great stones. Some weigh many, many tons.'

'That problem's solved, Lovejoy,' he said smoothly, 'by Mrs Heindrick.'

Now I did turn and look. This was the biggest breakthrough since the wheel. 'You mean you've thought up a way of inserting a forged artefact into an ancient archaeological site without leaving evidence of a break-in?'

'Yes. Next problem?'

'It's impossible.'

Heindrick glanced at his watch. 'Wrong. Your ex-colleague Jason—under a considerable armed guard, I might add—has just gone on ahead to arrange matters.'

I insisted, 'But he's had to lift at least one of the stones, or simulate . . .'

'No.' He was enjoying himself. Even Joe-alias-Kurak was smiling. 'I do promise you, Lovejoy. From the old Celtic times until tomorrow when the archaeological team arrives hotfoot in response to my summons, not a grain of peat, soil or stone will have been disturbed.'

'But that can't be done.'

'And the authorities, archaeologists, and you will all be honest, independent witnesses to see me draw out the very first gold torc, and place it in the hands of the coroner himself. Indeed,' he smirked, really whooping it up, 'the archaeologists themselves will have to cut down through the layers to assist its being brought to light.'

I gave that one up. So Lena had attributes other than taste, wealth, beauty, personality, attraction, style, sexual skill. To them that hath shall be given.

'Okay. It can be done if you say. But how do you get the other fourteen?'

'By the time we get the genuine sleeper out, it will be nearly dark—'

'Kurt will claim to have seen the shine of other gold items,' Lena cut in. 'An armed guard will be found for the night.'

'Your men?' I guessed.

'Right.'

'—Who will look away while Jason and Kurak lift the others. You will then have "authenticated" gold torcs.'

'Don't miss the two main points, Lovejoy darling.' Lena sounded strangely bitter. 'There will be an outcry. The whole world will be informed next day that an unknown number of torcs were stolen from a proven Bronze Age site, which provides us with the most sensational—and free—advertising.'

'You said two points.'

'Authenticity. The more scientific tests they do on the one genuine piece they possess, the more they lend authenticity for our fourteen.'

'Why put them all in the site, then?'

'Soil analyses, radioactivity tracer counts, chromatography and spectrographic scans, mycological screening.' Kurt sighed heavily. 'Your undeniable gift, Lovejoy, blinds you to the scientific lengths to which cynical antique dealers will go in trying to establish authenticity.

'And forever there will be a reference standard.' Lena's bitterness was back again. Even Kurt peered doubtfully at her. 'Our buyers will naturally refer to the only known genuine item from the Kilfinney Hoard.'

'It does have a certain . . . ring to it, no?' Kurt was in dreamland.

'Will you get customers?' I asked innocently.

'As long as tomorrow's miraculous discovery goes perfectly.'

'I've seen your kiln. I trust your people have had the sense to take it easy with the temperatures. And get the soil samples right.'

'Of course, Lovejoy.'

You can't really tarnish gold easily. The trick is to heat it low and slow, then cool it in soil of identical composition with the site where you intend to plant it. If you do it right, the magical metal will look as aged as you can get it, and those cynical nasty-minded archaeologists will find no traces of 'wrong' dust.

'My last worry's fingerprints.'

Kurt's eyes clouded momentarily and I thought, got you, you bloody knowall. 'Whose?' he asked me.

'The Celts. Think scientists forget them, mate? We are probably bigger and fatter than the Old People, so our fingerprints are different. First you wipe off your own forger's prints with a shammy leather (don't use cloth for heaven's sake or they'll detect the fibres you leave behind on the tips of the torc). Then you find some old geezer about ninety—the smaller the better, jockey-sized if you can—and make him wash his tiny withered hands (no scents in the soap, please) and rinse them well to remove soap traces. Dry his hands in air until they look the same as usual (don't let him touch anything, fibres again) and give him the torc to fondle. Take it from him in your shammy leather, and bury in the allotted place.'

'Lovejoy,' Kurt enunciated crisply as I concluded my explanation, 'you have just earned your fee. We'll see to it. Otherwise, I do assure you we have organized it perfectly.'

'And Jason's already put the sleepers there? *In situ?*'

'No.' Kurt lit a cigar with tantalizing deliberation. 'I said that he had gone ahead to arrange matters.'

'But *some*body has to do it,' I pointed out. The ensuing pause lasted a decade or two. My smile died. 'Erm, any idea who'll do it?'

'Place them underground for us, you mean?' He did a smoke ring, really thick and absolutely circular. 'Oh. That's you, Lovejoy.'

'No deal.' My voice had thickened, though I wasn't really terrified of going underground into some ancient frigging burial mound or whatever it was they'd chosen.

'Yes it is. Definitely a deal. Isn't it, Kurak?'

Kurak looked at me. 'Eesa deal.'

'Why can't Kurak do it?'

He put on theatrical astonishment. 'Why, Lovejoy! How simple you are, under that brash exterior! Because only you will know which of the fifteen torcs is the genuine sleeper. And it is very, very important that it is placed with perfect precision.'

'On my own? I do it on my own?'

'Ah no.' He gazed at the tip of his cigar, smiling. 'Kurak will go with you, to see fair play as you might say.'

I cleared my throat. 'I could still do it wrong deliberately.'

Kurt laughed at that, really fell about, shaking his head ruefully at the continuing folly of Mankind.

'You'll do it right, Lovejoy. You'll see why, when we get there. Won't he, Lena dearest?'

'Oh yes,' Lena said, 'he'll do it. Against all his principles, wishes, inclinations. He'll do it for us. Perfectly.'

Each syllable fell on my eardrums like the clap of doom. I'd been collected. 'Then congrats again,' I managed at last.

We rose, and Kurt said we must all have a quiet,

peaceful day, because tomorrow we had work to do. All I could think of was how the hell you put a gold torc into a hole without excavating into the bloody thing.

Lena wanted to show me the library afterwards. I was almost sure one of those marital signal-glances was exchanged between Lena and Kurt but paid it no heed. Everything was beyond me by this stage. What was one more problem?

She kept her arm linked through mine as I admired the books. Both of us were a bit tired by now. She said very little to keep the conversation going and seemed more listless than she ever had.

'Who keeps your leather bindings intact?'

She shrugged. 'Kurt sees to that. The maids, I suppose.'

I ran a finger on a book's spine hard enough to squeak. 'Why do they use lanolin in neatsfoot oil? A lot of American book collectors don't like the British Museum formula because of its beeswax. Maybe Kurt thinks it blocks the penetration. The old London restorers often just use Propert's saddle soap. You'd be surprised how effective it is—'

'Lovejoy.'

'—on these ponderous Victorian half-calfs when the hinges weaken—'

'Lovejoy.' She turned me round. I thought for one frantic moment she was going to start undressing again but it was only warning time. She leant against the shelving, staring absently at my face, oddly like some child not wanting to start the next compulsory lesson. 'You won't do anything silly, will you?'

'Who, me?'

'Kurt has plenty of men, armed men. They have cars, boats, horses, guns. They know the whole district, inch by inch.'

'What *is* this, Lena?'

Her eyes lifted to mine. 'There's no choice, Lovejoy. Understand that, please. You'll go along with Kurt's plan, or you will be simply lost in the countryside. Everybody will assume you've simply gone home. The point is, I want you around after this is over.'

'I'll go along. I'm not daft, love.'

'Then you'll be mine. For ever.'

I nodded. 'Your people collection.'

'Don't make it sound Purgatory, darling.'

'What I've experienced so far has been . . . bliss, Lena.'

'And don't sound so worried. Kurt understands. He won't mind our meeting again in the summerhouse late tonight.'

I swallowed. 'That's all right, then.'

'Incidentally,' she said as we resumed our strolling inspection. 'About your friends.'

'Mmmh?'

'Your two friends.'

'Did you know your library ladder's a genuine Taylor Patent?' I stopped us to examine its smooth leather-and-brass-studded exterior, lovely mint condition. 'It adapts into a long shelf-ladder. They cost a fortune nowadays. If you unclip it, you'll see the patent date and stamp on its hinge—'

'That dowdy woman and her weird relative.'

'Eh? Oh, them. They just gave me a lift.'

She smiled a wintry smile. 'That's all right, then,' she quipped. 'They left the hotel an hour ago. On the Dublin road, in a hired car.'

'Really?' I said absently. 'Incidentally, is it true that the Hunt Collection out on the Dublin road has the world's best collection of Methers? Those two-and-four-handled wooden drinking mugs are not all that uncommon. Lots of places have some pretty fine examples, so the Hunt Collection must be really something worth seeing . . .'

She let me prattle, watching me carefully not watching
her. My heart was in my boots, but I kept the chat going
on and on and on . . .

CHAPTER 21

Before making my famous non-escape I lay on my bed,
thinking of Shinny, of her lunatic suitor Gerald, of Lena,
of Kurt, of poor old Joxer, of Jason. But most of all about
antique dealers like good old Kurak/Joe. And money.

Way back in the days of yore, before priests got guitars
and charities went bent, people actually *were* what they
seemed. I mean, Caligula appeared somewhat antisocial,
so naturally you wanted to keep out of his way. And, right
up to comparatively recent times, town councils—
apparently composed of respectable, trusty gentlemen—
were respectable and trusty. And so on. Must have been
an odd world.

Phase Two happened very few years ago. Money did it,
going funny when politicians invented ever-dafter
schemes guaranteeing themselves undying places in
history. Well, they succeeded. Us poor goons got cyclic
inflation in exchange. Which, you remember, sent
everybody a little strange in the head. Blokes who were by
nature Above Thoughts Of Sordid Gain practically killed
in the hedgerows for inflation-index-linked pensions.
Women, never creatures to quibble about inessentials,
zoomed with unerring aim at anything possessing a
guaranteed value.

The Great Antiques Boom was born.

Those twenty years from 1958 to 1978 were the heyday,
and we are in its tail-off. The modern antiques scene is
the spreading train of sparks behind Haley's Comet—
apparently greater than the originating force but in fact

full of rubbish which deservingly is destined for outer
space. And let there be no mistake: your friendly
neighbourhood antique dealers were in ecstasy during
that G.A.B. They practically had a licence to print
money—and some did even that. Mostly they laughed in
their Jags and fluid-drive Rolls Royces and bought and
bought, triple-priced any antiques as a matter of course,
and howled with outrage if some elderly widow refused to
part with her grandmother's heirloom Sheraton commode
for less than a dud shekel.

But the end of the G.A.B. caught antique dealers on
the hop. Their flat world went round overnight. No
longer could you hire any old pantechnicon, load it to its
panelled ceiling in Coggeshall, Norwich, Sudbury,
Reading, and sell its load of 'old household furniture' in
any lay-by on the Dover Road for cash. Gone were the
days you could place a *Daily Mail* advert ('Wanted!
Antiques For America! Will collect! Pre-1930
Clothes . . . !') and expect the owners of rare antiques to
beat a path to your door. Suddenly, the supply of
antiques dried up.

The public had learned.

They learned that anybody on earth is perfectly
entitled to pop an heirloom into Christie's. That they
could play off one dealer's offer against another. That
they too could advertise. They learned how to use the
reference library. How to hang on, stall, even (forgive
me, please) lie a little or even a very great deal to
'authenticate' a shabby piece. The results were often
ludicrous, frequently shambolic, occasionally disastrous.
But mostly they paid off, in solid cash.

Antique dealers were appalled. Some went out of
business. Some even got a job. Still others became more
careful, and these survived. Oh, they did the usual—fake,
cheat, fabricate, steal, forge, pull the auction-ring gig in
every auction on earth, fiddle, pretend, lie, thieve, and

all that jazz. But survive they did, despite monumental ignorance, in the maelstrom. It was in that turmoil that the 'sleeper' scam came right back into its own.

Of course, in antiques there's nothing new (Tinker's joke, this: in the antiques game there is probably more newness than anybody dares suspect). And in any case, they say old wine is best.

There are as many scams as there are antiques. A scam's a lucrative illegal exploit based on deception more far-reaching than the trusty old con trick. The sleeper is one of the best and oldest scams. Michaelangelo himself used it in his time. So did Hitler with his paintings — though with rather less success. And even famous museums have dabbled in this ancient (but far from extinct) trick, especially when trading items with other august and honourable institutions. Remember this: no museum in the world is blame-free when it comes to owning up where its treasures came from and giving honest-to-God accounts of provenance — and here I'm not specially knocking the Boston Museum of Fine Arts about its famous 137-piece gold breastpiece, or that weird business they indulged in during December 1969 with that Raphael attribute portrait, or the British Museum, or the Washington Dumbarton Oaks 1960s purchase of Byzantine religious silvers found in Asia Minor by the peasants of Kumluca village. No, honestly I'm not. Nor am I knocking collectors. I mean, it's great that people care enough to crave possession, I always say, and lustful possessors have always been great preservers. But a collector's craving is very, very big stuff. They've even been known to kill in order to possess.

What I am getting at is this: Your actual *dealers* don't often kill. They'll do anything else in furtherance of their latest purchase's career. But kill? No. And the most desperate dealers are the legits, those with posh addresses off Piccadilly and dinky offices in Rome, yet even these

will not go about murdering. Terrible with reputations
and bankruptcies, but they somehow never reach for the
arsenic or the revolver.

I turned over, listening. Somebody was coming along
the corridor, one of their regular heavy-footed patrols.
The mansion was so well protected it was a rural Devil's
Island. I listened them out of earshot and thought on. If
antique dealers did not murder, and Kurak was really
only a certain kind of antique dealer with a superdooper
knack of pulling successful sleeper exploits, then Kurak
did not crisp Joxer, no? And Jason, also a dealer, was
therefore not above deception and a little honest thievery,
but he too was excluded.

Ergo, Lovejoy, look among the fine upstanding
collectors of this world for you real dyed-in-the-wool
killer, not among the crummy load of inept nerks who
constitute mankind's antique dealers. And that meant
the Heindricks.

Well, I'd escaped from the hotel. It was time to do the
same from Dotheboys Hall here. I swung off the bed,
ready to go.

My plan—such as it was, I thought in disgust—was to
steal down to the summerhouse at midnight to meet
Lena, and take off if the opportunity arose. Lena's
acquiescence had been full of pleasure, if somewhat
guarded. I'd had to assume she still believed me to be in
ignorance about those curtains in her circular rotating
elegant wooden summerhouse.

To escape down, you climb.

Once in desperation from hunger I'd done a couple of
jobs as a handyman's mate. Old Cedric was a jobbing
builder, and I'm still convinced he only took me on
because I was so useless. Still, Cedric and the world's
worst handyman's mate (me) installed a series of thrystor
switches, and automated a posh manor house down on

the estuary. It had automatic everything down to
cupboard doors and loo plugs. You could run that house
by flicking an eyelash. Which particular eyelash Lena'd
used while we loved in the summerhouse I wasn't sure,
but I wasn't dumb enough to believe that a woman
committing the ultimate indiscretion would fling open
the curtains to the gaze of all and sundry. Therefore Kurt
not only knew. The question was how far he walked the
well-trodden thoroughfare to Lena's heart . . .

It was obvious the circular summerhouse could be
openly seen from all top-floor windows, which was one
floor up. Ten past midnight, and the mansion cooling
into quiet the way these old places do. There was enough
light coming up the staircase from the hallway to let me
see. All I needed was to bungle my way into the staff
quarters or Kurt's bedroom. In either case there'd be
some painful explaining to do.

Double doors faced the top stair, which was a good
indication of a drawing-room rather than a bedroom.
Good panelled oak, maybe 1850, with the original
handles. Reluctantly I opened one blade of the door.
Even if you aren't really scared you can frighten yourself
by imagining all sorts. I slipped inside, closing the door
behind me and simply standing there, my chest thumping
and sweat on my forehead.

It wasn't as dark as all that. A slender rib of light
showed beneath a connecting door to the right. The three
high grey rectangles directly ahead must be the windows.
I felt my way towards the central one, hands slowly
sweeping ahead of me in case I damaged a Chien Lung
vase—more of a risk than getting caught in this place.

At first I thought it was a gun, mounted there on a
swivel tripod with armrest and two chrome levers. The
banked array of electronic gear, with its palpable arrays
of knobs and sliders, gave it away as some kind of complex
recording gear, maybe video-tape or the like. I stood as if

to operate the gun thing, feeling along the barrel. Too thick for a gun, but like a . . . telescope? I put my eye to one end. Nothing. Yet it was directed at the summerhouse or very close to it. Apart from the flowers and the kiln there was nothing else to see down there.

Video-tapes are thicker than others. Feeling along the shelf, I naturally guessed the last one, fallen flat, would be the most recent. I inched my way across to the screen, thanking various electronic gods that screens pick up any old trace of luminescence to show intruders where they are. The only noise was the deep click when it slotted in and connected. I had the sense to turn down all knobs, and only rotate them slowly one at a time as the screen began to glow.

It was Lena all right. And me. By the time I got the picture right we were half way there, and in glorious colour. Odd experience, watching your own body behaving in complete disregard of anyone. And you learn things, too. Lena looked as dazzling as I knew she was, but I was a revelation. I'd always assumed I was a gentle, considerate bloke to my birds, kind of polite. The screen Lovejoy was an animal.

Great. For a second I stood there in a fury, then switched if off and turned to go and almost started the whole lot crashing down by falling over a wire. My pathetic luck held. I made the door on hands and knees, regretfully feeling the carpet's knottage—number of knots to the inch, measured along the fringe, though properly you compare oriental carpets by the *count*: knots per square inch. It felt as if it would count out at 250, maybe a Kashan. Somebody moved out in the adjacent room, probably Kurt the movie-maker getting ready, so I scarpered into the corridor.

Well, it seemed everybody in the vicinity was expecting a new performance of the Great Snogging Picture Show II, so what the hell. I strolled confidently downstairs, passed my own landing, and on out of the main door. Naturally I made it look coy there, eeling outside after switching off the hall light. Give Kurt another smirk or two, that surreptitious touch. Let them think I hadn't guessed.

Breathing a regret to Lena, I moved off the gravel among the beds of bushes and flowers. A particularly vicious cluster of heathers gave me a nasty moment, cracking and swishing like hell, but they were between me and the kiln so there was no way to avoid them. Nobody was around. I made the kiln—still warm it was—and clambered up to its roof, shelling my jacket. The flue chimney was metal of some sort. I held on to it to lean across the space between the kiln and the wall. A six-foot gap, and the wall topped with a crust of broken glass embedded in concrete. My rolled-up jacket lay across the glass, which was the best I could do. The trouble is, my hands cut easily on anything.

I was just about to risk the leap when something scraped over the wall and I practically infarcted, thinking, Sod it. One of Kurt's armed men. Caught good and proper. I might make it to the summerhouse if I got my jacket and denied everything . . .

A voice whispered, 'Would that be yourself, Lovejoy?'

'Eh?' I froze. The darkness thickened above the wall. Somebody's head. 'Who is it?'

'Shush your noise, man. Is it yourself?'

Gerald. It was Gerald. 'What the hell are you doing here? Have you got a ladder? Grab my arm—'

'No, Lovejoy. Wait. It's the planting of some old trinkets they'll be doing, isn't it?'

'Yes.' How the hell did he know that?

'At Kilfinney?'

'Yes.'

'Sure, I knew it when I saw you wandering among those auld ruins.'

'You were there?' I'd have strangled the clown if I could have reached him. 'Then why the hell didn't you help when they nabbed me?'

'Ah, it's a terrible impatience you have on you, Lovejoy. Where's your interest in the scheme of your fellow men—?'

'Stuff that, you frigging lunatic.' My throat was raw from whispering. 'I'm imprisoned here. I want out. If you're not going to help, then shift, you burke.'

'What are the trinkets, Lovejoy? Those gold crusts the men were baking this morning?'

Oh hell. If he had seen the kiln fired on the gold torcs, he too must have seen me and Lena doing our stuff.

'Yes.'

'Then you play along with them. I've a plan.'

I hesitated fatally. 'You have? And leave us in the clear?'

He grew lyrical. 'As innocent as the snowflakes that, born in the high clouds of winter, descend to bless the earth with sweetness—'

I cursed him. 'What about me, though, you nerk? They want me to do the plant early tomorrow. Heindrick'll do the discovery bit.'

'Ah, there's a terrible temper you have, Lovejoy! But it's a grand scheme, right enough. Do it, Lovejoy.'

'Just as they say?'

'That's the thing.'

'But what about me being frigging safe?' I demanded.

'Ah, you mustn't let little things worry you, Lovejoy. I'll be there to see fair play, or Sinead'll give me a thick ear.'

'You sure?'

'On me auld mother's blessed—'

'Shut it. Is Shinny still here? They told me you'd gone to Dublin.'

'Sure where else would she be? Now you go back, Lovejoy, and leave it all to me.' The darkness where his head had been thinned.

'Gerald?' No answer, only that scraping. The swine had some sort of ladder there all the bloody time. He could have got me out. '*Gerald*!'

The gravel scuffed on the drive near the house balustrade. That would be Lena. I reached over, grabbed my jacket and made it to the summerhouse steps just as she flitted along the path.

Kurt would be warming up his ciné-cameras now. I wondered which was my best side on infra-red.

CHAPTER 22

The lough made a soughing noise before dawn. Earlier, it had rained for a couple of hours, coming on while Lena and I, erm, met as planned.

That night we all must have had only about three hours' sleep, and while it was still dark were on the road in an ordinary rather oldish dark blue saloon. A nice careful touch that, including the fishing gear ostentatiously loaded up for us on the roof rack. Me, Kurak who drove, and Kurt full of himself as always. He was all tweeds and raglan, the country gentleman out for early fishing. There are people who really love the desolate country dawn bit.

'Where are the real anglers?'

Heindrick smiled at my question as we parked away from the vacant parking space and got out. 'Ah, we'll be spared those, Lovejoy.'

'Back in East Anglia there'd be a hundred fishermen here at this hour.' I'd been hoping to find enough innocent bystanders to mask Gerald's presence. As dawn lightened the lake sky it became obvious there was no witness, no help, and no bloody Gerald either.

'Light, Kurak.'

Kurt hooded the torch glass and flashed twice across the lough, twice again in the direction of the castle ruins.

'That for Jason?' I asked.

'Possibly.'

'We burying the sleepers in the castle ruins?'

Kurt waggled a finger. 'Curiosity killed the cat, Lovejoy.' He was holding this case, heavier than lead.

Depressed at all this military-style organization, I plodded after Kurt as he led the way to the right, Joe following, still doing his phoney Slav act.

A horse neighed once, the noise coming from near the crannog. Something clopped nearer, up ahead. There were other people in the countryside, all of them hostile. I dwelled on Gerald and Shinny with bitterness. Nobody lets you down quite as ruinously as friends, do they? Friends are famous for desertion and betrayal.

'Ready, sor?'

One minute there had been the grey-green dawn, then suddenly there was this quiet bloke standing close by the wedge-shaped grave.

'This it?' I asked. They ignored me.

'Yes. Ready.'

'You'll come then, and mind your feet.'

And he took us away from the lough, away from the grave, over to our right about a hundred uneven paces. We were at the turf digging.

'All's clear, sor.'

'Very well.' Heindrick dismissed the guide with courtesy. He nodded and faded into the hillside. The three of us were left alone.

'What happens now?'

I didn't much care for what little I could see of the turf digging. Narrow slabs of the stuff were slanted in rows, forming a barrier. Standing in the excavated hollow we could not be seen from the road. Even the hillside did not overlook us. A darker patch was evident on the side nearest the Bronze Age wedge grave. And it dawned on me.

'I got it.'

'Spread the leather, Kurak.'

'Eees, m'sieu.'

Kurak unfolded a large chamois leather from its plastic bag. Heindrick began lifting the torcs in their individual chamois pouches from the case. Each was bagged in stapled plastic. He began counting them out on the spread.

I said, 'If you can't dig down or sideways into an archaeological site, you dig upwards. Am I right? You tunnel from below, starting some distance away. And plant the sleepers through a tube, a drillhole.'

Heindrick finished it for me. 'Plugging the drillhole, of course.'

'Having sucked the traces of drilling.'

'Vibration restores the dust to its even, pristine condition, Lovejoy.'

'Who does that?'

'Eeesa mee.' Kurak had uncovered a small boxed machine looking for all the world like a hurdy-gurdy without its support stick. It seemed handle-cranked and had a leather strap.

The sky was beginning to pale quite clearly now. Spatters of rain tapped us. The wind had shifted to the south. The dark oval in our hollow was now more distinct, about four feet across.

'That the tunnel?'

'Yes.'

'Is it that wide all the way?'

'Not quite.' Trust the malicious sod to be smiling.

'Got a diagram?'

'As far as we've been able to visualize the burial chamber.' Kurt brought out a paper and pencil torch.

'Done for us by a research archaeologist, for a fee.'

'Is he in on it?'

'There's that curiosity again, Lovejoy,' he reproved, indicating the diagram. 'The tunnel runs at the left side of the grave chamber's narrowest part. You will deposit the genuine torcs in the far right-hand recess.'

'My arms aren't that long.'

'You're provided with an extending arm. Kurak will carry that. The other torcs you will place beneath the adjacent compartment.'

'One more thing.'

'No, Lovejoy.' The swine patted my arm sympathetically. 'Just go.'

I needed to know. 'Who goes first?'

'You, Lovejoy.'

'Having Kurak between me and the exit? No, thanks.'

'Lovejoy.' Rain speckled Kurt's spectacles. He spoke with infinite patience. 'If this is done exactly to my order, we succeed. You get the price as we agreed, a torc. Plus other benefits. You come on the payroll, exactly like Kurak. This scam will make a fortune, for you and the rest. You join the wealthiest antique ring in the history of mankind. Or you proceed no further. Which?'

Good old Gerald, with his promise of help. Well, there were enough ancient graves about for people not to notice one extra.

Swallowing, I shelled my jacket, took the torch and stooped into the entrance. 'Let's go.' Kurak kept his hand partly raised in a chopping position. That was in case I made to flash the light anywhere else except into the tunnel.

From the level, the tunnel descended pretty sharply — too sharply for my liking, considering we were a million frigging miles from the grave. The aroma had a thick, curiously bittersweet character which made my throat clog up for a few moments. A tube ran along the

trodden peaty floor, of the kind you use for garden hoses.
Kurak gave me a push. I plopped on to all fours and
began to crawl as the tunnel narrowed into a cloy wetness.

'I'm going, I'm going for Chrissakes!'

'Eeesa time-a du goow, Lovejoy.'

'Shut your stupid teeth, Joe,' I grumbled. The tunnel's
closeness was bringing the sweat out on me. 'What's that
hissing?'

'Air. There's a battery pump back in the turf diggings.'
Kurak was Joe Bassington again, his corny accent gone.

'Here, Joe. Do they know who you are?'

'Sure.' But from the way he said it, I began to wonder.
Maybe Lena had procured his services by feeding him the
same sort of promises she'd given me. Women are famous
for that. It couldn't be that the duckegg actually believed
Lena and he were somehow to take over from Heindrick.
Nobody could be that thick, not even a bloke crazed by
Lena. I crawled on.

The tunnel narrowed further. I tried working out the
incline as we moved deeper underground. Why the hell
do they never teach you anything useful at school?
Teachers are idle swine. Maybe one in thirty or so? That
meant a depth of say ten feet after crawling a hundred
yards. In the damp brown-black pungency the torchlight
showed walls of rock and practically solid peat.
Remarkable how hard the rotten stuff was, compressed
into a fibrous woody texture. And wet, wet.

Carrying a torch when plodding on your hands and
knees is difficult. You need a hand to hold the thing, yet
you need that hand for your fourth corner, so to speak.
Alternating on my wrist and knuckles I moved lopsidedly
on. I could hear Joe pushing the gear ahead of himself,
the box and that tube thing slithering on the tunnel floor.

By counting the number of moves I'd made since I
crouched on hands and knees I reckoned we'd gone about
fifty yards, counting one foot per movement. That was

the point the tunnel suddenly compressed us further. To advance it meant a belly-crawl, elbows on the floor and wriggling like soldiers under fire. Grumbling at Joe — more of a whine now than a mutter — I led on, down into stickiness and mud, the roof such as it was showing more rock than peat. The hosepipe was still there, snaking ahead into the narrow black hole.

What I didn't care for was a sloppy dampness of the tunnel floor. As it narrowed it got wetter. I hesitated and pressed my weight on the torch rim. A moment later the bloody mark filled up with water. We were reaching the level of the lough. For an instant I panicked, moaning and quickly backing until my feet clonked on Joe.

'What is it for Chrissakes?'

'We're getting below water-level, Joe.'

'I'm not enjoying this either, Lovejoy. Get going. We're practically there.'

'Frigging hell. Can't we just leave them here and . . . and . . .'

'. . . And be buried in some bog?' He laughed, actually snorted a laugh, the nerk.

Ten paces further the tunnel angled up and to the right. At the dip it was about quarter filled with a stinking puddle of muddy soil. Everything Heindrick had given us was sealed, but I wasn't inclined to take chances and made Joe check the seals on every item after we'd sploshed through the dip. Only having one torch was a nuisance. Joe wanted me to pass it back for him to inspect the plastic wrappings, but I wasn't having any of that caper. The torch was mine and I was sticking to it, so I shone the light back between my legs until he said the covers were all still intact and we could go on.

It was no more than eight or nine yards, that short ascent. So steep was it that I actually slithered and had to pull along with a handhold. Then the tunnel stopped, and there I was mystified, staring at the end of a hole and wondering what to do.

'Above your nut, moron.'

'Eh?'

'It's obliquely angled, a four-inch stone plug.'

'I know, I *know*! Stands to reason it must be there.' I made to undo it but Joe's hand grabbed my leg.

'No! No! Turn off the air pipe first!'

'You stupid burke! We'll suffocate!'

'Not for a few minutes.'

'Why? Why?' I wasn't really panicking, but breath's important stuff.

'They might count the bacteria and fungi in the grave dust and on the remains. They circulate in the air. They're different species in the outside air than inside an old grave.'

'Who's going to think of *that*, you silly bugger?'

'Professionals,' he answered, cold. 'Switch that air pipe off.'

'So help me, Joe,' I swore, and turned the hose's end round. The hissing ceased. Straight away I felt myself gasping for breath even though I knew how daft I was being.

'Get on with it, Lovejoy, or we'll be here all day.' That did it.

The plug was supported by a latch like an old wooden gateway, except this latch was steel and slotted into sockets which were set in stone to either side. The space was about three feet by three. I lodged the torch against the wall. Joe had to rest his elbows just below me, his legs projecting down into the sloping tunnel, so merely passing the tube forward was a feat of skill. From it I took the expanding finger — only a crisscross of wood with a scissor grip at one end, and rubber tips at the other. Close the scissor grip and the crisscross extends, carrying whatever you've placed in its rubber-tipped 'fingers'.

'Hey, Joe. I'll have to do it blind.'

' 'Course you will, stupid. Have a shufti first, work out the length.'

Sensible. I began to realize how useful it was having a bloke as skilled as the Sleeper Man along.

'How?'

'From here to where you drop the sleeper's about nine feet. The finger's capable of twenty. So make a mark on the ratchet in that proportion. The angles are constant throughout, right?'

'Right,' I said blankly, thinking, Eh? In the end he did that while I unlatched the plug. I shone the torch, a good krypton beam.

The inside of any burial chamber's only pleasant in a museum. Seeing inside one for the first time since the Old People closed it is a frightener, really unnerving. We were near the apex of the triangular cavity. From there the ceiling—stone slabs laid crossways—widened. I could just see the edges of two of the compartments. These are kinds of booths which occupy the walls of the grave. The Old Peoples' mortal remains went in these recessed galleries until the place was sealed for ever. And ever. I found myself shaking.

'Lovejoy!' God knows why we were both whispering. There was no chance of being overheard even if we yelled our heads off.

'What?'

'Mind that plug! On to the chamois.'

Reverently I laid the stone plug on the spread leather, taking care not to rub the grave dust from its oval top surface, and whispered for Joe to pass up the sleepers. The fifth torc which he handed me from the case was the genuine one. It broke my heart to unwrap it and grasp it about its midriff by the expander. Joe tried to see my every movement but it was just not possible in such a confined space, in Indian file at that.

'Don't let it touch anything, Lovejoy.'

'You can trust me,' I said. Once I let myself think of Heindrick's threats I'd be finished, so I pretended confidence. I've always been good at lying, especially to myself.

It was surprisingly easy. I had to guess of course at the finish, as the luscious gold torc crept slowly out from the plughole and vanished from that eerie shadowy scene into the space of the grave. I hadn't allowed for the weight of the thing—you try holding a gold weight on the end of a nine-foot length with your fingers and you'll see how hard being a crook actually can be. Worse, I hadn't calculated for the extender's curve under the torc's weight. After cursing and struggling I thought what the hell and let the torc go. We heard a soft thud and Joe muttered an oath, but I was more concerned with bringing the extender back without reaming out the whole grave's interior. I told him it didn't matter, that I'd stuck it in the space Heindrick wanted.

After that the others were simple. I had a rest between each, exercising my hands to make sure I could do the others properly but it was only for show so Joe would bring back a good report to our master. It took longer to replace the plug than it had removing the wretched thing.

'That it?' I was close to panic and wanting to get out, but he insisted on passing me the mechanical vibrator on its flexible shaft. We had an ugly moment with Joe telling me it was absolutely safe and just to press the tapered end against the stone plug, and me whining for gawd's sake he'd electrocute both of us. In the end it functioned perfectly, juddering against the stone in a busy way until Joe reckoned the vibrations should have settled the grave's dust over any trace of our penetration.

'That's all, Lovejoy.'

Give Joe his due, he was a real pro. Though there we were underground and in the clear now our job was done, he would not budge until every piece of plastic, every trace of our presence, was carefully bagged in plastic — he'd even brought a pocket stapler to seal the bloody things. I was frantic to get out, whisper-yelling what if the frigging dip filled up with water and suchlike hysteria, all to no avail. He showed what a true pro he really was, calm and businesslike.

There was room for me to turn and crawl out head first. But he couldn't pass me, being simply stuck like a worm in its burrow. With a nod, he took hold of the tube in one hand, grabbed the case strap in his teeth, and began slithering backwards down the tunnel. Every yard he had to pause, pull down his jacket which kept rucking up his chest and impeding his elbow thrusts, but he kept calm and eeled along towards safety. I had a vested interest in his progress, but didn't feel like making humorous comments about the mess I was in.

That's how I remember Kurak, alias Joe Bassington: calm, mud-covered, strain showing on his face, but always edging on and on ahead of me in the torchlight. A real pro. Never once complained about the light in his eyes, knowing I would have worried about too much darkness. He even stuck his hands out to make sure my chin didn't risk going below the water-level at the dip. Great bloke, was Joe.

And when we got out, into the torrential downpour of a day hideously brilliant, bright and grey, Heindrick told us we'd been much faster than he had anticipated.

Joe only said, "Eeesa Lovejoy. Ee doo far well, m'sieu.'

'Good, good,' Heindrick said, all smiles. 'Shall we proceed homewards, Lovejoy? A late breakfast?'

'Right.' I scrambled from the turf workings and eyed the skyline. Still nobody to be seen, no Gerald, nobody. Great. My trusty helper had been rained off, the nerk.

'Oh, Lovejoy,' Heindrick called up. 'Your jacket's under the plastic. See you at the car. I'll just give Kurak his instructions. Tie up the loose ends, you understand.'

'You're the boss.'

Without another word I left them there in the turf diggings. I'd burrowed like a frigging earthworm, been scared stiff, practically buried, covered in mud, and left defenceless by my so-called friends. And now I was soaked through, exhausted and hungry. Great. I'd never felt so sorry for myself. We'd done it, though. Now all we had to do was act our way through our casual 'discovery' of the gold torcs, and it was done.

But it still gets to me that I never said thanks to Kurak, alias Joe Bassington.

CHAPTER 23

The last thing I expected was a house party. Two quartets of the Heindricks' friends were wading into a buffet when I cleaned up and rejoined Heindrick. Lena was in a shirtwaisted thing with bishop sleeves, fawns against white. On other older women it would have been a mile too young, but Lena carried it off. She brilliantly defeated two plump young Galway birds who thought they knew it all until she apologized for the Rumanian caviare and sweetly asked had they tried the metheglin. I liked them, but after Lena's broadside they only stood apart and muttered.

There wasn't an ounce of guile among the guests as far as you could tell. County set, wealthy and ruthlessly exclusive. I was introduced as Lovejoy the famous antiques expert, which is the only lie that ever makes me go red. Then I was treated like a refugee. When a smooth auntie-shaped woman discovered I hadn't seen the latest London Ayckbourn revival, the whole party realized I was simply contagious and drifted aside. I tried to nosh.

Eating posh grub is daunting: posh means microscopic, and everybody notices if you have more than one minuscule blob from a dish. We were given no time to eat properly—this also being diagnostic of a country set—but ample access to the hooch, a cunning move, considering our host's intentions. Some were already woozy when we lammed out in two big carloads. I drew four hairy blokes talking horses—and Jason as driver.

'Hey, Jase,' I said as we drove east among the traffic. 'See that Chelsea porcelain eel tureen Mrs Heindrick served the caviare from? Red anchor, original cover.' Worth a year's executive salary in 1967, its current value's mind-boggling. No response from Jason, and our companions were still on about nags. Bravely, I tried again. 'Mind you, Red Anchor fakes go big nowadays, eh? I hate animal shapes. Her Chelsea top-decorated strawberry-leaf teapot was definitely Raised Anchor Period. Worth twice the tureen. Don't you think Lena made a mistake?'

'Shurrup, Lovejoy. I'm driving.'

'Well, Jase, two different styles on one table and all that.' I shook my head regretfully. 'I'd have thought Lena might have avoided—'

'Gabby sod. I said I'm driving.'

Odd, horses having names just like people. These blokes in the back were nattering on as if nags were real individuals. Takes all sorts, I suppose. Jason negotiated a bend, allowing a car to overtake. We were three cars behind the Heindricks. More cars about now, early afternoon. One was a white Ford saloon. No dents, one bloke.

'If I'd been Lena,' I said, 'I'd have used that early Meissen Augsburg decorated gold-ground travelling service she has. Notice it in the hall case?' Ponderously I nudged him. 'Wouldn't you, Jase? The Indonesian mahogany table would have ballsed up the colour scheme, but there's a way round that—'

'I'm driving. Shut *up* or I'll—'

'Okay, okay,' I said, peeved.

He was puce by now, but it wasn't me that made him edgy in the first place. I'd only made him worse. I thought hard about that. The road forked and bent simultaneously. The white car was turning off on the branch marked 'Hospital'. Jason's left hand was on the wheel, but his little finger could have easily reached the flash lever. Anyway, something clicked and it wasn't Jason's sudden cough. I wondered if he'd read any good books lately, *Paradise Lost*, something like that. The bloke in the white car had. I was sure of that.

It went off exactly as planned.

The cars put us down by the lough. We were to walk to the top of Kicknadun Hill, from where the level exercise ground belonging to the stud farm could be seen on the western slope. I hung back, for a million reasons depressed and worried by it all. I was staring glumly at the crannog with the two Galway girls when the noise attracted our attention and we went to join in.

Heindrick's excited shouts, people yelling my name, and only me noticing that silent horseman standing so still on the skyline.

Then the plod across, and the whole charade. Spotting the gold torc's gleam by pencil flashlight shone down a tiny hole where Heindrick's stick had prodded between two great worn stones. Then Heindrick's dramatic race to the car to bring the authorities. Fortunately, about then Lena noticed two of her own estate workers riding on the hill. How lucky, we all agreed, and flagged them over to guard the find.

The classical sleeper scam: find, register, protect. All done.

It was at that point Jason asked me in a mutter where

did I think I was going.

'To have a look at the castle ruins.'

Jason was standing aside from the main excited mob, talking desultorily with Lena. She looked the part as always, the only woman I ever knew who became slender in Hebridean tweeds. He gave her a checking glance and she nodded imperceptibly. I was to be allowed to walk three hundred yards in open view. Only my chains were invisible.

'*Do* hurry back, Mr Lovejoy, if Kurt returns, won't you?' Lena said loudly, which was by way of announcing to her two men that she'd given permission.

'Not be long.'

But where *was* Joe? That's what was getting to me. I hadn't seen him since our escapade of today's rainy morning. Lena herself had driven the first car, Jason the second. No sign anywhere now of that relentlessly familiar Ford always on the outskirts of the action. No sign of Gerald or Shinny. I made a slight detour, taking in the turf diggings for old time's sake, hearing with bitterness the laughter and thrilled chattering of the Heindricks' guests gathered round the burial site. Everybody in friendly groups of self-interested grasping layabouts except me. Morosely I stared down into the excavated hollow of the turf diggings, and saw the idle nerk down there.

'Ah, 'tis a foine day, Lovejoy, sure enough!'

'You lazy bastard. Where the hell have you been?'

Gerald grinned up at me from his reclining position on an ex-army groundsheet. He even had that long thin canvas bag of fishing tackle with him.

'Ah, here and there.'

I climbed down. 'You promised you'd keep me safe. Do you know I was sent in there to . . . to . . . ?' I looked again. The mouth of the tunnel had gone, only a paler smudge where the drier peat had been replaced. Newly

cut peat slabs covered the tunnel's position. Within hours
the location would be practically untraceable. I felt ill.
That's the trouble with being a coward. Courage gives
everybody else a head start on you.

Gerald was quite unabashed. 'Did they let you go to see
those auld castle stones, Lovejoy?'

'Yes.'

'You'd better be off then, unless it's those three riders
over the hill you want chasing down to see what you're up
to.'

I'd seen nothing new, and I thought I'd been watching
the skyline now like a hawk.

'Christ.' I thought a second. 'Here, Gerald. Does one
have a white car?'

'No.' The bum was settling down for a kip, shuffling his
long endlessly-jointed limbs into a Chinese puzzle. 'That'll
be auld Fenner the printer. Has a cousin in Connemara
who plays a lovely fiddle. I remember one time—'

'What do I do?' I'd never felt so helpless. Everybody's
plan was working out except mine. The whole thing had
got away from me, without a cheep on my part.

'Ah, you go with them and tell your tale to the
government people. Do as Heindrick says.'

'Then what?'

'Escape, o'course. Like a thief in the night. Or just walk
out. Sinead will have a grand motor outside.' He grinned
drowsily. 'Then we come back here, break into the
grave—from the top like the honest men we are, and . . .'

Light dawned. 'Nick the torcs. Everybody assumes it's
local layabouts. And we have torcs, complete with
provenance?'

'You've hit it, Lovejoy. A darlin' idea. But we get the
spoils of war. Ah,' he said lyrically, 'think of all the grand
poetry I'll be writing with all that wealth!'

'With fifty per cent,' I corrected.

Gerald opened one eye. 'Ah, we all soldier on for poor

takings, Lovejoy, for the whilst. Anyway, it's the coroner's office you'll be talkin' to soon.'

'Here, Gerald. Seen Kurak?'

Both eyes open now. no smile. 'Isn't he back at the grand mansion?'

'No sign of him there when we left.' Anyway, no use worrying. It was one less rival, but I was no longer certain what the battle was about. If Lena's offer was genuine — and it was beginning to look like it — I'd soon be in clover. Maybe Joe had got the sack?

'I'll keep an eye out for him, Lovejoy,' said my trusty vigilante, his eyes closed in sleep. I shrugged and left him there.

The castle's ruins were still interesting me when they shouted for me from the grave mound down by the lake. The officials were arriving with Heindrick, two black cars in the distance. I went to swear the truth over my pack of lies.

Passing the turf diggings to join the others, there was no sign of Gerald. He'd vanished into thin air. I wished I could do that.

Official events seemed a lot more direct in the city than they'd be in good old shambolic East Anglia. For a start, the officials knew everybody by name and their bald-headed stout boss — their coroner, but God knows what powers he actually possesses — had to keep prising his way into small groups of spectators who seemed to want to talk about everything else. Horses were big in everybody's mind. The boring business of a zillion-year-old grave full of bones and trinkets was clearly a blot on the day. The official's only hope was to get a good natter going, to sabotage the dull proceedings.

We gave evidence against a fast-running verbal tide of gossip. My own heap of falsehoods was interrupted every second breath. Place names, I discovered, quite intrigued, would cause some shorthand lady to butt in ('Oh, Kilmallock's a lovely place! My cousin Sian's there . . .') which gave everybody else reason to say Croom was nicer still but sure wasn't it Mallow took the biscuit even if it was nearer Cork than the good Lord intended . . . How the boss geezer kept his rag I'll never know.

The Heindricks were in fine form, especially Lena. She killed all doubt about her status by casually mentioning that I'd been fetched over to decide which of her three Rembrandts were genuine. 'I am currently persuading him to stay longer.' She smiled, a thousand watts for each of us. 'His gift will be invaluable with my other Old Masters.' Everybody got the point. Heindrick was signed up as the actual finder, members of his posh house party excitedly taking turns to sign deposition forms saying exactly what they were doing when positively *tons* and tons of gold were actually *touched* by Kurt's walking stick honestly *miles* deep in that old burial mound . . .

I went for a pee, the way all suspects escape from courts these days. The trouble was Jason, standing patiently in the corridor with one of Heindrick's men.

'Leave the door open, Lovejoy.'

'Rude sod. Can't I just go to the loo?'

'The window's barred,' his assistant said. It was the turf-digging man, quiet and absolutely certain that Heindrick's will would be obeyed in all things. Jason wasn't having any and kept his eyes on me.

'Lovejoy's dangerous,' he said. 'You leave the door open or you wait.'

'Good, good,' Heindrick said from behind me in his sibilant voice. 'Well done, Jason. We can't be too careful, especially now.' He paused and smilingly reassured us that he wouldn't be much longer, for the sake of the girl clerk walking past carrying taped legal files. She shut the office door behind her. 'Once the torcs are out we'll need Lovejoy's presence even more. You two get him back to the house. He won't be needed here any more.'

'Here,' I began, but found myself propelled down the corridor and into the street. According to Gerald I was supposed to escape from here, leap into Shinny's waiting car, and—

They didn't quite put the elbow on me, seeing there was so many people about and the streets fairly active with traffic, but I was in the front passenger seat of Heindrick's Daimler with ugly speed. The turf man sat behind as Jason took the wheel. His eyes never left me.

'Mind that bus, Jason,' I yelped nervously.

'Mind your mouth, Lovejoy.'

The turf man pointed a finger at the windscreen, instructing me to look straight ahead.

'Okay, okay. Just go careful, mate, that's all.'

But I had seen what I wanted. Shinny's pale face, in a modest grey Austin parked across the road.

We left Sarsfield Bridge and the River Shannon behind and lammed off along the Ennis Road. I tried talking but Jason closed his ears and the turf man merely reached over to lock my door and leaned closer in case. I checked my safety-belt a hundred times or so, pulling it so tight I could hardly breathe. I got one reply from Jason, though, and it was that which made me decide he simply had to go.

It was while we were on the old north road to Ennis that it dawned on me that Jason was driving. *Jason* was driving. Not Joe. Relatively new and unproven Jason. Jason, who required to be accompanied by the silent watchful turf man to ensure his undying loyalty to the Heindricks. Not the trusty obedient doglike phoney Slav Joe Bassington. *Jason* was driving. No longer Kurak, the Sleeper Man, organizer of a thousand sleeper scams. Jason had displaced Kurak, Jason the ex-military officer. Who could be relied upon to organize, distribute, run an organization, now that the sleeper scam had been pulled.

I thought, Sod it, and asked my question.

'Here, Jase. Did Lena let on that she told me about Joe?'

He began his last minute on earth by saying nothing. Then he shrugged and said, 'Well, Joe was useless.' His last words.

Which made up my mind for me. Those words took it all out of my hands. 'Past tense, eh, Jase?' I said, and pressed the release of his safety-belt. He turned a puzzled expression on me as the belt's metal insertion flew across him and the belt snicked off. He managed to say, 'What—?' but by then I'd grabbed the wheel and turned us, and the car was going over and over.

Seat-belts are supposed to be great things, comfortable and safe. The trouble is they nearly break your neck saving your life. If you make it through the crash, you come round being strangled by the bloody thing.

The only way I could get out of the sickening petrol stench and that ominous grinding sound was by sliding from under the shoulder strap. I made it, shakily crawling out through the shattered windscreen and across the ground until I guessed I'd got clear. Funny, but only then did I realize the motor-horn was blaring.

Twenty yards, maybe. Unsteadily I moved another few yards and sat to focus on today's good deed. Jason was sounding the horn, his chest pressing forward into the steering-wheel for all the world as if he was rummaging for something under the dashboard. Except his face was a smear of blood and he was so still. That's the trouble with undying loyalty. It doesn't last.

The car was a crumpled write-off. Car designers these days say it's a good idea making them so they squash on impact, God knows why. Like saying sausages should have a standard dose of salmonella.

I felt nauseated so I turned to retch a bit and saw the

turf man. He was the reason there'd been no windscreen.
A good thirty yards from where the car had slammed into
the projecting rock, he lay awkwardly with hunched
shoulders.

'Lovejoy? Lovejoy? Oh my *God*!'

'Aye, love.' I peered up. Shinny was above us on the
roadside. I couldn't see her car but its thrumming engine
was audible under that horrible constant horn. 'There's
been an accident.'

She slithered down beside me. 'Dear God. I've no
equipment with me. Are you hurt? Tell me, tell me. That
dreadful noise. Oh my God . . .'

'See if you can help them, love,' I said nobly, doing my
sinking act. 'I had my safety-belt on. Jason didn't. My
poor old mate . . .'

'Stay absolutely still, darling. Oh my God!'

'Be careful, Shinny, love,' I called anxiously after her.
'There's petrol escaping. It might explode. The ignition,
you see . . .'

I felt sore all over, but still made her car quite quickly.
She gave a scream of alarm when she heard me pull away,
but that's women every time. Always thinking of
themselves. It was me in difficulties, not her.

CHAPTER 24

I drove like a maniac. For once I was ahead of the game.
Everywhere you looked were advantages. One, Jason was
out of the way—maybe only temporarily, because he
might not have croaked, but for sure he'd not be chasing.
Two, so was the turf man. Three, the Heindricks were
still occupied with the lawyers and officials. Four, they
didn't know I was free. Five, I had a car, and they
wouldn't recognize it because it was Shinny's. Six, time

was getting on . . .

Playing crafty, I stayed on the N24 Tipperary road heading east, leaving the more direct T57. It doesn't look far on a map but I was well in sight of the Galtee hills before I was able to cut back on the Hospital road, leaving the T36 Kilamllock fork on my left. All that took time, but it helped me to calm down and stop feeling ill from what I'd done. Like a fool, I explained aloud to the interior of Shinny's car that it had been forced on me. If only other people didn't drag me into their bloodsoaked wars I'd be able to stay holy and pure and unsullied as I normally was. Shinny's car, a little grey Austin saloon, was scented by her. The sweet woman's handbag lay on the passenger seat. She was a lovely creature. No binoculars or weapons in the glove compartment, though, which proved she was as thoughtless as ever.

I'd worked out that if I followed the road which ran a few miles to the west of the lough I could somehow reach the lane which curled round the west side of that low hill which overlooked the water and the clusters of archaeological sites. There would be the guards, of course. From there I could snake down . . .

There were two guards. One was the rider from the castle ruins, the other a stockier bloke with leather patches sewn to his jacket elbows. Two saddled horses were idling nearby the grave mound.

They were smoking, talking, occasionally looking around, but making the mistake of keeping an eye on the distant road rather than the terrain. That was just as well because I'd learned enough of these country blokes' ways to realize they could spot a flea on a ferret without even looking. Nobody near the turf diggings, thank God, and the castle ruins partly screened that shoulder of the hill.

Keeping to the blind side, I ran as fast as possible, actually a slow clumsy plod, over the uneven tussocky

ground. Horse tracks showed me the way to go. That
castle rider had used this way more than once lately. It
was surprisingly easy but a bit knackering, moving at a
low crouch and watching in case another of Heindrick's
men showed up. Thick as always, I had never tried to
discover how big Kurt's team actually was. I'd always
assumed I was too much of a coward to take them on—
and I was right. Hide, or run like hell, yes. But no to a
dust-up, every single time. I made the turf diggings
unseen, and was fairly certain no other riders were
lurking about the landscape.

There could be no mistake about where the tunnel's
mouth was, even though now turfs were stacked across it.
The big question was, how far in had they arranged the
roof fall, and whether they'd done it with explosives of
some sort. Risking detection, I gave a long gaze from the
edge of the dug recess towards the lough. Between me
and the grave site where the horses and men waited a
small area of roughening was visible, but I couldn't
remember if it had been there before. The site of a fall-
in? Or some unexcavated Bronze Age goings-on?

I pulled off my jacket and started lifting the peat turfs
off. They were semi-dry. Clever move, that, showing
they'd been dug up for quite a time and therefore unlikely
to have been put there recently. It looks easy but isn't.
Hurrying didn't help, and the tools which were stacked to
one side proved too difficult to use. You had to have
learned the knack. I even tried levering with one of the
long straight steel poles which the diggers use for marking
distances, but finished up swearing and cussing. My heart
was thumping, not all from exertion. I went on, stacking
the peat blocks slantwards on their narrow edges along
other more weathered slabs. They were surprisingly
lightweight, lighter even than wood.

Every twenty peats I paused to climb the few yards to
the rim to suss out the riders. No cars still, no new

battalions. Then back to the pungent aroma below, shifting the peats one by one to clear an opening. The idea was to make a crawlway into the top of the tunnel mouth. There'd be no sense in humping the whole lot. That would only mean more backbreak replacing them when I got out.

The fall just inside the mouth should not have amazed me, though it did. Loose rock mingled with soil and a crumbly peaty stuff had tumbled into the tunnel now. No tool marks on the rock. All in all a careful job, an infilling which would in time resemble the rest of the ground, giving no hint of the tunnel beyond. And just enough rock to make authentic peat-diggers move away from the tunnel line. Good military thinking.

A thin spade thing helped. It had a sort of useless sideways wooden finger at right angles from the haft, but I was past caring by then and had chucked up the idea of carefully sussing out the lie of the land. If the murderous sods found me, well, they found me. Presumably the city officials would send a Garda along to see fair play. I hoped.

The fall was about four feet thick. I got through the top end, working on the principle it was probably easiest and looser stuff there, less compression weight. The first gust of air from inside, when the turf spade penetrated without resistance, fetched out at me fœtid and stenching. It made me gag. I returned to don my jacket—no clues for the passers-by from clever old Lovejoy—took a breath of fresh rainsoaked smog and returned immediately to drag away more peaty earth and crawled inside. There had been no sign in the diggings of that life-giving air hose and its clever little battery-driven pump so I was up the traditional creek once I tumbled headfirst into the tunnel's gloom. What good is technology that's out of reach to those who need it?

'Joe?' I called. 'You there, Joe?'

My eyes were hardly adjusted to the brownblack gloaming before I started crawling forward. Every few yards I paused, wondering what the hell I was up to, and shouted Joe's name. Me being daft me as usual, I hadn't the sense to work out distances, so my progress was judged by the deepening darkness.

Shinny's car, besides lacking every possible amenity and utensil, had also lacked torch, rope, jemmy, crawlers, oxygen cylinders and pickaxes. Typical of a woman. They always crack on about their usefulness, God knows what for. Answers on a postcard. I was at the point where the tunnel narrowed and descended at an angle towards the wet bit, and grumbling under my breath at the stupidity of me and everyone else when I stopped crawling. I screamed then. A rock in my way had groaned, a long hoarse low moan of grief and loneliness and pain and desolation.

'Joe? Joe? That you, Joe?'

'Lovejoy?' the rock groaned.

'You frigging lunatic!' I yelled at his head. He was trapped somehow because he wasn't moving and other rocks and earth were piled on him, pressing his shoulders to the tunnel floor. 'You selfish fucking pig!' I went on screeching abuse at him till my breath gave out. 'You frightened me to frigging death, you stupid Cockney sod! Why didn't you let on you were in here? You silly goon!'

He whispered, 'It's my legs, my back, I think, Lovejoy.'

'Do you realize the festering mess I'm in?' I yelled at him. 'I could be safe out of here, you stupid burke—'

'Ta for coming back, mate.'

'Shut your stupid teeth. Where're you stuck?'

'Dunno. Me length, I think.'

I felt round him as far as I could. He was partly turned on his side, face prone. Supine, and his mouth would have filled with earth and suffocated him. Did I hear a rumble of earth along the tunnel?

'Where the hell are your arms?'

'Pinned.'

'Got anything, tools, ropes, light?'

'No.' His voice was a weak whisper. 'Mr Heindrick said it was best not to take anything.'

'What did he send you back for?'

'Disconnect the air hose. I should have remembered it myself, Lovejoy. He was really great about it, didn't lose his temper, just said to do it straight away.' His tone became anxious. 'You don't think he'll be mad because of the fall-in?'

I thought, I don't believe this. I don't *believe* he's frigging real. That pair of maniacal killers had got Joe to rig the best sleeper scam in antique history, then heaved a tunnel on him, breaking his back and walling him up, burying the poor gullible sod alive—and he still spoke reverently of them?

'Aye, Joe. Sure. Great pair,' I said. 'Look. No explosion or anything, just before the sky fell?'

'Explosion?' He honestly sounded puzzled. 'No. Just the noise of the rockslip.'

Thank God for that. 'I'll scoop beside your chest and top shoulder, Joe, right? Can you move your fingers?'

'Bit. Did Lena—Mrs Heindrick notice I wasn't back on time?'

'She was worried sick, Joe,' I lied, scrabbling the dross aside and shoving it behind me like a mole, thinking, Love is simply a kind of optic atrophy. The capacity for self-deception is infinite under the stress of love.

'I knew she would,' the cretin said, reassured.

There were definitely rumbles now from somewhere. Frantically I clawed the stuff away from him. That wasn't difficult. The problem was what to do with the mounds which kept accumulating between my legs and beside my thighs. The bloody stuff was everywhere. The stupid earth just stayed wherever you pushed it. What the hell did miners do, for heaven's sake? His arm came free a million years later. That meant between us we had enough muscle to prise his weight off his under arm.

Joe himself hit on the notion of trying to push the earth aside at the wall rather than shuffling it along towards the entrance, and him again who said the way to pull him free when the time came to try was for me to brace against the tunnel sides with my back arched and knees pressing against the opposite wall. He explained that his arms had more strength than mine, but then all Cockneys are arrogant swine. I'd be a plug against which he could pull. And he came free, sixth go, practically crippling me for life with the strain.

It was then I noticed I couldn't see at all.

'Joe?' I said, nervous and getting that damp fearish feel.

'Ta, Lovejoy,' Joe said. 'I can't move me back or me legs, mate. Sorry, but you'll have to—'

'Joe. Can you see anything?'

'No.'

I wondered about his eyes. Maybe pressure sends you temporarily blind. 'No pallor past me?'

A pause, grunt of exertion as he lifted his head. 'No.'

'Unless it's got dark since I came in here, something's blocked the entrance.'

We moved on, me feet first and Joe following head first using the strength of our two pairs of arms. Something stopped me, a pole or something. Breathlessly I halted, a leg either side of the damned thing.

'Hang on, Joe.' I felt with a hand over my back.

Steel, vertical. It came out of the tunnel roof and into the floor. It hadn't been there when I crawled in, couldn't have been. I tried pushing, pulling, lifting. Not a hint of movement. I scrunged up, put my feet against it, braced my hands on Joe's shoulders and pushed until Joe moaned with pain.

'Joe, mate,' I said at last, my teeth chattering, 'we're caged in. Somebody'd driven a frigging great bar through the tunnel.'

'Vertical?' He sounded so cool, the thick burke.

'Of course it's vertical, you loon! They drove it down so of *course* it's frigging vertical. It's half-inch steel. We're in a dungeon with one frigging bar!'

'The tunnel here is about a foot and a half diameter,' he mused. 'No way round it, eh, Lovejoy?'

'No.' It came out as a long moaning whine.

'No tools,' Joe mused. 'Nothing. Any chance of using a piece of stone to lever it out?'

I was hysterical. 'It's frigging rigid, you crass burke.'

'Hang on. You got anything, anything at all?'

'No.' I whimpered, practically screaming, babbling.

'You can't have nothing, Lovejoy,' he mumbled. 'I've got nothing because I planned to have nothing. You're so scatterbrained, Lovejoy, you must have something. Car keys, coins, anything. Can you reach your pockets?'

'I changed my trousers at the big house.' And I'd left Shinny's keys in the car. 'A violin string, for Christ's sake.' So we could play the violin, if we had a violin.

'Like that joke from the Depression, Lovejoy. If we had some bacon we could have eggs and bacon if we had some eggs.' He was doing his best.

'Wait.' The trouble was the air. If two men breathed at so many breaths per minute, how long before they croak in a tunnel say, eighty yards long by eighteen inches? 'Joe. Any loose earth against you?'

'We've brought a ton.' It had shovelled along in front of Joe as we'd manoeuvred him.

'I need a ton. Push it here.' I pushed it down under my belly, handful by handful, until a great wadge of soil was splayed against the metal bar.

'What're we doing, Lovejoy?'

'Getting out, you ignorant Cockney nerk. Close your

ears. I'm going to pee and make some mud.' I added politely, 'Excuse me, please.'

Five minutes later I'd made two vows. The first was to try to control my terror, keep cool and work on no matter what. The second was to donate a trillion quid to medical research so they find a way to let blokes pee in a horizontal position. It took me ages to squirt even a useful drop out. Grimacing, I ploshed my hand up and down in the loose earth bowl I'd fashioned, until the mess was thick and gruesomely squashy. Then I set to work, the E string looped round the metal bar, low down where the mud was.

'What's the noise, Lovejoy?'

'Sawing. Mud saw. It's how the ancient Han Chinese sawed jade.' I moved the metal string slowly, making certain there was mud where the E string moved across the bar. Hurry, and the metal string would break. Go too slow and we'd asphyxiate down here. Just right, and the wet soil would erode its way through anything. *Wheem*, the metal went.

'Mud saw? Are you kidding?'

'The mud's the saw, you burke. The Chinese cut opal, jade, stone, damned near anything, with a bent cane and string. But it takes time.'

A pause again. Maybe crumbs of reason were knocking about his thick skull. 'We got enough, Lovejoy?'

'Time?' *Wheem, wheem.*

'Air.'

'Fingers crossed. Keep me awake for God's sake. Don't let me nod off.'

'Lovejoy.' That reflective voice meant he was working things out, maybe for the first time. 'You don't trust Mr and Mrs Heindrick, do you?'

'Trust nobody. Save your breath, gabby sod.' *Wheem, wheem.*

'We're going to be partners,' Joe confessed, really quite

proudly. 'Them and me.'

'Oh, aye?' Such close partners that they decided to kill you, Joe, I thought, sawing away. Once Heindrick overheard me address loyal servant Kurak as Joe—as we entered the tunnel to lay the sleepers in the grave—Heindrick had decided to flop a landslip on to Joe, seal the tunnel and drive away. Oh, he wouldn't have done every little thing himself: orders to kill at a distance are so much less disquieting. So Lovejoy's carelessness had put Joe where he was. And, Joe, you may not realize it, but I'll bet you too are on a series of video films for Kurt's late-night viewing. *Wheem, wheem.*

'Lena and me are going to—' His voice was thick, drowsier. I felt a twinge—well, actually a wholesale cramp—of panic at the idea of being alone.

'Hey, Joe. Remember that sleeper gig somebody pulled in Worcester a few years back? Was that you?' More mud, and *wheem, wheem*. My forearm muscles were stiffer, worn out.

He roused, chuckled. 'Sheffield plate? Yeah. Josh Hancock, 1755, a saucepan.'

'Honest? You old devil! People my way said it was the Manchester men. They're pretty good—'

'Them?' Awake now, he delivered a few choice opinions on the merits of the Mancunian sleeper man. 'We cleaned up on that.'

'And who did that cinder job over Cambridge way last summer?'

'That was me too.'

'You? How many pictures was it? Somebody said it was half of them—' A plosh of mud, then pull the string across the metal. *Wheem, wheem.*

'Lovejoy,' he said solemnly, 'we had the whole bloody lot copied—best repros money could buy. Then we sleepered the lot. The whole collection!'

'Go on!' My fingers were sore as hell, and I had to rip

strips off my shirt and use them as finger loops before continuing. 'Didn't you burn the whole manor house?'

Joe chuckled. 'Scared ourselves to death. The old squire's lady—eighty-two if she was a day—was upstairs. The firemen got her out in time.'

'So all your fakes went up in smoke, and—'

'—And the whole collection's been sleepered. Next year they get discovered.'

'Congrats, Joe. Really great.'

We kept each other going, reminiscing over the great scams of the past and filling in for each other bits of news. We talked of the fake 'originals' in the antique postage stamp markets. We invented a guessing game, telling of the best fakers we knew and arguing over awarding points. Two for the best true story, one point for a draw and nil for losing. We covered the great Tompion clock scandal, the Tom Keating trial for his fake Samuel Palmers, the long, long story of the Louis XV giltwood console tables which those world-famous London auctioneers did over with such apparent transparent ignorance for a fortune. We cackled and joked about the phoney South London collections of Daguerreotypes. I revealed all about the set of Roman legion's surgical instruments, on display in a Midland museum, which I'd broken my little index finger making a twelvemonth ago. And the saga of Jason's scam with the phoney *Paradise Lost*. And the best way of semi-ageing pearls just so their radiance can just be rescued. And the perennial argument about how the new synthetics are doing down the trust in antique diamonds because nowadays anybody can fake an antique brooch if their fingers are nimble enough. And the stupidities of recycled glass forgeries. And how to age papers and new parchment. How the sapphire glaze can be copied on modern reproductions. How to age wood and simulate Cuban mahogany. How to . . . how to . . .

A hand on my shoulder. I'd nodded off and Joe was shaking me awake.

'Okay, Joe.' By now the air must be fœtid, horrible, and I couldn't tell it from fresh. I had to feel again to locate the groove in the metal bar. No good cutting at a new place when the bar was part way through in the centre.

'You were saying about the thumbprints, Lovejoy.'

'Aye.' *Wheem, wheem* my E string went. I seemed to have been doing this all my life, bent as far as the tunnel would allow and hauling on alternate ends of the string. Pack the groove with more muddy mess, fix the string carefully in the groove and *wheem, wheem.* 'Aye, Joe. After that Elizabeth Barrett Browning manuscript "Prometheus Bound" was sold for over eleven thousand quid—it had her thumbprints, remember?—every bloody crummy book on sale anywhere had bloody thumb-prints . . .'

I'd no idea how long it was, but Joe was suddenly shaking me and urging me to have a go and kick at the bar. I took a hell of a time explaining that the E string kept passing through the bar and I couldn't find the grove before it dawned on me that I'd cut through.

'You've been doing the top for donkey's years, Lovejoy. It might break with a kick. You did the bottom hours ago.'

That was news to me. We counted 'One, two, three' and I kicked. Something scraped all up my calf, right through the skin. I wept deliriously real awakening pain, but realized then that there was space where the bar should have been, and I was blubbering and slithering and dragging Joe after me and him saying, 'Great, Lovejoy, great, eh?'

And I felt air.

CHAPTER 25

Rain and cold, mud, chill wind. The lot. But beautiful air, rasping like lung ice in the chest. Fingers bleeding, leg stinging and shoeful of blood, but that air.

I'd dragged Joe out on his face. With my last erg, turned his face sideways so he now projected from the peat barrier as if he'd been fired from a cannon and come through the wall. And the peats that had seemed so light now weighed a ton. He looked unconscious.

A figure moved on the rim of the diggings, and looked down.

'Jaysus! Is there no killin' you two?'

My luck, to find the castle rider. I'd hoped for enough solitude to somehow drag Joe over the hillside to Shinny's car and escape him, to hospital maybe. Surely there'd be a hospital in the town called Hospital? I glanced at Joe for help, but he'd clearly switched off, the selfish sod. If only he weren't so big I'd have got him away by now. You'd think giants like him would naturally go on a diet as a matter of course, thoughtless burke.

'Give me a minute, mate.' I wanted it to sound terse but it came out a bleat of terror.

'Back in there, the both of yuz.'

'Please, mate. Do a deal? Them golds—'

He grinned down at me from the bleak skyline. 'Mr Heindrick's the boss. Kurak's too much muscle. Back into that tunnel.'

Where he'd give me both barrels this time, to make sure. I felt like it was the end of the world.

'Look, mate,' I wheedled. 'It's Joe they want dead. Not me.'

'Both of yuz.'

'Let me go,' I blubbered. 'Do Joe, but let me go. Lena said me and her were partners—'

He chuckled. 'You and Kitchener's army. Every boyo in the West's ridden that lane. We call them Lena's cowboy pictures on the estate.'

Get up and kick him, Joe, I prayed, but he slept on. Sleeper man in more ways than one. The castle rider shrugged, raised his shotgun with that ugly practised speed, hardly seeking aim.

'Have it here, then, me boy.'

I screeched, 'No!' and flung myself sideways hoping to shield myself with Joe, though there was nowhere to run. My arms folded themselves about my head as something thunked up above. Silencer? But nothing hit me. And no bang. I was only in the same old agony, no pain added for once.

Wincing, I peered out between my arms. He was up there looking puzzled, stockstill and legs apart, plucking at a stick near his collar. He turned to his left, moving the shotgun with him. Another thunk sounded. Another stick, black against the grey underclouded sky, joined the first. The shotgun fell, and the castle rider lay sideways into the air. I watched, stunned, as he flopped into the turf pit a yard away. Peat spattered my face. He was still. The two arrows projecting from his neck had broken in the fall. Their fractured ends were ever so clean, varnished a bright translucent acid-oaken yellow. They proved there was a bright safe world still in existence somewhere out of this drab wet brown-greenery.

'Glory be to God!' Gerald was up on the rim. 'Where did you come from?' He cast a look around, then climbed down with all those jointed limbs. He examined the castle rider's body.

'That's wasn't me screaming,' I explained. 'It was Joe just before he passed out.'

'Sure it was. I recognized the voice,' Gerald said

diplomatically. 'He looks done for.'

'Maybe a broken back. Anybody else about?'

'Just this blackguard, God rest his poor soul.'

'We'll have to hurry, eh?'

'Not so's you'd notice.' He winked and began to slot his bow and quiver of arrows into that long thin canvas case. 'Somebody lodged an appeal against the Heindricks.'

'Another cousin?' I guessed.

'Aren't you the amazin' one, Lovejoy! How'd you guess that? It's me cousin Sean's boy Liam. A terrible Wexford man, to be sure, God forgive him, but goin' for a lawyer and wantin' to take on every judge in Munster—'

'Got any tools, Gerald? Hammer, chisel.' His surprise didn't stop me asking. 'I've a little job to do before we get the torcs.'

'Long job? We haven't many hours.'

I saw again those small ledges of rock supporting the last wall slab of the burial chamber. 'No, not long.'

'I'll see what I can find.'

'You take Joe to hospital. I've Shinny's car over the hill.'

'I saw it.'

I wasn't surprised. He seemed to have seen everything since we started. I hadn't.

'You know,' I said. 'I thought that bag was for fishing stuff.'

'And hurt them little innocent watery souls?' He paused to look at the castle rider. 'We'll put him in the tunnel before we go. Two good arrows wasted. D'you know the price of them things? 'Tis a scandal, a scandal. You'll wait here?'

'Promise,' I said, and meant it.

I'd misjudged Gerald.

CHAPTER 26

That last hour changed me for life.

Gerald was indefatigable. His multi-hinged limbs all angles and his prattling tongue never silent two seconds together, he did countless journeys across the hillside, and made a stretcher from those horribly familiar steel marker-poles tied with twine so we could hump Joe's recumbent mass over the hill. The arrangement was for Gerald to drive Joe to hospital while I finished a small task that was on my mind.

I was near dropping and had to ask for a rest when finally we tottered within sight of Shinny's crate. Gerald was all for sprinting on, but I had the heavy end and insisted.

'Here,' I puffed. 'What the hell's that glass thing?'

A shining bubble was on the track next to the car.

'My bubble car.' He sounded really proud.

So he had spoken the truth when I'd asked about the glass bubble on the van roof at Caitlin and Donald's house in Drogheda. I remembered the shrill whine of an engine.

'I kept hearing scooters,' I said.

He was enraged. 'Scooters? You evil black-hearted Englishman! Don't you know that bubble cars are the engineering wonder of the age and scooters are nothing but cardboard cut-out Heath-Robinson toys that shame the purest principles of engineering poetry—'

I sighed. Resourceful he might be, but he was still a nut in my book.

'Lift,' I said.

He kept up his tirade all the way to the car.

I watched the car go and returned reluctantly to the

turf digging. Leaving the dead castle rider there like a dead guard at a tomb made me feel ill, but there was nothing for it. Everything was out of my hands now. Once I decided that, it went like clockwork, maybe twenty minutes or even less. I went the length of the tunnel. Gerald had somehow purloined all the equipment everybody else seemed to lack. He'd found a hammer from somewhere for me, and a chisel that weighed a ton, and one of those tiny disposable torches that last for ever.

Though I say it myself I did a marvellous job underneath the burial chamber. I chiselled away the underlip from one side of the last slab completely, packing the chippings into the space created to give it some slender support. Then I did the other side but going cautiously, inch by inch. The great cross-slab formed the last paving of the burial chamber, and in turn it supported the place where the two converging walls met to form that characteristic wedge shape.

Heindrick's original tunnellers had cut away a great deal to make enough tunnel space, so in a sense they'd done me a favour. There wasn't much to do to make the whole structure unsafe. I scrabbled out in a panic only when there came a slight grating sound above me as the great slabs shifted and settled, their first movement for millennia. Gerald talked a soft welcome in my earhole before I even knew the swine had returned. He fell about when I nearly infarcted in fright, a great joke of the kind only imbeciles like him appreciate. When I came down through the superstrata I explained we'd have to go canny breaking in to lift the gold torcs out.

'I've made it a bit unsafe,' I told him apologetically.

'Ah, it's terrible careless y'are,' he gave back without batting an eyelid. 'How've you done that?'

'Anybody standing on the apex slab'll go through.'

'Won't that bring down the sides and the top monolith? Them graves are nothing more than a card house.'

'Afraid it might. How much do you reckon they weigh?'

'Them stones? Ton, maybe ton and a half.'

'Good heavens,' I said evenly. 'I do hope there isn't an accident.'

We broke into the chamber from above as dusk fell. Oddly, I noticed the two saddled horses idling patiently in the distance. The other guard seemed to have gone. Gerald said nothing about them so I was inclined to keep mum too. He seemed boss, full of plans and way ahead of me. Just how full I'd yet to discover. I may be good at antiques, but I'm dud on people.

Gerald had not done too badly this far and me and Joe were alive to prove it. But that evening he did us proud, with a pulley-operated metal claw which fixed on connecting rods fetched from his bow case. We—he, rather—lifted the gold torcs one by one from the chamber. I was really proud of their placing, pointing the krypton beam time after time to show him exactly how perfectly I'd positioned them. The ignorant sod was too stupid to appreciate my skill.

'Ah, Lovejoy,' he said sadly, sprawled out across the gap we had made by simply pulling a stone from the entrance roofing. 'Ah, what's the matter now? The sleeper game's the sleeper game. Different, y'see. This is your honest-to-God grave robbery.'

'Yes, but—'

'It won't count,' he insisted sadly, bringing out another torc in the metal claw and holding the pulley's nylon rope taut as he did so. 'Not in the annals and records of the great sleeper tricks of criminal history.'

'But you must admit—'

'No, Lovejoy. We're undoing all your great work. Nil out of ten, boyo.'

We left one torc on the dangerous slab at the grave chamber's apex. By then I was worn out. Gerald was still lively as a cricket, and got a thrill out of pretending every five seconds that the other guard was creeping up on us, the goon, just to see me leap and panic. Despite his tomfoolery we did the final gory job pretty well, making quite a good finish.

We—mostly Gerald—put the castle rider into the tunnel, walled it up with debris, closed the tunnel mouth with layers of peat, the whilst singing some old Gaelic thing ('An auld peat-layer's song from the Dark Ages, Lovejoy!')

The final insult was that he hadn't returned in Shinny's motor and we had to drive off in his bubble car. The worst ride I've ever had. He thought he was giving me a real treat, and praised its speed.

'We need to get away fast,' I complained, my teeth rattling in my head from the vibration. I'd never been so near the ground without lying down. 'For when they find the tunnel. And the castle riders, erm . . .'

'Sure, Lovejoy, we're not to blame if wicked people go digging tunnels under the countryside!'

'They know I was in the Heindricks' group.'

'Ah, but you stayed in town all day, Lovejoy.' He nearly turned the bloody machine over, laughing like a drain. How he managed to crumple all those limbs in that driver's seat I'll never know.

'No, Gerald,' I explained to the moron. 'I came back to the lough. In the tunnel. At the turf diggings—'

'*No*, Lovejoy,' he corrected. 'Don't you remember? You stayed with the rest of us. We all went shopping.'

'Who's "us"?'

'Me cousin Brian. Our Terence's three. Auntie Mary and her husband's brother Donald . . .'

'Right,' I said lamely. 'I'll need a list, okay?'

CHAPTER 27

Funny thing about women. They have this knack of putting you on the defensive, as if you start out guilty when they're in the right over everything. They're born with it. Normally it always unsettles me, though I manage by ignoring any guilt I might possess. Sometimes it doesn't work. That last night with Shinny was one of them, even though it was celebration time.

Gerald and I had driven eastwards in his daft van through Tipperary as far as the Irish Sea and then doglegged up to Dublin. There, on a waste ground in the city's outskirts, we gazed at the fourteen torcs gleaming on the unfolded leather sheet in his van.

'Well, boyo,' he said softly, 'isn't that the poetic sight?'

'What now?'

'I take the genuine torc to be authenticated. The rest get valued.'

'Authenticated? Not by a trained archaeologist?' Police were in my thoughts.

He grinned. 'My cousin Sebastian's one. Wouldn't it be time he earned his keep, now?'

'Then we'll market the rest on the sly?'

'Sure it's a terrible criminal mind you have, Lovejoy,' but he was grinning. 'Which is it's the true torc?'

'That.' I pointed instantly and waited while he wrapped it with reverence in a separate leather. 'Wait, Gerald. What's the split?'

'Equal?'

'Agreed. But look. Kurt Heindrick promised me one repro torc as payment.'

I'm not a greedy bloke, but fair's fair. We argued a bit, really quite mildly but meaning it. Gerald said payment for what. I countered that without my divvie sense there could be no sleeper scam at all.

'Like just now,' I insisted. 'How would you have known which torc to show Sebastian if I hadn't pointed it out just now?'

We settled—some more reluctantly than the rest—on my taking one from the delectable row of gold crescents. 'Only until we all meet after Sebastian's given us the certificate of authenticity, after his tests,' Gerald warned. 'Then we argue it out, you, and me and Sinead.'

'All right.'

He made me turn my back, mistrustful sod, face the toffee shop across the road and pick one without looking, on account of their possible slight variation in size. Which only goes to show how people trust people. I uttered a few harsh expletives on his attitude, which delighted him.

'Sebastian's tests will take three days, Lovejoy,' he said, wrapping the rest carefully. 'Look after Shinny till then, you wicked Englishman.'

'See you, then.'

He drove off, me waving at the clattering smoking hulk. I crossed the road as he'd instructed to catch the bus, smiling at the weight in my jacket pocket.

He'd told me to be at this restaurant dead on eight. I wasn't fooled any more—or thought I wasn't. Gerald was really a ball of fire, just made of hinged bits of angle-iron.

Shinny and I reached the restaurant simultaneously. There were a few awkward minutes looking at one another through candle flames while she asked what had gone on and I made blundering explanations praising Gerald to the skies.

'He's got the torcs,' I explained. 'A valuation by weight.'

She smiled. 'Couldn't you have done that, Lovejoy?'

'To the last farthing, but you know. Partner's foibles.'

'Yes.' She seemed sadder than yesterday's bunting.

'Gerald got a message to me through Kathleen. She's—'

'A cousin?'

'Mmmh. Our Patrick's side of the family. Joe's in hospital.'

'He might make it?'

'Oh, he will, Lovejoy. Gerald will take care of the bills and everything. He already has a job for him when he comes out.'

'What if he's maimed for life?'

'Trust Gerald.'

'If you say.' Though I couldn't see Joe doing anything but the con trick. Once a sleeper man, always a sleeper man. 'Erm, were you all right, love?' I cleared my throat and watched the waiters for a bit. 'I had to, erm, borrow your car after . . . that accident.'

'Of course you had, darling.' She touched my hand sadly. 'I understand.'

I didn't think she did but let it pass.

'Erm, Jason and the other bloke. Were they both . . . ?'

'Both. I waved down a motor and they phoned the ambulance.'

Thoughts of what might have been sometimes make you go green, so I focused on grub and gelt. We ordered a mound of food then I asked the question uppermost in my mind.

'Will Gerald be okay with those torcs? They're worth a fortune.'

'Trust Gerald.' She held my hand and gazed at me with those eyes through the golden flames between us. 'You can't beat an Irishman in a shilling race.'

We drove to the strand to watch the Howth lights and walked the dark streets. She was in the mood for reminiscing and talked of her childhood abroad, the dresses she hated and how shivering cold she'd been at school. I made her laugh once by telling her to teach me

that Gaelic turf-cutter's song Gerald had sung while at
the turf diggings. She fell about, helpless. I had to hold
her up.

'Gerald? Him? Oh, Lovejoy, darling! Gerald hasn't a
word of the Gaelic. He makes everything up. Everything.
All the time. Don't you understand anything at all?'

So Gerald was a non-Gaelic Gael as well as non-poetic
poet.

I mused, for her sad soul's sake, 'What else is he not?
Better tell me now before our partnership really gets
under way.'

She laughed at that so much she cried.

We walked over the little river and into somebody's
garden. She was on their steps while I dithered at the
gate.

'Come in, Lovejoy.'

Keys clinked. The door opened and she was silhouetted
there, looking down the steps at me as the hallway light
came on.

'Er, is it all right, Shinny?'

'There's nobody here, darling. It's my cousin
Maureen's. She's away for three days.'

I went up the steps. 'Caitlin's side of the family? Sean's?
Patrick's?'

'Mary's. You know, Mrs Heindrick's head maid.'

And there was I assuming Gerald always knew where to
be by a kind of instinct.

'Tell her not to mix the porcelain styles in future,' I
said severely. 'I was saying to Jason only the other day that
Meissen Augsburg would have been ideal—'

'*Lovejoy!*' the bandsaw said, but I was already putting
my torc in the kitchen's sugar tin, shoving it deep in the
sugar. I found some plaster to stick its lid on tight.

'Safety, mavourneen,' I said. 'In case we sleep heavy,
alannah.'

She rounded on me and hauled me close. 'Lovejoy,' she

said fiercely. 'If you start your silly rubbish tonight I'll—'

She was pulling my jacket off, then my shirt, then handing me along the corridor.

'Mind my arm, mavourneen.'

'One more word out of you,' she said in fury. 'One word, that's all.'

She slammed me into a bedroom on the first floor where an electric fire already burned. She swung me round to face her and kicked the door shut with a thud that shook the whole house.

'Ready?' she said, arms akimbo.

'I think so,' I said doubtfully.

'Right,' she said, shelling her coat. 'Get 'em off.'

Once, during the night, I thought I heard a familiar whining scooter engine, but Shinny's lovely cool breast was in my hand still, so I wrapped my legs over her and went back to sleep.

She was gone.

You will have experienced those moments of disorientation when you wake up assuming you are at home or somewhere, and suddenly every single sense screams *different! different!* and for a sick moment you feel utterly scared and lost. It was like that, opening my eyes into bright ten o'clock daylight with strangeness all around and the big double bed crumpled and . . . and . . .

And Shinny gone.

I shot up, heart banging, dashed into every room thinking of the Gardai and the Fraud Squad and Interpol and Sherlock Holmes, but there was only this envelope.

I thought, This is bloody rubbish. She can't have left, just when we'd become lifelong partners. The note was on the back of a shopping list.

Darling Lovejoy,

    I'm gone with Gerald. I can hear you saying as you

read this that women always settle for what they can get. Maybe we are really like that. I don't know. I do wish I could have got you for keeps, but you will never be the sort.

Gerald wishes you good luck and says to tell you we'll do the sleepers proud. Last night's paper is in the kitchen. Gerald said not to show it you till now.

All my love, darling,

Shinny.

The paper had a front page chunk about a gentleman and his wife being seriously injured while involved in an amateur archaeological excavation in the west. The wedge grave had fallen in, the floor crumbling under their weight. In fact, there was doubt whether they would even survive. Gardai were making extensive enquiries. Two local men were missing, with some of the torcs. The Heindricks were highly respected pillars of the community, and there were lessons for us all in the sad events surrounding the accident. Poor them. I didn't bother reading the rest, and thought of Shinny.

Of course I should have spotted it. Gerald was in partnership with Joe — maybe always had been. He, Joe and Joxer had been in collusion all the time. And of course Shinny. They had all gone along with the Heindricks as a team within a team, to con the conners. I should have known. An Irish poet in East Anglia would have been coals to Newcastle, but a Dublin-trained nurse could arrive, work at a hospital and serve as go-between for Joxer and Gerald. A plan cool enough for Jason, the Heindricks and me to have missed the truth completely. No wonder Gerald didn't much care how deep his arrows went. And Shinny had the strength to leave me high and dry. As I'd said, I couldn't imagine Joe doing anything else but antiques con tricks. Once a sleeper man always a sleeper man. They could manage without me. Of all, I was superfluous. Tears came to my eyes. Honestly. Tears.

Me. At my age.

And Shinny, lovely eyes sad across the gold candle flames, had said it too: You can't beat an Irishman in a shilling race.

I'd been had. I'd been done.

Shinny and her team had conned me, conned the Heindricks, and played us all off against each other. Last night's love had been farewell, a kiss before flying.

Worse, I was broke, Not a bean.

Except . . .

CHAPTER 28

You won't believe this, but all morning I mooned about the place touching the bed and looking for traces of her and suchlike daftness. Love is a hell of a thing. I felt I would never smile again. I went to find the sugar tin in the kitchen. Gone. Good old Shinny had snatched it as she ran.

The trouble is, I thought, watching the children cross the road towards the school, love has to be made or you've got none. Like antiques. And 'made' means *made*, formed, laboriously worked into being in that creative act that is the terrible and utter act of loving.

You can't do it alone. Try, and all you achieve is a longing, a feeling, desire, hope, fondness. Certainly, to love somebody she has to be there to be loved. I was heartbroken.

Well, almost.

I made some tepid tea, drank it as a kind of St Giles bowl, and watched the women go past with their prams towards the shops near the green where the buses turn at the top of the road.

There wasn't a crust in the house, not a penny. Shinny

had taken every groat. Not that I'd had much. And
Shinny had paid for last night's supper in the posh
restaurant by St Stephen's Green. Still, it showed she was
thinking of her present and future comfort, which is
practically every bird's fulltime occupation.

About midday I brewed up again, worse even than
before, thinking. I was a long way from Dublin's centre,
and me with not even the bus fare. The train from the
level crossing would cost a mint because fares always do.
Stay here and starve to death? Or move about in hope?

Nothing else for it.

I heaved a sigh, rose and went back into the bedroom.
The gold torc, glowing with its ancient splendour, was
still underneath the bed where I'd slipped it after lofting
it from the sugar tin during the night. Loving Shinny to
exhaustion had been a pleasurable duty to protect the
torc.

The rare eighteenth-century old flat iron which I'd
substituted for it in the sugar tin wasn't to be sneezed at.
The rarer ones—Abraham Darby of Coalbrookdale,
incidentally, as that one had been—are almost priceless
now, real collector's items. I was very, very narked that
Shinny had taken it, thieving bitch. Even if she'd thought
the tin contained a gold repro, it was still me she was
stealing from. Well, all right, it still belonged to the
householder Maureen, but I felt annoyed with Shinny. *I*
could have nicked the flat iron instead of her. That's
women for you.

I slipped the torc into my pocket. As long as I gave the
whole coat to the archaeologist, he'd be able to
spectrograph his way to the undeniable truth—that in my
hand was the original gold torc. It had been easy to pick it
out simply by its vibes, even while Gerald watched me and
I gaped innocently at the toffee shop. Of course, sad that
Gerald and Shinny had only umpteen reproductions, but
gold's worth its own weight. They wouldn't starve. Just get

a nasty shock when they found everybody laughed at the claim that at least one of their torcs was genuine. Still, people shouldn't go trying to defraud friends.

To equal things up, I decided to look round the house. There was a small Henry oil on the wall, faded from stupid placing on the wall facing the window where the sunlight would hit. It was suffering from craquelure because of coal fires in the same room. Careless old Maureen.

The painting came free of its frame quite well without a scratch. I borrowed a pillowcase and folded it over the painting. (Tip: never wrap a painted canvas up with string directly. Fingers are kindest and therefore best for carrying.) Then I borrowed a small white-metal 'bronze', 1911 or so when they were all the rage and everybody wanted one of those stalwart heroes leading a prancing nag for the mantelpiece.

Patricia Harvest, the plump lustful sexpot from Goldhanger, like all antique dealers, couldn't tell white-metal from dandruff, so I'd get at least half the fare home from her. She was sure to be in the main hotel where the antiques fair was being held. After all, I'd promised to meet her there without dreaming I would actually turn up. In fact, thinking of her winning ways made me feel quite warm inside again.

Finally, I borrowed a small carriage clock from the kitchen. No longer going, but walnut-cased clocks, especially those with typical Belgo-French corner pillars, are highly sought nowadays even though they aren't much before 1870. Funny how fashions go in collecting. It fitted neatly in my pocket.

I found the right hotel sixth go. Bloody telephones, never any use.

Mrs Patricia Harvest was in suite 108, bless her greedy little heart.

'Pat?' I said, all casual. 'Lovejoy here, darlin'. As promised.'

'Patricia,' she corrected. 'Lovejoy?' She was already breathing hard. 'Darling! At last! I've been waiting and *waiting*. Where are you?'

'That's me at the door now,' I said prophetically. 'Be prepared to (a) pay for a taxi at the hotel, (b) rape me in your circular bed, and (c) make a fortune with me at that antiques fair. Okay?'

'Oooh, darling,' she said, practically groaning.

Before departing with my loot, I totted up my expectations on a scrap of paper lying around. When I turned it over I realized it was Shinny's farewell letter. I hadn't meant to be so casual about it all, still busy being heartbroken for life, but the trouble with heartbreak is it's not much use. Yet that thieving swine Gerald had nicked all my gold torcs. I felt like strangling him, but hunting the bastard down might leave me full of arrows in some desolate bog. It was either revenge, or immediate solace in Pat Harvest's sexy wealth.

What was it I'd said? Sooner or later someone *has* to chuck in the sponge on vengeance and settle for forgiveness. Otherwise we're all at war for ever and life's nothing but a succession of holocausts.

But why should that somebody be me?

Then I thought of Sal, Joxer, the two duckeggs off the motorway bridge, Jason and his oppo, how close I'd come to it. And suddenly there were reasons it had to be me. Wait for all the other idle sods in the universe to walk away from revenge and you wait for ever. Besides, I remembered the ugly thunk of Gerald's arrows as they hit the castle rider. I might even win the torc back, but there's no pockets in shrouds.

And there were other antiques waiting, to get to know and to love.

Patricia would be delighted to see me. She always was,

being so clueless about antiques. And I'd let her see my latest purchases, a valuable Henry oil, and an original Celtic torc, for a consideration. She'd agree, of course. Patricia's considerations were famous and very, very considerate.

The trouble with Paul Henry as an artist was that he copied his own Irish paintings, which causes a bit of turmoil when connoisseurs glimpse one of his. There's always this row about provenance, too, though I'd have to play that one off the cuff. But nobody achieved that green like him, and those white cottages — always too stark when you look too closely at the brushwork — melt into the lovely landscape when you step back.

I wondered if anybody had tried to forge them yet. Maybe Pat — sorry, Patricia — was still friendly with that faker in Goldhanger and we could do a deal. I'd have to watch his technique, though. Him and his lunatic use of yellow ochre and umbers. In this game you can't be too careful . . .

I slammed the door and stepped out, whistling, heartbreak forgotten.

Bestselling Thriller/Suspense

☐ Voices on the Wind	Evelyn Anthony	£2.50
☐ See You Later, Alligator	William F. Buckley	£2.50
☐ Hell is Always Today	Jack Higgins	£1.75
☐ Brought in Dead	Harry Patterson	£1.95
☐ The Graveyard Shift	Harry Patterson	£1.95
☐ Maxwell's Train	Christopher Hyde	£2.50
☐ Russian Spring	Dennis Jones	£2.50
☐ Nightbloom	Herbert Lieberman	£2.50
☐ Basikasingo	John Matthews	£2.95
☐ The Secret Lovers	Charles McCarry	£2.50
☐ Fletch	Gregory Mcdonald	£1.95
☐ Green Monday	Michael M. Thomas	£2.95
☐ Someone Else's Money	Michael M. Thomas	£2.50
☐ Albatross	Evelyn Anthony	£2.50
☐ The Avenue of the Dead	Evelyn Anthony	£2.50

ARROW BOOKS, BOOKSERVICE BY POST, PO BOX 29, DOUGLAS, ISLE OF MAN, BRITISH ISLES

NAME ....

ADDRESS ....

....

....

Please enclose a cheque or postal order made out to Arrow Books Ltd. for the amount due and allow the following for postage and packing.

U.K. CUSTOMERS: Please allow 22p per book to a maximum of £3.00.

B.F.P.O. & EIRE: Please allow 22p per book to a maximum of £3.00.

OVERSEAS CUSTOMERS: Please allow 22p per book.

Whilst every effort is made to keep prices low it is sometimes necessary to increase cover prices at short notice. Arrow Books reserve the right to show new retail prices on covers which may differ from those previously advertised in the text or elsewhere.